Overflight

Overflight

A NOVEL BY

Charles Neider

NEW HORIZON PRESS
Far Hills, New Jersey

Distributed by
Macmillan Publishing Company, New York

Library of Congress Cataloging-in-Publication Data
Neider, Charles, 1915-
Overflight.

I. Title.
PS3564.E26808 1986 813'.54 86-18248
ISBN 0-88282-026-5

BOOKS BY CHARLES NEIDER

FICTION
Overflight
Naked Eye
The Authentic Death of Hendry Jones
The White Citadel

NON-FICTION
Beyond Cape Horn: Travels in the Antarctic
Edge of the World: Ross Island, Antarctica
Susy: A Childhood
Mark Twain
The Frozen Sea: A Study of Franz Kafka

BOOKS EDITED BY CHARLES NEIDER
Antarctica
Papa, by Susy Clemens
The Selected Letters of Mark Twain
The Comic Mark Twain Reader
The Autobiography of Mark Twain

ACKNOWLEDGMENTS

It gives me great pleasure to thank two gracious institutions which were my hosts when I began writing this book: The Center for Advanced Study in the Behavioral Sciences at Stanford, and The University of California at Santa Cruz.

Preface

It is unusual for an author to write a preface to his own novel. A novel is supposed to be sovereign, standing without help. In the present case the novel's locale, together with some of the events (the two, locale and events, are here inextricably related), are so extraordinary in their extreme exoticism that a few words of preparation for the reader may not be amiss, and may even be welcome.

Henry James wrote prefaces to some of his novels but they were designed for an edition of *revised* novels. Thomas Mann wrote a whole book about one of his novels (*Dr. Faustus*), titled *The Story of a Novel,* but it was done after the novel's publication and reception. This was near the end of his career, and he was a great writer and could do as he pleased, without the risk of losing a large, devoted audience.

All of the characters and most of the events of *Overflight* are fictional. What is not dreamed up is the background, the continent of Antarctica, which, as a writer and humanist, I had an unparalleled opportunity to observe at first hand. I also was granted two experiences, the euphoria Antarctica often inspires, and the mixture of fear, awe and despair it generates when things suddenly go wrong. The helicopter crash in *Overfight* is based largely but by no means entirely on an unforgettable and deeply traumatic experience I had in the place the crash occurs in the novel. Because I had the good luck to experience the continent and the equally good one to survive the near-fatal crash, I was able to write a novel which, so far as I know, is at this time (April 1986) the only one with a completely authentic Antarctic background.

Antarctica has long attracted the attention of writers, some of them noted ones. Poe devoted part of his *The Narrative of Arthur Gordon Pym* to the continent. In *Pym* the continent is a *hot* place! Jules Verne wrote a sequel to *Pym*. The author of a distant era who dealt most faithfully with the Antarctic—not with the continent but with the Southern Ocean that rings it—was the poet Coleridge in *The Rime of the Ancient Mariner*. I think he must have got his acute sense of that strange ocean from reading James Cook's two volumes about his circumnavigating the globe. Cook was the first to cross the Antarctic Circle, which he did three times. But these and many other attempts to project a fictional image or sense of Antarctica failed because the authors lacked the opportunity to live and travel there. Antarctica is *the* intemperate continent, unlike all others.

How did I come to write *Overflight?* But before answering this question, let me give you a sense of the place by quoting the "backgrounder" article I wrote for the October 19-25, 1985 issue of *TV Guide*.

Antarctic memories. The sun that never sets in summer, circling counterclockwise like a demon, round and round, capable of searing you at 3 A.M. as it bounces off the ice. The Adelie penguins caught in a blizzard, heads in plumage, letting themselves be snow covered, too Antarctic-smart to try to buck it. The heavenly dry sky, so deeply azure, yet containing tints of lemon, lime at the zenith.

Fear? You bet: sometimes right in my marrow. I wouldn't want to be caught dead camping out or trekking with somebody who's not afraid of the place, for that person might show poor judgment in a pinch and cost me my limbs if not my life. Mostly, though, you seem to wear a Chinese mask of stoicism while in the Antarctic. And on the whole you feel cozily secure. If you didn't, you couldn't function, much less enjoy the place.

Dangerous? In some ways not as dangerous as a great city, a city of meaningless rapes and killings. Aside from sudden changes in weather, the worst enemies in Antarctica are ignorance, stupidity, vain pride. Beware of extrapolating the rules of the temperate region to Antarctica; Antarctica has laws of its own. No land mammals, no reptiles, practically no insects, no noxious plants to bother you. It's often said that Antarctica is a hostile place. I disagree. It's magnificently neutral. Tough? Yes. But the living ecosystems are remarkably fragile. Trample on a bit of lichen, and it may take a long, long time for it to recover in a place of such thin life margins.

And of such beauty. It's by far the most beautiful place I've ever seen. The word "noble" comes to mind when you're viewing it. Awe, humility and a euphoria that recalls the feelings of immortality of childhood: these are other important emotions there.

"How *is* it up there?" I'm sometimes asked. Well, it isn't *up* there, it's *down* there. Up, down: from outer space it's all relative. It's relative on earth too. In the remote, geological past, the magnetic poles have occasionally flipped polarity. If that were to happen today, all our compasses would point south.

"How are the polar bears?" There are no polar bears and no indigenous land animals (except a tiny mite and a wingless fly) as there are in the Arctic. There's an almost total absence of indigenous life. Antarctica was a part of the southern supercontinent, Gondwanaland, some sixty to seventy million years ago and, for the last forty million years, has been the most remote large landmass on our planet. It's the only great landmass that never harbored a native human population, so it's the only such land you can visit without a colonialistic sense of guilt—no natives were molested there, enslaved, expropriated, murdered, extinguished.

A contrast. The North Pole is situated on a sea surrounded by great landmasses: North America, Asia, Greenland. The South Pole (altitude: 9300 feet) sits atop a high inland plateau of ice at the center of a continent surrounded by the Southern Ocean—the confluence of the Atlantic, Pacific and Indian Oceans—with characteristics of its own.

The coldest, windiest, driest, highest, most dangerous and most beautiful continent. Beautiful? White ice? (Locked up in the Antarctic are some ninety percent of the world's ice and two-thirds of the world's fresh water.) But the ice isn't just white, it's full of pastel subtleties: rose, pink, prune, pale green—and then suddenly electric, cobalt blue. And the textures are infinite: ripples, waves, soft ice, crevasses, hummocks, a variety of snow covers. Exotic? It's the only continent on earth that pulses, expanding in the austral winter, shrinking in the austral summer.

In winter the ocean freezes for hundreds of miles around the continent's perimeter, almost doubling Antarctica's size. And there are vast mountain ranges and strange, windy, cold, dry valleys that deglaciated long ago.

We're talking about a continent that's larger than the United States and Mexico combined; that occupies more than twenty-five percent of the landmass south of the equator; one of whose ice shelves (the Ross Ice Shelf) is up to 1400 feet thick and about the size of France. Solitude? About three thousand temporary inhabitants during the height of the working (summer) season. You feel graced to be able to take a deep breath so far from the rest of the gang teeming the planet.

How do you get to Antarctica? Aside from a few expensive tourist tours that briefly and mostly touch the northern extremities of the Antarctic Peninsula region south of South America, you don't, unless your government sends you there. In our own case, the National Science Foundation is the Antarctic's doorkeeper. I'm not a scientist. I went as a writer and a humanist to sense what it's like to live and work there, and to glimpse how the Antarctic affects our minds, senses, emotions, and mysteriously expands and regenerates us. All three times I flew to Christchurch, New Zealand, where I got suited up, then proceeded by Navy HC-130 to an ice airfield near McMurdo Station on Ross Island, Antarctica.

What do people *do* in Antarctica? The scientists work in labs or in the field. The logistics personnel help them prepare for camping, set up field camps for them, transport them. Recreation? You read, listen to music, hang out at the bars. The physical-fitness craze that has swept the United States in recent years has reached Antarctica, significantly reducing the bar population. For more extreme tastes there's the Vanda Swim Club, involving breaking through the ice crust of Lake Vanda in one of the Dry Valleys and taking a dip in the nude. And there's the 300 Club for those who, when the temperature is −100° Fahrenheit or lower, race outside from a sauna for a run around the Pole. The club's name refers to the temperature difference of 300°.

Cold? Carbon dioxide, a gas, becomes dry ice at about −77° Fahrenheit. Vostok Station, a small Soviet base on the great plateau, is the world's coldest recorded place. Recently it experienced a temperature of −128.6° Fahrenheit.

People ask, "How do you stand the cold?" You're tempted to reply, "Heroically." Actually, you dress for it. Still, I've been miserably cold on several occasions. The worst was in a near-fatal helicopter crash close to the summit of the southernmost active volcano, the huge, white Mt. Erebus, higher than Fuji or Vesuvius, and with one of the world's three fire lakes in its crater.

The four of us survived, at −31° Fahrenheit, in an Air Force survival tent (designed for two persons) at an altitude of 12,200 feet for some ten hours before we were spotted by a helicopter and then rescued. And my three companions had forgotten to bring their own survival gear. Vain pride? Taking the continent for granted? Putting too much faith in the helicopter's high technology? Still, we were found, and without irreversible damage. Was it luck, or a miracle?

Man is fragile in that place. But, as I have said, the place is fragile, too. When the pressure mounts and mounts to exploit for mineral and gas and oil reserves, will this, the last great common on earth, survive? Its great beauty, its suggestion of being marvelously extraterrestrial, its awesomeness, its pristine nobility—will these remain? For the sake of our posterity, for the sake of our planet, let us hope they do.

I fell in love with Antarctica the first time I went there (under the sponsorship of the United States Navy), and it seemed a wonderful opportunity for a literary person to come to grips with an almost untouched literary frontier. So many frontiers had already closed, yet here was one still pristine, and particularly suiting my inclinations because it invited me to write about landscape, seascape and exotic life forms like penguins and whales. The theme of sea and land presenting forceful challenges to human existence and enterprise was a familiar one to me. Fifteen years earlier, in 1954, I had edited a large volume, *Man Against Nature,* which contained, among other things, excerpts from nonfiction narratives by Amundsen, Byrd, Scott and Shackleton, early and great Antarctic explorers. The continent had been recorded intelligently by these men, especially by Scott, and later by waves of scientists, but it still lay fresh and waiting for a novelist. No need to envy James's Europe, Joyce's Dublin, Hemingway's Africa, Faulkner's South.

While hoping for an opportunity to meet Antarctica at its heart—that is, to have central, profound experiences such as aren't easily come by in our day of high technology (a world apart from the time of sledges, dogs, skis, manhauling), I proceeded, during the Navy visit and a subsequent one sponsored by the National Science Foundation, to gather materials for a nonfiction book, which would result in the publication of *Edge of the World: Ross Island, Antarctica*. But on January 9, 1971, a day I am not likely to forget, I was involved in the spectacular helicopter crash. *That* brought me close to the heart of the continent—too close, perhaps, there being a good chance of my and my three companions not surviving the experience.

But to return to the question: Why did I write the novel? Answer: because I had a superb opportunity to do it authentically. Because it was one chance in a lifetime to do it *first* (I liked the idea of an American getting the jump on the British, who had had a long head start), and to do it in such a way that it could not easily be improved on. Because the setting was so extreme as to be almost unbelievable, almost dream-like (or should I say nightmare-like?), yet I was in a position, if I was humble and worked hard, to make it believable. Because story and setting were so exotic that they did fair justice to the spectacular, exotic continent. Because fiction can, with luck, reach a much larger and broader audience than nonfiction, and I hoped to raise the public's consciousness regarding the endangered continent to which I was increasingly devoted. Because I wanted to see what would happen, and, in a sense to experience it, if the crash had been even more extreme, with fatal consequences. And because I had been graced by love for the continent and by my survival, and it seemed not enough to let it go at that, it felt necessary to pay my dues in a way other (but not necessarily greater) than nonfiction books.

Princeton, New Jersey
April 18, 1986

Overflight

1

I was at McMurdo Station, the American base on Ross Island in Antarctica, when I received a radio communication from Kiwi Airways of New Zealand. It suggested that I be the flight commentator for their Flight Five Zero, scheduled for 29 November 1979 to commemorate the fiftieth anniversary of Richard E. Byrd's flight over the South Pole. It stated that I was the right person for the assignment because, like Byrd, I was a Virginian, and because I knew Antarctica from extensive personal experience.

It took me about fifteen minutes to decide to accept the assignment. How pathetically we intuit our destinies. Which is probably just as well. If we knew much more, many of us would opt out. But what would be the point of a human race all roses? What would heaven have to offer then? And wouldn't there be a lot of nastiness about giving up the ghost?

Fifteen minutes to make a decision which changed my life. But then it's so often like that. You decide to cross the street, and are hit by a car. You take someone as a lover, and for the rest of your life have herpes. How cozy it must be for the gods to watch us strut the stage and take so many pratfalls. But how boring it must be to be immortal, fixed for eternity, and to realize there's no possibility of change.

Yet somewhere in my mind lurks a flickering memory of a premonition of disaster. The flight as scheduled was too "right," even the number assigned to it, Five Zero. And I was too "right" for the job. When things are that right, brother, sister, smell a rat. Yet we are always straining for just such a moment of "rightness." Down, premonition! Down, base suspicion which spoils the seeming rightness of things! We must have our tragedies. Dear gods, what on earth would we do without them?

Right for the job? Well, not entirely. Flight Five Zero was unique in that it was commemorative but otherwise it wasn't. It was to be the last such flight of the season, purely tourist in nature and not strictly necessary. Originating in Auckland, the flights were roundtrip, nonstop, turnaround, with McMurdo as the destination waypoint. At times I was so worried about them that I thought of them as a form of Russian roulette.

The New Zealanders were blithely assuming that nothing could go wrong with their DC10's in Antarctica, or that if something unpleasant should happen, such as a forced landing, the Americans would provide the search and rescue. But the Americans, in the form of the Navy (the Antarctic logistic support force for the scientists), lacked a sufficient search and rescue capability to deal with such a large-scale eventuality.

Both crew and passengers of the tourist flights wore spring or summer clothes, natural for the season in New Zealand. Yet despite such clothes, the flights carried not a particle of Antarctic survival gear.

Who among us is so secure in self-opinion as to be immune to applause? As for me, a teacher by profession, accepting the assignment meant that I would be speaking about a subject I loved, and to an eager audience. And so I discounted, or submerged, my private worries as I made the decision.

All too human? Unfortunately yes. But what else is there? Perfection? Too long a wait. Time is always running out.

You may be thinking, "Well, in that case he deserves whatever he got." But I may have gotten more than you suspect. I suggest you reserve judgment.

My name is Joel Stevenson. I was raised in Richmond, went to William and Mary, and got my doctorate at Berkeley. I'm a professor of American history at the University of Virginia. I was born in the year of Byrd's flight.

2

I was scheduled to leave McMurdo on a Navy C130 for Christchurch, New Zealand at 1 A.M. of 28 November.

The evening of the 27th, stopping at the McMurdo wardroom for a couple of beers, I ran into Billy Blackburn, one of the C130 pilots, and stood with him at the bar. The wardroom, part of an old Jamesway hut, was small, crowded, overwarm, brownish, dimly lit. The bar was high. On the wall behind it was a huge pinup of a young woman with seductive eyes, large breasts and red pubic hair.

Blackburn gave the impression of being of middle height like myself but was taller. He was a strong, popular personality at McMurdo. Seeing him always heightened my vitality. I suppose you could say I loved him and that if I weren't exclusively heterosexual I might have been passionate about him. Who knows the limits of one's own sexuality? He was a handsome guy, very trim although in his mid-thirties, and in a way quite unpredictable. He had the reputation of being a superb pilot.

We had hardly got to talking when he said, "Do you know there are at least three irregularities on that Kiwi flight you're taking?"

"Kiwi" refers to New Zealand or a New Zealander.

"No. What?"

He said that none of the three pilots assigned to the flight had flown to Antarctica before, and reminded me that it was a universal rule for aircraft, both military and civilian, that no pilot commands an Antarctic flight who hasn't previously flown to

Antarctica, usually as a copilot. He added that, as a matter of fact, not a single member of the flight crew had visited Antarctica.

Furthermore, at the route qualification briefing eighteen days ago none of the three pilots had been shown their nav track on a topographical map, especially the last leg, from Cape Hallett to McMurdo. The nav track was the computer flight track, which the aircraft followed automatically. The special importance of the last leg stemmed from the fact that McMurdo was the southernmost waypoint.

Going east to west, you have Mt. Terror, Mt. Terra Nova, Mt. Erebus and Mt. Bird, all on Ross Island. West of Ross Island you have McMurdo Sound. And west of the Sound you have the Western Mountains. So the only safe approach to McMurdo if you're coming from the north is down the Sound. The New Zealanders were not able to show their tourists anything in detail from a DC10 as low as even 6,000 feet, so they usually dropped to 1,500 or 2,000 feet to let them see McMurdo, Scott Base, the Ross Ice Shelf, Cape Royds, Cape Evans, and so on.

But you always have those Ross Island mountains to think about, especially Mt. Erebus, which is almost 12,500 feet high. Now suppose you have poor visibility. Or let's say you have bad visibility, a really big cloud cover, thick, massive. Let's not even talk about the real killer, a whiteout. How do you know what you're doing without a map that shows you the high ground, especially if you're brand-new to the place? Obviously you don't.

Blackburn said that the airline's own flight rules required that a flight to Antarctica must have two captains and one first officer, yet my flight had one captain and two first officers. There was a large difference in flight hours between a captain and a first officer.

"But why these irregularities?" I asked.

"Entropy, Doc," he replied. "Things running down. The bureaucratic clock missing more and more beats. You still going to take that flight? Sure you are. We're all gamblers down here. We're nuts to be here, especially the pilots. But we're not as crazy as you are. We have no choice, once we've asked for this duty, and come down here, and learned the reality. Goodby romanticism. Not that I'm knocking it, you understand. I like to be a cowboy as much as anybody. But *you* keep coming of your own free will, as if you love the place. Good luck, son. One of these days we're going to kiss your ass farewell."

My reaction to what I learned was a desire to back out—first, I didn't care to endanger myself unnecessarily, and second, it was distasteful to be associated with anything ignorant, bungling—in a word, unprofessional. But the momentum of events in Antarctica, as in a war, can be a great hindrance to sensible action, a powerful force distorting one's instinct for self-preservation.

"How do you know all this?" I asked.

"I got it from Sam Ogilvie himself, the captain."

Blackburn had returned from New Zealand four days before. I knew he had many pilot contacts there.

"Has he or the other two pilots complained to the airline?"

"No."

"How come?"

"Because the flights are considered foolproof, failsafe. And the pilots would be making waves and crying chicken—not healthy for their careers in the company."

"Is Ogilvie worried?"

"No."

"And the others?"

"Not a bit. They should be."

I now behaved with apathy regarding the irregularities, as if I had had no wish to back out of the flight, and as if they involved someone else, some person for whom I had little or no empathy. Still, I seem to recall a fleeting moment of cunning. I felt I ought to take some defensive action, but I'm not sure if this recollection is genuine.

As it turned out, my reaction was delayed until I reached Christchurch. But then, possibly because of the delay, it was strong, almost imperious, and there was a strange taste of mystery about it. As you will see.

As for the authenticity of what Blackburn had told me, I

trusted him implicitly. He was incapable of petty, vague or false rumors.

He paused a moment, then said, "Down here Erebus is a big fact of life for a pilot. Ask any of them. We're spooked by that mountain."

We were silent awhile.

Then Catherine Waterhouse, one of two Navy doctors at McMurdo, dropped in and joined us. She and Blackburn were fond of each other. She was quite beautiful, intelligent, had a good figure, was thirty-three and single. She and I were always rather formal with each other. I had known her about six weeks. This was her first season in Antarctica. It would have been hard to believe that very soon we would fall in love, but under circumstances so bizarre that I've found myself shaking my head in disbelief when I've recalled them.

She too was drinking beer.

Suddenly Blackburn asked me, "Where'd you get these clothes?"

I was wearing khaki cords and a khaki shirt. I had hung my red parka and black cap on a wooden hook in the cold anteroom.

"Army and navy store."

"I'll be damned if you wear khaki," he said emphatically. "From now on you're gonna wear Navy greens."

He quickly unbuttoned and removed his shirt and handed it to me. It had LCDR BLACKBURN printed over the right breast pocket and VXESIX over the left one.

Catherine Waterhouse laughed.

I said, "Billy, you don't want to do that."

"*Fuck* you if you don't want to wear my shirt," he said angrily, surprising me.

I said, "Hell, Billy, you know I feel honored."

"You hummer, I'll get you a dozen of 'em. You're a *Navy* man now."

We exchanged shirts. I was proud to have his. It fitted me perfectly. It was much heavier than mine. Later I discovered it took pressing well, and the buttons were sewed on to last for eternity. It always feels good to wear it, for it brings back Billy sharply to my mind. I treasure Billy, my memories of him have enriched my life.

Some Coast Guard officers, loosening up, started laughing a lot, a number of Kiwis were shooting craps, and soon there was a fair amount of profanity abroad.

Blackburn, right foot thrust forward solidly and with a stamping sound, torso leaning strongly forward, eyes not lingering on anything or anybody, sang leather-voiced. I remember "There She Goes," "Half of a Photograph," "I Can't Help it if I'm Still in Love With You," "I Really Don't Want to Know," "Half as Much," and "There Stands the Glass."

Kate Waterhouse gleamed with admiration for him.

I myself couldn't listen to him and watch him without becoming mesmerized. He was handsome, athletic, had a powerful neck. His eyes were as serious and devoted as if he were singing hymns. He never paused between songs, only stamped his right foot hard and thrust it forward solidly and leaned forward to signal the beginning of a new one, and lowered his chin a moment until it almost touched his chest.

Meanwhile he held his glass high. His eyes, half-glazed, burned with a sacred light (bourbon), almost extinguished now. The powerful voice never faltered or cracked. His repertory was delightfully extensive.

He started throwing coins onto the floor, shouting, "Sweepers! Sweepers! Get the hell out of here!"

Hank Dana slammed coins onto the floor.

I slammed coins onto the floor.

Kate Waterhouse slammed coins onto the floor.

Blackburn threw a dollar bill down.

A Navy commander who had just come in threw down a dollar bill.

A Kiwi threw down some Kiwi money, both coins and paper.

Hank Dana, related (so he said) to Richard Henry Dana, author of *Two Years Before the Mast,* kept wildly side-kicking coins and bills under the bar, often missing them, and grinning apple-cheeked, with a pointed gray chin, his eyes sometimes lost in folds of skin, and saying something sober now and then and managing to look sober some of the time.

Blackburn said loudly, "We need somebody impartial to collect the sweepers as a gift to this new bartender here."

The bartender, an enlisted man, smiled and said nothing.

"Doc, you're elected!" Blackburn shouted to me.

There were shouts of "All *right*!" and "Right on!"

I gathered the sweepers on my hands and knees, added a dollar bill, Blackburn placed the money in a glass and set the glass on the bar. The bartender looked pleased, uncertain, shy—his expression kept changing.

Then Hank Dana, saying he'd be back in a minute, ran outside and quickly returned with Blackburn's portable tape recorder and some cassettes, and played some old songs, and somebody said, "Hank, what in hell happened to your head?"

Dana's dark head was gray on the right temple, there was dirt on his right shoulder and right thigh, and his right hand was bleeding.

He grabbed a brown paper towel and clenched it in a fist and wouldn't let anybody examine his hand.

Finally he admitted he had slipped.

"What a slide to second it was! I slid completely across the street!" he said.

We all laughed.

"But nobody saw me!" he said very rapidly. "There were no witnesses! I looked around and checked that out!"

There was a lot of shouting and laughter. How good it was to be in that small, overheated room.

It makes me want to cry to think about it. Hank Dana got killed in a helicopter crash the next season, and Billy Blackburn was riding in the cabin and got badly burned. Although he had plastic surgery, he doesn't look the same. And something has gone out of his voice, I hope not permanently.

Sometimes I feel so very, very old, as if I've overstayed my time. Too many things to remember. Forgive me for talking like this momentarily. You will see this is an upbeat story.

3

At 9:30 P.M. a young man, one of the general field assistants, drove up to the Lodge in a truck and took me, my overnight bag and my orange survival bag to the small plywood bus booth near Mac Center, the center of Navy operations at McMurdo. I waited alone in the unheated structure, which shook heavily under the powerful southeasterly ripping through the base. This was the prevailing wind here. It came off the great polar plateau and swept across the vast Ross Ice Shelf before reaching Ross Island. The booth would have blown away if it hadn't been guywired down.

I began to feel very cold despite my Antarctic clothes. Wondering impatiently when the bus would come, I went outside but the wind was viciously cold. The sun, now in the southwest, was as brilliant as ever. It never set at this time of year. It just went round and round counterclockwise, due east at 6 A.M., due north at noon, due west at 6 P.M., due south at midnight. It was enough to make even a sunworshipper like myself angry at times. Waking up in the middle of the night, and seeing it ready to burn my skin off, I sometimes would grumble silently, "Why don't you just quit for a while. You're overdoing it."

Retreating into the booth, I recalled one of my several affairs with the southeasterly.

I was hiking alone to Scott Base, the New Zealand station, on an overcast evening. Scott is about two and a half miles east of McMurdo. The temperature was 4° Fahrenheit, the wind velocity at McMurdo ten knots. But in the Gap, which I was climbing, were head winds of twenty knots or more, which brought the effective temperature down to $-35°$ or lower. I had the neck and ear flaps of my black pile-lined cap down but side gusts burned my eyes, causing them to run copiously. When I put up my parka hood I discovered I couldn't secure it; one of the drawstrings was missing. The southeasterly kept blowing the hood back over my shoulders. Finally I let it stay there, raising my hand occasionally to shield my left eye, which felt frozen.

I was wearing bear paws, huge fur-lined leather gauntlets, over my regular gloves. Whenever I removed them to adjust the hood, my hands burned and went numb in their double gloves (khaki woolen insert and black leather shell). Feeling tired and sleepy, I found myself thinking how nice it would be to sit down for just a bit.

A voice in my head said, "Do it, Joel, do it! And close your eyes for a couple of seconds, rest them, poor things! You'll feel ever so much better!"

Another voice said, "Yes, Joel, do it and it will be lull, lull, lullaby, and sometime later they'll find you, hard as a rock."

Luckily, I managed to heed the second voice.

About five minutes later Father Crawford, a priest from Christchurch, wearing Navy fatigues, joined me in the plywood booth. Then a stout, tall lieutenant commander from personnel came in, followed by a frosty professor of international relations at Yale, who in my presence at the Chalet one afternoon had made some veiled disparaging remarks about my school (Tom Jefferson's place). I hadn't taken the bait.

A large Navy truck drove up. The back of it had a canvas top and sides. The four of us got in and sat in pairs on opposite benches. As we climbed eastward to the Gap I glimpsed McMurdo slipping away behind us. The road heading northward beyond the Gap had been torn up badly by meltwater. The driver was going fast. All of us except the Yale professor, who was hatless (macho about being able to endure cold), held on to arched wooden beams above our heads to keep our skulls from smashing into them, and once we flew into the air and came down hard on the wooden benches.

On our right, east of us, Ross Island, black rock and white snow, sloped away to the bluish Ross Ice Shelf which stretched out flat and immense to the horizon. The shelf is the size of France. On our left was a mottled, flinty, dark, volcanic hill of pumice-like stuff swept clean of snow and marked by regular vertical ridges which were shaped as if they had been made by bulldozers. A hill further along on our left was furry with snow and on our right, somewhat ahead of us, far below on the white shore, was Scott Base, looking tiny with its antennas and green huts.

Suddenly we went over what felt like a boulder, and the Yale professor's head cracked against a beam. He looked intensely startled, wide-eyed, alert and in pain. Grabbing hold of the beam with one hand, with the other he explored the top of his head, which was bleeding slightly.

"Oh," I thought, "the just vengeance of heaven."

We heard the moaning, barking and yipping of the Scott Base huskies as we were descending the steep road slippery with brittle shards of volcanic rock. We became aware of the pressure ice at the coast's edge, its angular, uplifted, helter-skelter, vaguely frightening forms tinted with delicate blues and greens. Skuas were wheeling above the shoreline. Far out on the ice, almost indiscernible, was a cluster of specks: Williams Field.

The truck stopped between two trackmasters. Our gear was put in one. We entered the other and lumbered southeastward across the ice shelf, which at close range one could see was uneven, wavy and minutely crevassed. At Willy, as the field was generally called, we made our way to the galley hut and dined at a small table. Father Crawford, much interested in the history I was writing, asked questions about it. It concerned American activities in Antarctica beginning with Byrd's first Antarctic expedition, 1928-30, which introduced the regular use of aircraft on the continent.

Some time between one and one-thirty we boarded a ski-equipped Herc, short for Hercules C130, the huge four-engine turboprop aircraft which was designed to serve as a troop carrier, known at McMurdo as the work horse of Antarctica. The last thing I saw before boarding was beautiful, blue-white Mt. Erebus, the largest and most active volcano in Antarctica, one of the largest in the world and one of the very few which contains a red-hot lava lake in its crater. Because of its breadth it gives the impression of being much lower than it really is.

It looked now serene, gentle, innocent. Clad as if in ermine, its pockets of blue-gray shadow resembling ermine tails, it suggested the kind of female breast that remains shapely even when a woman is on her back. A high steam plume flowing from its crater blew to the northwest, showing that the southeasterly had a high ceiling.

You can't see Erebus from McMurdo unless you climb Observation Hill or some other high point, but from Willy Field you can see it well, as also from Scott Base. I recalled the many wonderful times I had gone sledging on the Ross Ice Shelf with the dogs, the Scott Base huskies, when I lived at Scott, and the hundreds of splendid views of Erebus I had then. Gazing at the mountain lovingly now, I would never have dreamed that before long I would be obsessively convinced it had great evil lurking in its molten heart.

During the long, wearing night (the Herc's noisy cabin wasn't sound-proofed) I visited the flight deck, where my friend Sandy Pomfret, the pilot, told me things about Flight Five Zero. Again I was disturbed. Although they were not irregularities, they were certainly shortcomings, at least to an experienced Antarctic pilot.

He said that at the route qualification briefing the pilots had not been told about whiteout conditions and how they might be anticipated with an overcast sky and with snow-covered or ice-covered terrain. Nor had they been informed of the procedure for trying to land on Willy's ice runway and skiways in case of a forced landing, or the emergency circumstances which might require such a landing, or the best way of trying to survive on the ice, or the altimeter adjustments to minimum safe altitudes which have to be made in the Antarctic because of the low barometric pressures there.

With these shortcomings and with the irregularities in mind, and working on a mysterious, powerful hunch, one not to be denied—put it down to a sixth or a seventh sense, and its mysteriousness to my infrequent communication with it—I made an eccentric decision as soon as I left the Herc and entered the Christchurch airport. Being eccentric myself, at any rate as compared with some of my academic colleagues, I was not particularly bothered by its eccentricity.

If only I had known what that intuition portended, which is to say if only I had been godlike instead of merely human. No, not merely. I have no wish to put us down. There's more than a divine spark in us still. I believe in us despite what happened, or maybe because of it.

Normally I would go to the USARP (pronounced you-sarp) depot just outside the Christchurch airport, deposit my Antarctic clothes and my survival bag and don spring clothes fetched from a stored suitcase which I had left on my way to McMurdo. (USARP stands for United States Antarctic Research Program.) I decided now not to go there. Instead, I would wear most of my Antarctic clothes (special longjohns, wool shirt, heavy trousers, heavy boots) and carry my survival bag with me.

But the idea of traveling in such clothes in the late New Zealand spring was outlandish, so I went to the depot after all and put on the semblance of spring clothes—a lightweight shirt, a madras tie, a light woolen jacket. I put a stick of deodorant into a trouser pocket. I stuffed my Antarctic shirt, cap and parka into my now heavy survival bag, made of thick canvas, with a strong zipper, and two canvas grips for handles.

So now, as I trusted, I gave the appearance of being lightly clad, but was ready in case of a forced landing. I would be unable to avoid an immense amount of sweating but if I could endure the discomfort of camping out in Antarctica I could suffer being overheated for a time. I would use the deodorant to counter the perspiration.

There was no separate room for privacy in the large depot warehouse. The workers, all of whom recognized me, paid no special attention to me, but when I started to leave the place with my survival bag I noticed raised eyebrows and significant exchanged glances.

Finally one of them asked, "What are you taking that for?"

Laughing, I said the first thing that popped into my head, "The mystery of human behavior is beyond me," and walked out.

They probably put me down as one of those nutty professors you see on the TV soaps. But if I had to be eccentric against my nature, I would. There was no way I was going to disregard my powerful hunch.

Between flights I checked my overnight bag and survival bag and went for what I planned to be a long walk in the direction of the city. Open fields. Hills. Exotic nature smells intermingled with the smells of traffic. I walked with long strides, enjoying the sudden change from winter to late spring, early summer.

Soon I wished I didn't have my longjohns on. Sweat was bathing my back and chest, trickling down my face. I loosened my tie, unbuttoned my collar, but nothing helped, I was too strangely dressed for this weather. Nothing to do but turn back, enter the White Heron Lodge, wash up in the men's room and use the deodorant stick generously.

4

Upon arriving at Auckland Airport I checked in at the Gateway Lodge. It was mid-afternoon. The city of Auckland was a half-hour or more away, depending on the traffic. Tired, sleepy, hot, fresh from Antarctica, I had no wish to take on a modern city.

I remember asking the attractive, gray-haired woman as I registered, "Gateway to this world or the next?"

She smiled and replied, "Oh, that depends on you, sir."

I looked up, thinking her witty.

"Oh, I'm sorry, sir," she said. "I didn't quite hear you at first. Very much to this world, sir. You sound like a minister. They're always joking like that. I suppose it's part of the trade."

"No, I'm a historian," I said. "We have our own occupational hazards."

"How nice," she said, apparently not listening carefully.

She didn't seem to notice my orange survival bag (sea bag). Nor did anyone take particular notice of it as I carried it to my room.

I walked in the neighborhood of the Lodge, got overheated, showered, then napped for about an hour. I hadn't gotten much sleep on the flight from McMurdo to Christchurch.

In the lobby I overheard some foreign tourists discussing the Antarctic flight they would take tomorrow. One, an ascetic looking Japanese man in his fifties, I guessed, with a fine little mustache, was openly worried, not about the destination waypoint but because the craft was a DC10. His bald head seemed to be crammed with figures. He noted in meticulous English for an audience of three Japanese and three or four Caucasians that in

May of this year a DC10 had crashed in Chicago after an engine fell off, killing 273 people, and that in October another had crashed in fog on a Mexico City runway, killing seventy-one of the eighty-seven persons aboard.

As for my own feelings about the DC10's, I had flown in the aircraft several times recently and if I had any worries about them, they were obscured by those stronger, fresher and more immediate ones I had about the flight's special shortcomings.

During dinner at the Lodge I had New Zealand chowder (tua tua, crayfish and lemonfish), and whitebait for the entree, with McWilliams sauterne, rather sweet, a little like May wine. Glancing across the room, I recognized a woman named Pamela Mansfield, whom I had met in Christchurch some six weeks earlier (in mid-October), the night before I flew to McMurdo. She was with a gray-haired stout man now who looked to be a professional type.

At first I thought I would go over and say hello but something cautioned me not to. When our eyes met, she pretended not to recognize me. I didn't blame her, she had good cause. I'll explain later, in its place, why she pretended not to know me. I didn't try to meet her gaze again.

After dinner I went out for a stroll. Auckland was not at all like late spring at 55°, although the previous week its temperature had been in the high seventies, but it was expansive, and rich with November greens. I stared at the trees, at the women, especially at the children, and tried to ignore the traffic, which was both on the ground and in flight. Back at the Lodge, gazing at the swimming pool, I enjoyed the soft, moist, perfumed air, which unfortunately was spiced with the tang of jet fuel. Its moistness was very different from the harshly dry air of Antarctica, the world's largest and driest desert, where dehydration is often something to contend with when you are camping out.

Wanting to be fresh tomorrow, to shine as flight commentator, I decided to turn in early. If there's one thing I can't abide in myself it's botchwork. I soaked a long time in a hot tub. I awoke during the night, went to a window and looked out at the swimming pool, at the pool lights, the black sky. I remembered McMurdo, the Western Mountains, Mt. Erebus, knowing it was daylight there. At Williams Field I had slogged across the slushy ice to the waiting Herc. I had looked forward to seeing New Zealand, its spring, its young women. Young women and spring felt strangely remote from me now. Nor did I react to the night as I had expected. After my first visit to Antarctica I had been startled by the beauty of a dark night and by the relief of having the night overhead after a bright day. Perhaps spiritually I was still in Antarctica now.

At 7 A.M. I reported to the airline offices, where I met the cabin crew of thirteen (pursers, flight stewards and hostesses) and the flight deck crew of five (the captain, two first officers and two flight engineers). There would be 249 of us on the flight, mostly New Zealanders but also a sprinkling of Americans, Canadians, Japanese and Australians. I had worried needlessly about my Antarctic clothes and orange survival bag. No one seemed to notice them. I stashed my overnight bag and my survival bag on a low shelf at the very rear of the plane.

Before we took off I went to the rear again to check my gear. It was in place. Returning to the flight deck, I was surprised to spot Pamela Mansfield in the main cabin, chatting animatedly with her male companion. She saw me, looked startled, but still pretended not to know me.

I was introduced to the crowded, complex looking flight deck. The captain sat on the left (port) seat, the copilot on the right (starboard) one. I sat behind the captain. The flight engineer sat behind and at a right angle to the copilot. Between my seat and the flight engineer's was a seat for an observer, meant for a visitor or one of the cockpit crew not on active duty. Having flown often in many kinds of aircraft, military and civilian, I quickly oriented myself and felt comfortable.

The captain, Sam Ogilvie, was tall, lean, attractive and in his late thirties or early forties. He had dark brown straight hair, blue eyes and an oval face which looked very youthful, perhaps because he had such a light beard. I thought it must require very little shaving, mostly around the chin. His sideburns were wispy, like a boy's. He looked self-confident and intelligent. He was on the formal side, not only with me but with his colleagues too. He did not laugh easily, and when he did there was something hung-up about it.

In chatting with him I was relieved to learn that the previous evening, on the floor of his home study (all the flight crew lived in Auckland), he had carefully plotted our flight track on an atlas and on a large topographical map, both of which he had brought on board.

The copilot with whom I interacted most, Kelly Duncan, was in his mid-thirties, as I judged, had a dark complexion, keen gray eyes, an aquiline nose and, like myself, a poor bite, caused by the unusual thrust of his lower jaw. He too seemed bright. Although less formal than Ogilvie, he was formal, at any rate with me.

The flight plan called for us to overfly the Auckland Islands, the Balleny Islands and Cape Hallett. Ross Island is situated at a latitude of almost 78°. Volcanic in origin, it is roughly triangular in shape, about forty-five miles wide and an equal distance long. Mt. Erebus is twenty-two miles north of McMurdo.

We would circle McMurdo, which is roughly 840 miles from the Pole, turn north, fly over Cape Hallett and Campbell Island and proceed to Christchurch, our first landing point, where I would leave the flight. Technically, ours was a non-scheduled domestic scenic flight. It would be roughly equivalent to a non-stop flight between New York City and Wilmington, North Carolina via Quito, Ecuador.

We were a widebodied jet with two wing engines and an engine mounted in the tail fin. Our wings were swept back rakishly at an angle of thirty-five degrees. Sometimes, as when landing or taking off, the DC10 could seem squat, fat, ungainly, but when viewed from the side while airborne it could look trim, even beautiful, suggesting an exotic long fish which had surfaced from the bottom of a sea and taken flight. The cockpit windows were its eyes. The cabin windows strung behind them were rare and delicate nerve ends.

We took off precisely at 8:30 A.M. Flying south, after awhile you see below you the roughest waters on earth: the Southern Ocean. The earth's rotation from west to east forms westerlies in the southern high latitudes, and the winds, because they have no large landmasses to hinder them, circumnavigate the globe freely, creating eastward currents and the infamous fierce weather.

At first, looking for ice, you see only gray water. Then stray icebergs in a black sea come into view, then stretches of pack ice, and finally sections of the continental ice sheet. You suspect the water is very cold. The southernmost parts are colder than the freezing point of fresh water, some of them being as low as 29° Fahrenheit.

The longest part of the southbound flight, almost five hours, was uneventful. For me the most important event was my talk from the flight deck about Antarctica, the Ross Island sector, Richard E. Byrd, and his historic flight over the South Pole exactly fifty years before that day.

It was not until we reached the air approaches to Ross Island that the trouble began, first in the form of a tremendous, thick cloud cover.

5

It was now 1:30 P.M., exactly five hours after liftoff, and we were in cruising flight at 33,000 feet about 150 miles north of McMurdo. The weather was brilliant but we saw increasing cloud cover below and ahead of us as we moved rapidly southward.

The second copilot and the second flight engineer were not in the cockpit at this time and they did not enter it during the subsequent events. There were two visitors in the cockpit, a woman and a man. Airline policy encouraged such visits.

Kelly Duncan, the copilot, made contact with the Mac Center forecaster on the high frequency radio.

"If you have copied our latest weather," the forecaster said, "we have a low overcast in the area at about 2,000 feet. And right now we're having some snow. But our visibility is still about forty miles."

Duncan said we wanted to descend to 18,000. The forecaster approved, adding that the clear areas were some seventy-five to a hundred miles to the northwest of McMurdo.

"Doesn't look very promising, does it?" the captain, Sam Ogilvie, said as we began our descent toward McMurdo Sound.

"No, it doesn't," Kelly Duncan said.

"Oh, goodness," the seated woman said, "do you think we'll be able to see Scott Base?"

"Oh sure," Ogilvie said.

The forecaster said, "Within a range of forty miles of McMurdo we have a radar that will, if you like . . . we can let you down to 1,500 on radar vectors."

"This is the captain, ladies and gents," Ogilvie said on the public address system. "We're going initially to 18,000. The cloud cover in the McMurdo area has increased. But the visibility is forty miles, so ground visibility is good. We'll take advantage of the radar facilities at McMurdo for letdown. That should take us below the cloud and give us a view of the McMurdo area. It's always possible this will change, of course, but we're hopeful we'll be able to give you a look at McMurdo today. Thank you."

By the time we were about 115 miles from McMurdo the weather had worsened a great deal. There was a massive cloud cover below us. The forecaster, who was at McMurdo, instructed Duncan, the copilot, to try to contact the Ice Tower, which was the control tower at Williams Field, and he gave him a channel frequency number. Duncan tried. Then the captain tried, but he also failed.

I thought, "Now Joel, stop being an alarmist. Ogilvie is a bright guy. He'll just turn back, as any sensible person would, when he sees how nasty the weather here can be."

Let me say a few words about the DC10's radio communications so that you won't find any of the ensuing events puzzling. The forecaster, or Mac Center, could hear us because he picked up our high frequency (HF) radio waves as they bounced off the ionosphere high above the earth. But he couldn't see us. The Ice Tower, on the other hand, with its very high frequency (VHF) radio, had the capability of seeing us on its radarscope once we were within about forty miles of it. However, communications between us and the Ice Tower were limited to a line of sight. They could not cope with such barriers as the curvature of the earth or intervening high ground. The HF system too had its limitations. It was usually disrupted and sometimes blacked out during sunspot activity, which affected the ionosphere's ability to reflect radio waves, especially in the polar regions, which contain the magnetic poles.

When we were about eighty miles from McMurdo, Kelly Duncan tried again to reach the Ice Tower and again failed. Below us was a vast sea of clouds. There was no sign of Ross Island or the Western Mountains or Mt. Discovery a little south of Ross Island.

At about sixty-five miles from McMurdo, Duncan again failed. If anything, the weather had thickened. The only visibility was behind us and on our flanks, and even that wasn't good.

"I'll have to do an orbit here, I think," Ogilvie said. "Actually it's clear out here if we can get down. Tell him we'd like a further descent. We have contact on the ground and we could if necessary descend doing an orbit."

Duncan told the forecaster we were about forty-five miles north of McMurdo and would descend VMC (visual meteorological conditions). He said we were vacating 18,000.

I thought Duncan was stretching it a bit by saying we would descend VMC. It's true we now had some blue patches in the cloud cover but there was not one to the south of us, where we were heading at about 300 miles an hour.

Ogilvie said he would descend to 10,000.

"I'll do an orbit here to get down, I think," he added.

"Captain," I said, "with all due respect, don't you think we ought to stay up until we're sure what we've got? Our failure to raise the Ice Tower may mean we're off course and have got something between us and the Tower. Erebus is lurking out there somewhere."

"Thank you for your opinion, professor," Ogilvie said drily. "I assure you we're absolutely on course. This is a superb machine."

And he took the DC10 out of the nav mode (automatic, computerized flight), put it on heading select (manual flight, relatively speaking) and began the orbit. We banked to the right.

Ogilvie had given me every sign of being a bright man but I saw now that he might lack wisdom, a characteristic even more valuable than intelligence, for without it intelligence is often lost in blindness and fanaticism, and on some occasions is programmed to self-destruct. The more that events were overtaking us, the more I sensed that Erebus was indeed close to us, waiting to do us harm. All my premonitions seemed to be rushing posthaste to fulfillment. But I still had nothing rational to go on. I had a feeling that some indisputable proof was going to present itself. Would it do so in time?

Kelly Duncan now finally reached the Ice Tower. He said we were descending through 13,000 with the intention of going to 10,000 and were requesting a radar letdown through the cloud.

The Ice Tower approved.

"There you go, professor," Ogilvie said. "So much for our not being able to raise the Ice Tower."

Shortly afterwards we lost the Tower. We never regained it.

"Lost contact when we got down a bit lower," Don Player, the flight engineer, remarked.

We began to spiral downwards clockwise, going north, then east while maintaining our speed.

Although our failure with VHF had a great deal to do with what happened to us subsequently, it didn't have the slightest effect on the flight deck crew, as far as I could tell. Throughout the events which I witnessed, they remained calm and self-confident.

I knew that the VHF system was immune to disruptions caused by weather or sunspot activity and therefore I could not help wondering if some high ground, lying between us and the Ice Tower, might be preventing us from making and maintaining contact with each other. Don Player's remark, "Lost contact when we got down a bit lower," struck a chord in me. It seemed to me that he was on target without knowing it. But why did we make contact at the beginning of the orbit?

Suddenly I thought I knew why: because we had moved west, away from the obstacle in our path. And then when we swung around to the east and lost altitude, we lost the Ice Tower because we put the obstacle between us again.

What could the obstacle be? Presumably we were over the entrance to McMurdo Sound, and there was no high ground there. Where were we then? In the northern approaches to Ross Island? And could the obstacle be Mt. Bird? Or Mt. Erebus? If so, most likely it was Erebus because Erebus was so high.

I tried to explain my fears to Ogilvie but it was useless.

Events were moving too rapidly and he was preoccupied with doing the orbit. But he had time to say, "Are you a radio expert too, professor?"

He had a point. So I kept my silence after that but only for a while, for I had a point too: my life, and his, and the lives of all the others on the plane. And if I was no radio expert, at least I knew something about Antarctica and the region we were flying in. I thought it insane to lose altitude so close to Ross Island without knowing visually where we were, especially as we lacked VHF contact with the ground. For some reason I thought of Pamela Mansfield in the cabin, ignorant of what was happening in the cockpit, and I felt guilty toward her.

Actually, although I was alarmed, I was fascinated by nature's inventiveness, her ability to bring a human tragedy slowly but definitely to fruition, to gather the components until they formed a critical mass that exploded like a bag of pus bursting.

"Captain again, ladies and gents," Ogilvie said. "We're carrying out an orbit and circling our present position. We'll be descending to an altitude below cloud so we can proceed to McMurdo. Thank you."

At 10,000 feet Ogilvie told Duncan, "I've got to stay VMC here, so I'll be doing another orbit."

Duncan informed the forecaster that we were at 10,000 and were thirty-five miles north of McMurdo. The forecaster instructed him to keep trying the Ice Tower.

Duncan tried and failed.

"Tell him we can make a visual descent and a visual approach to McMurdo," Ogilvie said.

We were now at about 9,000 feet.

"We're not picking up the VHF channels that they use here," Ogilvie said. "We're VMC around this way, so I'm going to do another turn in."

We began our second orbit, this time going counterclockwise, spiralling downward and maintaining our speed.

6

Now I must introduce you to Beaufort Island, a landmark of volcanic origin which has an important place in my story. I hope to give you a good sense of the island and a feeling for the lay of the land in its vicinity. The crucial relevance of all this will be apparent to you all too soon.

Beaufort Island lies twelve miles north of Cape Bird, the northernmost extremity of Ross Island. It's about three and a half miles long in a north-south direction, and one and a quarter miles wide at its widest point. Its shape suggests a comma if you look at it from the air while heading north. Its western side has a long iceslope which ends in seacliffs up to fifty feet high. Its eastern side is steep, bare and rocky. Its summit is at an altitude of 2,250 feet.

Although I had never made a landfall on the island, I was reasonably familiar with its contours and location, for I had flown past it at low altitude by helicopter to and from the icebreaker *South Wind,* a Coast Guard cutter on which I had lived for a time. These flights occurred when the ship was northwest of the island in the Ross Sea and heading south toward McMurdo Sound, where its mission was to break ice in preparation for resupplying McMurdo Station by tanker and freighter.

Also, I had had several occasions to fly by helicopter to Cape Bird and Cape Crozier. So I had seen Beaufort in the round, as it were. There were two further reasons for my being aware of it. It's the only island of its size close to Ross Island, and it's one of the most important breeding grounds for penguins in the whole area. As a matter of fact, it's a specially protected area because of its Emperor and Adelie penguin rookeries. Trespass and overflight are forbidden by international agreement.

There's nothing remarkable about Beaufort Island, yet because it's in the Antarctic it shares the great beauty one so often encounters there. I remember flying to the *South Wind* one mild midnight. A broad blue sky flecked by transparent cirrus clouds mirrored in the unruffled indigo sea. A milky patch across the horizon. Beaufort, lying in the middle distance, looking gentle, almost tender, in the low sun, its iceslope resembling a pearly silken animal skin, its icecliff gleaming like floodlit chalk. In the foreground the tiny vessel steaming toward an opening between two large icefields suggesting crinkled lily pads. And a wonderful sweetness everywhere. I tell you, such scenes have the power of haunting you.

Now, Cape Bird juts out northward from the rest of Ross Island. Seen from the air, it suggests a turtle's neck and head. On its west is Wohlschlag Bay, an indentation of the Sound. On the east, facing the Ross Sea, is Lewis Bay. It's the latter which especially concerns us, for the northern iceslopes of Mt. Erebus descend to meet this bay with a high icecliff. The distance between Beaufort Island and the icecliff is roughly thirty statute miles.

I can now go on telling you my story.

We were turning westward to begin the completion of our second orbit. The DC10, which had been steadily losing altitude, was at around 7,000 feet.

"There you go! There's some land ahead!" Kelly Duncan, the copilot, said.

He was right. The land was due west of us. Staring past the complex instrument panel, we studied it through the front double windshield. We were all relieved to see it, whatever it was. It had been hard on the cockpit crew, and on me as well, to have no visibility for so long. But the visibility was still poor and we couldn't make out whether the land was a cape or a peninsula or an island. What was it?

Sam Ogilvie, the captain, said with assurance, "Great! It's part of Victoria Land, on the western side of the Sound. We're right on target!"

A moment or two later, at about 6,500 feet, reaching for the nav control, he said, "I'll arm the nav again," meaning that he was going to put the DC10 back on the computerized flight track.

And then Kelly Duncan told the forecaster, "We're now at 6,000, descending to 2,000 and we're VMC."

There was a change of visitors to the cockpit.

The cockpit crew were very cocky now. But something disturbed me. I wasn't as sure as Ogilvie that the land was part of Victoria Land. There was something vaguely familiar about it.

At around 5,000 feet we were heading due south again, having completed our second orbit. And now something else troubled me. *There was absolutely nothing visible ahead of us*. No land, no sea, no ice, no sky, no shadows, no horizon. Whiteness, milkiness. Like having milk fill all the vitreous of your eyeballs. Up? Down? Slow? Fast? Nothing familiar to us. A cockpit hovering in nowhere, the everywhere of potential disaster.

I knew the Sound landmarks. We should have been seeing at least some of them. I felt certain we were embracing a whiteout. When I told Ogilvie what I thought, he derided the notion. I wondered what he knew about a whiteout. I urged him to pull up until we could make sure where we were.

"Not to worry, professor," he said confidently. "I *know* where we are. Everything's a-okay."

His response convinced me he had no conception of how dangerous a whiteout can be, especially to an airborne plane.

Still feeling there was something familiar about the land we had sighted, I leaned over Kelly Duncan's shoulder and craned to have another look, this time through his windshield, the starboard (right) one. It was uncomfortable to do. I had to cram into the small space between the flight engineer's seat and Duncan's. And between Duncan's seat and Ogilvie's was a long control and instrument box, which I had to avoid hitting. Kelly Duncan also studied the land.

The visibility (which in that weather kept changing for us because we were in rapid forward and downward motion), was a bit better now. I could make out that the land was an island. I could see its sheer, ribbed, bare cliffs thrust some 2,000 feet, I judged, out of the dense blue pack ice dappled mildly with sunlight.

An island? Considering our position, which was just north of Ross Island, I asked myself, "What island can it be?" There was only one possible answer, yet my mind balked even though the island's eastern contours were now tantalizingly familiar. And then in a rush its identity came to me. I would have recognized it as Beaufort much sooner if I had seen it from above or from the west, for I was more familiar with those views, especially the western one.

How glad I was to see it after all the cloud cover we had been dealing with! Which is an indication of how insane one's brain can be in certain circumstances. It took three or four seconds longer before the true meaning of what I had just seen (the island had slipped out of view), swept over me with a flash of panic which pulsed through my body and made my feet feel as heavy as lead.

Beaufort Island was west of us. But it should have been east if we were safely over the Sound, as Sam Ogilvie thought. This meant that we were on a direct collision course with a lower slope of Mt. Erebus.

We were moving south at 259 knots, near our minimum speed, or about 280 miles an hour, close to five miles a minute. We were about twenty miles from the Lewis Bay icecliff, I thought. If we continued on our present course we had no more than four to five minutes before impact.

There was still absolutely nothing to be seen ahead of us.

How do you sound calm and urgent at the same time? That's what I tried to do. I was standing just aft of the control and instrument box.

"Captain," I said, "that land we sighted is Beaufort Island. I've just recognized it. We're on the wrong side of it. On the east instead of the west. If we were over the Sound we'd see the western side, a *low* iceslope, not high, bare cliffs. We're dangerously off course.''

Ogilvie studied the chart, then said, ''You're wrong, professor. It's Dunlop Island, on the western side of the Sound.''

''But Dunlop is only about a hundred feet high,'' I countered. ''Beaufort is at least 2,000. That was a high island we passed, with bare cliffs. If you doubt me, let's go back and have another look.''

''Professor, let me tell you something. You don't know a damn thing about this plane's technology. Our nav system is the finest in the world. We fly between Auckland and Honolulu and are off target at destination by no more than a mile either side. We're over the Sound.''

''I tell you that was Beaufort,'' I said. ''We're in a whiteout. That's why we can't see Erebus, can't see a horizon, have no definition, can't see anything. We're on a direct collision course with Erebus! Let's pull up and get out of this!''

''Nonsense, professor,'' Ogilvie said coldly. ''There's absolutely nothing directly ahead of us. The radar screen is empty.''

''Then there's something wrong with the radar!'' I said spontaneously with great excitement.

So much for my trying to sound calm.

Sam Ogilvie laughed. Then Kelly Duncan and Don Player laughed, and then the two flight deck visitors. There was a chorus of laughter, it seemed to me. I felt my cheeks reddening.

Finally grasping the hopelessness of my situation—to Ogilvie, and probably to Duncan and Player as well, I was obviously an outsider, a Yank intruder on a Yank-made craft, on a Kiwi flight commemorating a Yank, and I was an ignoramus regarding the DC10's technology, and even worse: a coward—I abruptly left the flight deck and walked rapidly toward the rear of the plane.

The passengers, thinking perhaps they were about to reach their journey's climax, looked radiant. And how innocent they looked! It struck me they were like communicants in the care of high priests in the cockpit, or like children being led to some dark place by a pied piper. Some were taking photos through windows. Others were chatting over cocktails. One or two were writing in notebooks. An older man and a young woman were kissing passionately, which seemed to me remarkable behavior in the circumstances. I hoped they weren't Americans. No one was napping that I could see even though there were elderly people aboard.

Afraid that my stride might cause panic, I slowed down to what I thought was a casual yet businesslike walk. In the main cabin three or four people each tried to engage me in conversation, among them the woman I had known as Pamela or April Mansfield and who seemed finally to recognize me.

"In a moment, please, in a moment," I said to each without pausing, pretending now not to know her.

I ought to have been more careful about what I said, even during a crisis. Those words would rise to haunt me later.

Luckily the tail section was empty. The passengers had congregated in the main cabin. I was able to do my thing in private. Although I realized that my time had almost run out, and though my hands trembled in their eagerness to work and my brain was feverish with the desire to save itself, I urged myself to do everything very slowly, like a lazy bureaucratic clerk soldiering on the job. I unzipped my orange survival bag and, in slow motion as in a nightmare, withdrew the heavy woolen shirt, which I put on over my lightweight one and madras tie, letting the tails hang free. Then I drew forth my black pile-lined cap and put it on.

When I saw that my hands were beginning to hurry and fumble—they were the servants not only of my mind but of my frightened, heavily beating heart—I somehow found a place from which to say, "Joel, be graceful. You're probably dead anyway, so you've got nothing to lose but your self-respect, your only real capital."

Next I donned my heavy, very red parka, the hood of which was stiffened with wire and edged with wolverine fur.

To my surprise, one of the rear lavatory doors opened and a boy of about thirteen or fourteen came out, tall, rangy, dark-haired, gray-eyed, rather handsome in an English way, very intelligent looking and seeming mature for his age except that he absently checked his fly with his left hand. Instead of showing surprise at seeing me in Antarctic clothes, he responded with a clean, charming smile and looked very pleased, as if he thought I was part of a little show that was about to be put on for him and his fellow tourists. He observed me in silence. I was silent too.

Perhaps I'm giving a false impression in describing him minutely in this way. Actually I noticed him only fleetingly. Yet later I remembered him painfully well.

Trying to disregard him, and knowing that the human head loses a great deal of heat because of the large number of blood vessels in it, I put the hood up over my cap, attempting to arrange it so as to keep my side vision. Last, but extremely important—for I feared a fire would break out and with burned hands your chances of survival are almost non-existent—I began putting on my double gloves, the khaki woolen liner and black leather shell. I avoided using my bear paws, because, being huge mitts, they would prevent me from effectively employing my hands.

At that moment, a tall, slender woman in her late thirties or early forties, also dark-haired, also gray-eyed, and resembling the boy in his look of intelligence—she was beautiful, with marvelous high cheekbones and a lovely clean jawline—stepped out of an adjoining lavatory without seeing me. Her figure was trim, youthful, and she wore beautifully tailored pearl-gray slacks. Her mannish white shirt was tucked inside them. She adjusted her hair with an attractive, characteristically feminine gesture, and although she hadn't noticed me, I felt that the gesture was meant for me. I was immediately suffused with a pleasant emotion, one that felt strangely like love. Later I would be convinced somehow, and I still am, that the moment in which she walked out like that, stirring a life-enhancing feeling in me, played a role in my survival.

And then she saw me in my flaming red parka, my red hood edged with long-haired wolverine fur, my black gloves which I was just putting on, and she gasped as if in horror. Her long-fingered dry hand went instinctively to her mouth to censor a scream. I saw terror in her eyes.

That's the last I remember of the flight.

7

I awoke to find myself covered with snow. My gloved hands were inside my parka sleeves. My long, parka hood tunnel was closed. I withdrew my hands and opened the hood. Raising myself on an elbow, I saw I was on an iceslope above a bay full of pack ice. The sky was milky. A wind was blowing downslope.

I was convinced I was one of a party of nine men who had gone exploring and been caught in a blizzard. I seemed to remember hiking toward our camp or where, in the poor visibility, we took our camp to be, and finding ourselves on a steep iceslope without crampons and with only a couple of ice axes among us. The storm worsened, making the visibility really bad. I must have headed for a large sastrugus, in the lee of which I had hoped to find some shelter from the raging wind.

A sastrugus is a wind-caused wave or ridge in ice. Sastrugi come in all sizes and in bunches and are parallel to the direction of the prevailing wind.

Heading for the sastrugus was the last I remembered. I must have lost consciousness or fallen asleep immediately after lying down. But before that I had unconsciously drawn my gloved hands inside the parka sleeves and closed my hood tunnel. I had been covered by snowdrift. I surmised I had slept four or five hours, long enough for the storm to subside. As far as I could tell, I was free of frostbite.

Thinking our camp was further down the iceslope, I decided to head there. But when I tried to stand I discovered I was too stiff to do it, so I started downslope on my hands and knees. My body felt sore all over. I was exhausted, weak and very hungry.

Then I saw three men at a distance, striding away from me. The sun, which had just come out from behind clouds and which hung typically low above the horizon, was directly over the bay. The thin cirrus clouds still in front of it caused giant golden spokes to stream from it like immense flares. The men cast wavering long shadows onto the rough, wavy, glistening ice with its patches of powder snow.

But although they were in silhouette, I could make out details. Yellow parkas, baggy, oversized, heavy woolen trousers—clothes worn by Kiwis. (American parkas are red; the Americans didn't wear such trousers.) They carried alpine rope and ice axes and wore crampons. I assumed they were the three mountaineers of the survival training team at Scott Base and that they had come to look for us. I wondered where my companions were and if they were all right.

I called "Hey!" three or four times but my voice was weak and the wind strong and gusty. At first I was too embarrassed to shout "Help!" It seemed a melodramatic thing to do, and I was in pretty good shape, I thought. But when I saw them leaving me behind rapidly with long, crampon-strengthened, downslope, powerful strides, I summoned up strength and shouted "Help!" a couple of times, my voice cracking the second time.

One of them glanced back but couldn't see me. I waved to get his attention. He told the others, and all three hurried upslope, looking awkward now in their crampons, as if they had swollen feet. I could make out that they were young, still in their twenties.

"Hi. I'm Joel Stevenson. Very glad to see you," I said, managing a smile.

"I don't believe this! Do you realize you're the only survivor?" one of them said urgently.

"What! All eight dead?" I cried.

"What did you say?" he asked quickly.

I repeated slowly, "All eight dead?"

They looked strangely at me and at each other.

Then another one said quietly, "You mean 248 dead, don't you?"

"What?" I asked.

After a moment I asked, "Why are yawl here? Did you come to look for us?"

"We were sent to check for survivors."

"Why Kiwis?"

"It was a Kiwi plane. This is dangerous ice. We're mountaineers. We've had ice experience."

My mind was too tired to grapple with the weird questions they raised.

They were dressed similarly, were about the same height and were heavily bearded. If it weren't for the difference in beard color I might absentmindedly have taken them for triplets. They squatted near me.

"Thank God there's at least *one* survivor!" the one with the blond beard said.

"It's a bloody miracle!" another one said.

"A double miracle!" said the third, who had a red beard.

"You very cold? Been shivering violently? Been falling?" one of them asked.

"No."

"*Feel* cold?"

"Naturally."

He asked this because in deep hypothermia you no longer shiver, no longer feel cold.

"I doubt I'm suffering from hypothermia," I said.

"Any serious injuries? Been coughing blood? Anything broken?" the brown beard asked.

"Not as far as I know."

"Why you crawling then?"

"I tried to stand. Couldn't. Too stiff."

"Any bad frostbite?"

"I don't think so."

They peered at my face, checked my ears, found no frostbite and kept telling each other how extraordinary it was.

"How come you're wearing these clothes?" the red beard asked.

"What's wrong with them?"

"Why aren't you wearing summer clothes?"

I laughed.

"Why aren't *you* wearing them?" I responded.

They stared at me. I stared back, trying to comprehend why he had asked such a question.

"Think you can stand and walk with help?"

"Yes."

"Should we try to carry you?"

"Better to walk, I think."

"We have a couple of hundred yards to go."

"Let's give it a try."

"Good man," said one of them.

"A helluva lot better than you," another one joshed.

All three laughed. Their laughter was infectious. I joined them. I was aware of their alert, fast eyes, extremely clean, the eyes of persons in the best of physical shape. I thought, "People on excellent terms with their bodies: self-assured, a bit authoritative."

"What time is it?" I asked.

One of them glanced at his watch. "Almost twelve fifteen. What time you have?"

"Couple of minutes past two," I replied. I studied the second hand. "My watch stopped."

"That's a little after one, Ross Island time," he said. "New Zealand is on daylight. That was the time of the crash."

"What crash? Where are we?" I asked.

"Northern side of Erebus."

"Is that Cape Bird?"

"Yes."

I could see Beaufort Island.

The blond-bearded one said to the black hand-radio with the fat stubby antenna which hung from his neck, ''Gentle Eight, this is the Kiwi search team. We have found one survivor. Joel Stevenson. Repeat: we have found one survivor. Joel Stevenson. Crawling on hands and knees. But he thinks he can stand and walk with help. True condition unknown. We may have a case of deep hypothermia. Please lower the cabin temperature. We'll warm him ourselves on board. Better have an ambulance at McMurdo. Will you meet us at the rendezvous? Soon as possible, please.''

He was referring to the action of hypothermia, often misunderstood. The body's core temperature, vital to life, begins to drop. A drop of only ten or twelve degrees can cause death. The body begins to restrict the flow of blood to the extremities, ready to sacrifice them to maintain life. It is the extremities that grow colder first, so their blood vessels become constricted and accept less blood. In deep hypothermia a too-sudden warming of the whole body can be fatal. Blood is drawn from the core to the very cold extremities, is chilled by them and is then returned to the core, where it chills the core further, causing collapse and death.

''Well, let's get you to the helo,'' the red-bearded one said.

Helo (pronounced *heelo*; for helicopter) was a term commonly used in the Ross Island region.

They helped me to my feet. Two of them gripped my arms. We walked downslope. Occasionally there was a reverberating roar as part of the icecliff calved off into the pack-iced bay, hurling up high plumes of seawater like steam. Nor was Erebus still. Now and then it grunted with a bass so profound it shook the icescape.

''We looked all over,'' the brown-bearded one said. ''We looked only for survivors. We didn't try to find the two black boxes. We just meant to go in and out. In a break of the weather. It's been very bad here. Where'd you come from?''

I stopped, turned around and pointed.

''There's a large sastrugus up there. I must have fallen in the lee of it and gotten covered by snowdrift.''

"You were lucky not to fall into a crevasse. This is crevasse country. How long were you in the snow?"

"Four or five hours, I think."

"More like twenty-three."

"No," I said.

"When did you last shave?"

"This morning."

"Feel your stubble. You shaved yesterday, mate. What day is this?"

"The twenty-eighth."

"It's the thirtieth."

"No," I said.

"True, mate, true."

"Look at the wreckage. Doesn't it mean anything to you?" red beard asked.

I said nothing.

Later he told me I behaved as if I hadn't heard the question, and that although I glanced occasionally at the blackened wreckage nearby, I didn't seem to respond as if I saw it, nor did I seem to smell the penetrating odor of aviation fuel. He said I was an extraordinary sight on all fours, like an animal just out of its burrow, my head and back snowcovered, the vast sweep of the iceslope and its antler-furry powder snow behind me, the barren, black ribs of the Fang, reaching to 10,000 feet and even higher, just barely showing above the slope, the dreadful, blackened, fuel-stench wreckage on my right, behind me a large crevasse which I had luckily avoided. Erebus's craters could not be seen from where we were.

For my part, during their appraisal of me I saw that something very serious was troubling them. They looked haunted, spooked at times, on the verge of tears or of being sick, as if they had just seen something horrible.

I could feel the stiffness in my body loosening as we proceeded downslope. The helo, a Huey, was already hovering as we neared the small, natural flat place in the iceslope which served as its landing pad.

8

It turned out I was wrong about the landing pad. Apparently I had imagined its existence. The helo didn't try to land, it just hovered close to the iceslope. It was easy for the mountaineers to climb aboard. But I was too stiff. I had to be almost lifted aboard by them, with help from the frowning, clean-shaven young American crewman in the cabin. I caught a glimpse of the American pilots staring at me from the cockpit.

The cabin temperature had already dropped. I belted myself into a seat on the port side, taking care to secure the belt on the outside of my parka, not the inside. It was easy to overlook what seemed like a small detail, only to discover that your life could depend on it. Two men I had known had burned to death in a helo crash a couple of years before. People on either side of them had gotten out. Why hadn't they? It was suspected they had gotten overheated in the cabin, unzipped their parkas, belted themselves, and zipped up their parkas again when an open hatch had chilled the cabin. When the emergency came, they hadn't been able to get at their seat belts under the zipped-up parkas in time.

The Kiwis now checked my hands and again were surprised to find no signs of frostbite. They insisted on examining my feet. I let them remove my boots and socks. They looked perplexed when they found no frostbite. We had to communicate by shouting because the engine and rotors were so noisy. One of the Kiwis asked the crewman to warm the cabin. They wanted to speak with me, but without communication helmets it was too difficult, we would soon have become hoarse. Anyway, I was on the verge of trembling with hunger. Was there something I could eat? Rummaging in a survival bag, one of the mountaineers fished out a chocolate bar. The crewman handed me a cup of hot coffee. He and the Kiwis kept staring at me. My hand trembling, I bit the chocolate, trying not to wolf it, trying to hide my hunger, ashamed of it for some reason.

I recalled reading about the extreme hunger of Robert Falcon Scott and his companions during the farthest southing of his Discovery Expedition at the turn of the century, when Edward Wilson and Ernest Shackleton regularly had food nightmares: they were sitting at a table loaded with food, but their arms were tied; they picked up a dish, which slipped and broke; they lifted a bit of food to their mouths, and fell off a precipice; they spent all their time shouting at waiters who ignored them; by the time a sirloin of beef reached them it was only ashes.

The party's thoughts and conversations were inexorably interwoven with the subject of food except for a half hour or so after supper. The worst time was during the day's march, the manhauling of sledges on the immense, crevassed expanse under the tremendous blue sky, so dry the blue suggested black. The matter of food was reduced to minute, trivial details. How many paces did you make per minute? How many before lunch? You began to count. And to lose count. What was left in the pemmican bag? Exactly how much could be used for tonight's hoosh? How much pemmican was there on the ship, back at Hut Point on Ross Island? What gorgeous streaks of yellow fat the ship's pemmican contained! How marvelous the fresh seal meat on the ship had been, and the thick soup, and the thicker porridge! But what was such food when compared with London restaurant fare? You remembered declining a particularly succulent dish in England. What an extraordinary thing to have done! You must have been a very different person back in those mythical days.

Robert Falcon Scott was an Antarctic hero of mine, a greater one to me even than Richard E. Byrd despite the fact that Byrd and I were both Virginians. Inasmuch as Scott will play a strange and complex, even mysterious, role in my story, let me introduce you to him. He was a Royal Navy man. He had become a cadet at thirteen, a midshipman at fifteen and a full lieutenant at twenty-three. He was reticent, sensitive, intelligent and moody.

Early in November of 1911 he and four companions (Wilson, Bowers, Oates and Evans) began an immense trek towards the Pole, for the most part manhauling their sledge. Scott hoped to be the discoverer of the Pole. But when he reached the Pole on January 18, 1912 he found he had been bested by Roald Amundsen, the Norwegian explorer, by only about a month. The return journey of Scott and his companions was beset by illness, hunger and blizzards. Evans died in mid-February at the foot of the Beardmore Glacier. In mid-March, Oates walked out of the tent into a blizzard in the hope of saving those more physically fit, and was never seen again. Scott, Wilson and Bowers pitched their final camp only eleven miles from One Ton Depot on the Ross Ice Shelf (about a hundred and fifty miles from what is now McMurdo Station) but were hopelessly blizzarded in.

In the great naval tradition of keeping logs under the most adverse conditions, Scott kept writing his journal until close to the end. Also, he wrote several letters to friends and colleagues explaining what had gone wrong and crediting his sledging companions with noble behavior under heartbreaking conditions. He referred to himself and his companions as dead men but showed no self-pity and little self-concern in either the journals or the letters. His outlook remained broad to the end.

In mid-November of 1912 a search party discovered the tent, containing his body and those of Wilson and Bowers, as well as his records, letters and journals. On the sledge were thirty-five pounds of geological specimens, gathered on the Beardmore Glacier, which the party had declined to abandon despite the fact that for a long time they had been exhausting themselves in manhauling.

Now on the helo, hoarding my piece of chocolate, I sucked on it and wanted to ask for more but was ashamed to. The wrapper on the chocolate said Ghirardelli. Where had the Kiwis gotten it? I hadn't seen Ghirardelli chocolate at McMurdo—or, for that matter, anywhere else in the Antarctic. It reminded me of Ghirardelli Square in San Francisco, of the chocolate factory there, where you could stare at vats of the stuff being stirred by machines, and of the candy shop in the front of the factory, where I had watched grownups eating immense sundaes in broad daylight. I recalled views of the bay, of Alcatraz, of Golden Gate Park, the opera house, Union Square. In my memory the city was misted over by a golden fog but I wasn't homesick for it. Though I had just come through a survival ordeal, I was happy to be in Antarctica.

I went over our flight track in my mind. We had flown out over Lewis Bay, then gone west and crossed the saddle between Mounts Erebus and Bird, which at its lowest point is about 2,500 feet high. We had continued westward over Wohlschlag Bay, then headed south down the eastern side of McMurdo Sound, hugging the shore of Ross Island, that stretch of icecliffs, glacial snouts and bare capes which is probably the most historic in the whole continent. Sipping the coffee, I studied the icescape outside my hatch.

Huge crevasses like machete blades. We could have fallen into them and never been found. More crevasses, large, small, part of the glaciers sliding eternally down Erebus. Cape Royds, with Shackleton's hut, in which I had lived, partly to observe the Adelies in the world's southernmost penguin rookery. Remembered views from the hut: the black cape's seaside end; the guano-tan rookery on some last hills to the left; the lilac-white Sound beyond; the Western Mountains; and some piedmont glaciers at the eastern edge of Victoria Land, stretching and gleaming along the horizon and looking unbelievably close in the crystal air that deceived you about distances.

The feather-strewn north shore of Pony Lake. Dead Adelie chicks whose stomachs had been pierced by skua beaks. A few dead adult penguins. Some dead skuas. (The skua is a powerful, aggressive, gull-like bird which partially feeds on penguin eggs and chicks.) Some skeletons of both. The shore's rocks and soil were thinly crusted over in places by a whitish substance that I took to be salt from evaporated spume and scud blown inland from the Sound when the latter was icefree.

The Adelie eyes looked unreal, jewels stuck in black velvet. Their beaks were mottled brown, like tortoise shell. Pale blue eggs. Gray chicks with spindly necks, whose heads wobbled uncertainly as the beaks opened wide for a meal of regurgitated fish and krill. In the rookery were hard, guano-crusted trails between black boulders. Some of the birds nested high up on boulder conglomerate that suggested giant loaves of bread mashed upon each other. From places in the rookery you could see the birds backgrounded by Erebus the volcano, a white plume flying from its crest.

Shackleton's hut was said to be haunted ever since about 1915. It was claimed you could hear the sound of hobnailed boots at night. Dankness, yes. Smells of a stable and fishy rot, yes. Cans of arrowroot, ox tongue, scarlet runners, kidney soup, calavances, gooseberries, tripe, cod roes, yes. And other paraphernalia of the old days. But I had failed to encounter ghosts or nightmares or interesting dreams. In fact, I hadn't even dreamed in the hut, as far as I could remember.

Cape Evans below me now—and Scott's last hut, to which he had never returned from the polar trek, the hut I had also lived in (and I had observed the skuas nearby in the world's southernmost rookery). The hut was crowded. I felt crowded in it, lying in a sleeping bag on a cot. My head was close to two cases of Fry's Pure Concentrated Cocoa. Everything was more or less as it was left at the end. Lying on my side, I stared at rows of enameled metalware hanging from hooks; at many chipped pitchers; at the galley stove and chimney, which had rusted badly. All the colors blended: mahogany, mauve, rust. I heard sounds as of distant thunder. The sky was still cloudless. I wondered if the cannonading was caused by snowslides on the Erebus slopes or by gurgling of magma in the great throat.

I was much aware of Erebus then. Hiking toward Land's End, as I drew near, the glare of Erebus's skirts, slopes, falls and glaciers became almost unbearable despite my double-gradient sunglasses. The falls and glaciers suggested thousands of brilliantly illuminated lily pads. I was increasingly aware of the aesthetic realities, source and chief of which was Erebus: stark, beautiful, commanding. Erebus is a shield volcano, with broadly rounded, gently sloping sides, not conical like Mt. Fuji (Fuji's magma is more viscous, which is why a cone formed). In size Erebus is one of the world's major volcanoes, with an elevation greater than that of Fuji or Etna or Vesuvius.

I finished the chocolate and coffee, and dozed off. When I awoke I remembered everything: Beaufort Island, the whiteout, my argument with Ogilvie about our position with regard to Beaufort, the laughter in the cockpit at my expense, my hurrying to the rear of the plane, the boy who emerged from the lavatory, then the woman. The notion of eight companions lost in a blizzard was now a fading nightmare.

"Did the DC10 crash?" I asked the blond Kiwi.

He nodded. I felt horror rising in me.

"Many survivors?"

He raised a forefinger, pointed it at me.

"Only me?"

He nodded.

Raising his thumb, he glanced at his companions. They too understood I had regained my memory.

"Why *me*?" I wondered in horror. "Why *me*? Why was *I* spared?"

I was furious with Ogilvie. But he had killed himself too. He had depended on his radar. Surely the radar hadn't malfunctioned. If it had, he would have known it. But then why had the screen not shown the Erebus terrain? And now I felt sorry for him, for Kelly Duncan, for the rest of the crew, and guilty toward them all. All those people killed. I felt contaminated, contagious, nasty. How *had* I survived the impact? And the cold?

I felt ashamed, as if I had done something dishonorable. And I felt guilty toward Pamela Mansfield, toward the other passengers in the DC10's main cabin who had tried at the last moment to speak with me, toward the beautiful woman in the plane's tail section who had stared at me in horror. I recalled Pamela's refusing to recognize me in the dining room of the Gateway Lodge, and my pretending not to know her on the DC10. That she had refused to know me until just before the disaster added to my guilt. It reminded me of how badly I had behaved toward her one night in Warner's Hotel in Christchurch.

Two voices were arguing in my head.

"He didn't share his gear!" one said. "And now all are dead! Except him."

"There wasn't enough time! He had only enough to help himself!"

"The passengers asked to speak with him. 'In a moment,' he said slyly, knowing they were about to die. And he was sly about where he was rushing—to save *his* skin."

"The captain refused pointblank to heed his warnings! No one could have done better under the circumstances!"

"Mind of a murderer!"

"But the dreadful circumstances!"

"He'll pay a dreadful price!"

"Oh Pamela," I thought, "how could I have behaved so badly toward you in my room that night? But can you see that you were ridiculous too? Or was it only I? I know that only I behaved badly, and in that awful way. Sexually."

While I was wrestling with this private dialogue, the helo landed near the Chalet, and there was Kate Waterhouse, waiting for me in Navy fatigues and staring strangely at me, as if I wasn't real. It was as if I had gone rummaging in the house of the dead, become a citizen there, and then wandered out ghostlike to disturb the real world. I was hurt by her glance. I wanted to be taken back, to belong. But I was wrong—her tone was warm, almost motherly.

"I'm so grateful you're back," she said softly. "It must be impossible for you to make any sense of what happened."

"I feel . . ."

"Oh, I'm so glad to see you!"

The blond mountaineer stepped to my side and said, "May

I—I have something urgent to tell you. May I see you later? We have to be debriefed now.''

I glanced at Kate.

''If you keep it to a half-hour,'' she said to him. ''He'll be in the Dispensary.''

''I appreciate that,'' he said.

''Please get into the ambulance,'' she said to me.

I guessed she thought I might be too badly hurt to make it on my own to the Dispensary, which was in the middle of the station, downtown, you might say, just across a broad scarred path from the Personnel Building, which housed the chow hall. Whenever I thought of that hilly, rocky, cindery path crossed by the stream you jumped over, I recalled the silvery rivulets streaming down it from the summer meltwater flowing from the snows above the base. How gay that shining silver looked! Whenever I thought of the Dispensary I remembered the heavy double door, like warehouse refrigerator doors, at the entrance on a wooden platform above several wooden steps, and the sign ordering you to leave your boots in the anteroom to spare the Dispensary's linoleum floor from the ravages of volcanic grit.

But before I could enter the ambulance three figures came up, seemingly from nowhere. Each one of them embraced me: Dave Breslin (the USARP rep (representative) at McMurdo), Billy Blackburn, and Captain Schuyler Westcott, the commander of the Navy task force. They seemed on the verge of tears.

''You old hummer,'' Blackburn said.

''Good to see you alive, Doc,'' said Westcott, staring at me.

Breslin, a thin, tall, dark-bearded man, was frowning heavily.

''Why are you wearing Antarctic clothes?'' Westcott asked. ''Did you think the plane might crash?''

''I had some worries about it, yes.''

''Billy here has told me about the irregularities. Why did you crash?''

''I don't know.''

''Why were you off course?''

''I don't know. The radar didn't show anything in front of us, yet it didn't malfunction.''

"How do you explain your survival?"

"I can't. Are you asking me to justify it?"

"*What*! For God's sake, Doc!"

"You hummer, I warned you not to take that flight," Blackburn said. "Why did you have to find out what it was like?"

An enlisted man drove Kate and me to the rear of the Dispensary. When we were inside I saw it was empty. She asked, "How do you feel?" I said I was sore, weak, hungry.

"What's this about your being confused and disoriented?"

"I lost my memory, part of it anyway, for a while."

"Do you remember everything now?"

"Yes."

"Good! I'm going to examine you. Please undress."

She checked my blood pressure, pulse, listened to my back and chest, examined my hands and feet, tested my eye reflexes, knee reflexes. She said my back had several large bruises. There were also three bruises on my thighs.

"It's extraordinary," she said. "You seem fine. I mean relatively speaking. I want you here for observation for a while. You be good to yourself. Understand?"

There were four beds. I put on a hospital gown and got into the bed farthest from the windows. An attendant brought me a bowl of oatmeal and a glass of warm milk Kate had ordered.

"You're starving me," I complained to her.

She said, "Joel, it feels so good to see you alive." She was blushing. "I didn't realize how much you mean to me until I thought you were dead."

Too surprised and embarrassed to know what to say, I spooned the oatmeal.

As she was leaving, Billy Blackburn came in and sat on my bed. When I mentioned earlier that he was handsome, athletic and had a strong neck and full throat, I should have added that his ears were a bit like flags and that he sometimes wore a vague expression. But I knew he was much more intelligent than he looked, and anyway, I loved him. I recalled the evening in the wardroom when he had warned me about Flight Five Zero, and his singing then, and the sweepers, and Hank Dana's slide to second. The evening seemed prehistoric. I felt I would never, ever, be the person I had been then. I had suffered a tremendous air change, the chief sign of which, for me, was a great, restless, nagging guilt.

9

Before Billy Blackburn and I could chat, Schuyler Westcott and Dave Breslin came in, drew up chairs and joined us. Westcott, wearing Navy fatigues, was about my height and weight. He was a precise man, with wavy brown hair parted exactly in the middle, as if with a micrometer. His jaw was lean, his eyebrows were very hairy.

"Dr. Gould wants to know if he can visit you," he said to me.

"Of course he may."

"The Senator too?"

"But of course."

Gould was Laurence McKinley Gould, who had been science leader and second-in-command of Richard E. Byrd's first Antarctic expedition. The Senator was Harry F. Byrd, Jr. of Virginia, Byrd's nephew. Gould and I were good friends. I had met the Senator once or twice. I remembered now that Gould and Senator Byrd had come to McMurdo to mark the fiftieth anniversary of Richard E. Byrd's south polar flight by retracing the explorer's route in a C130.

"Did they go to the Pole?" I asked.

"The flight was scratched because of the SAR," Westcott said. "We had a little ceremony at the statue. They're returning to Christchurch tomorrow."

SAR, rhyming with "far," stands for "Search and Rescue." Byrd's statue was near the Chalet.

"Did you know you were off course?" Westcott asked me abruptly.

"Toward the end. We were on the wrong side of Beaufort Island. East of it instead of west. I warned Ogilvie—the captain—

but he ignored me. He mistook Beaufort for Dunlop, a much lower island the other side of the Sound."

"And you say nothing showed up on the radar as you closed in on the mountain?"

"Ogilvie said there was nothing. I didn't see the screen myself."

"Could the radar have been malfunctioning?"

"He gave no indication it was. On the contrary. We had a whiteout. I warned him about it. It seemed to mean nothing to him. We had no contact with the Ice Tower. I warned him we were on a collision course with Erebus."

"What did he say?"

"He said, 'Nonsense, there's absolutely nothing ahead of us. The radar screen is empty.' "

"He said that?"

"It's a direct quote."

"How can the radar show nothing? What do you make of it, Billy?"

"The pilots would have known if it was malfunctioning," Blackburn said. He laughed. "Maybe something spooked it. Let's hope the black boxes are found. They should give us some answers."

"And so what did *you* say?" Westcott asked me.

" 'Then there's something wrong with the radar!' "

"He must have loved that," Blackburn said.

"He laughed at me. So did the others in the cockpit. At that point I quit arguing. I went to the rear of the plane and put on Antarctic clothes."

"Were you sure you were going to crash?" Westcott asked.

"Pretty sure."

"Did you expect to survive?"

"I don't know. I just did what I could."

"Did you choose the tail section deliberately?"

"I knew I had the best chance there."

"People are saying it was probably pilot error," Westcott said.

"That's the first thing they always think of," said Blackburn.

"With a first-rate inertial navigation system on board? Not likely. Scapegoat the pilots, they can't talk back, they're conveniently dead."

"Hmm," said Westcott. "Why did this have to happen on *my* tour of duty?"

After a pause he said, "The news about you being the only survivor is already out. Instant celebrity. Hope you don't let it turn your head."

Another pause.

"Doc, Kate says you're in great shape—physically," he said. "But you've had a bad shock. Heavy. Dave here thinks maybe we should ship you out to the States so you can get some professional counselling. I hear survivors often need it. Some of the commercial airlines now offer it to their crash employees. What do you think?"

"It would be very hard on my project but if I thought I needed psychiatric help I'd go without a protest," I said. "I'm okay. I'll be back at work in a day or two."

"Let's think about it," Breslin said.

"I tell you I'm all right," I said.

He said nothing more, just kept frowning in the way I had noticed at the helo pad. I took him for a typical D.C. bureaucrat, eager to unload me to cover his ass should anything happen to me. I felt menaced by his silence.

"If it was up to me I'd hang onto you. A lot of people are going to want to interview you," said Westcott.

He and Breslin left after a few more minutes.

"If they try to ship you out you can fight 'em," Blackburn said. "You got clout. Gould will back you. Won't he?"

"I hope so," I said.

I asked Blackburn questions about the SAR. Who can plumb the mind's recesses? From having been amnesiac about what had happened to Flight Five Zero, and unable to see the wreckage when I looked at it, now I was thirsty for every detail. What I learned was:

Mac Center had expected to sight Five Zero first at 1,500 feet above the Sound at around 1 P.M. local time. When the DC10 failed to show up, it was thought the captain might have flown westward for sightseeing purposes to take advantage of the clear weather over the Dry Valleys. Mac Center tried to reach Five Zero on several radio frequencies and asked airborne planes in the area to make contact with it. Checks were also made with outlying camps in the hope that somebody had spotted it.

At around 2 P.M. Mac Center radioed Kiwi Airways in Auckland that Five Zero hadn't been heard from for more than an hour and that consequently the station's SAR planes were being put on standby. Helos in the field were recalled to McMurdo. A Kiwi survival training team in the Dry Valleys (the same that rescued me) was alerted to return to Scott Base. A U.S. Air Force C141 Starlifter heading for Christchurch was asked to overfly the planned return route of Five Zero.

At 4:30 a full SAR mission was launched. But the weather balked. Eventually two C130's and two helicopters searched the general vicinity of Beaufort Island and Lewis Bay, the last known position given by Five Zero. They covered a search pattern of several hundred square miles but were hampered by poor visibility, in some places by no surface visibility at all. Meanwhile the McMurdo chow hall was being set up as an emergency hospital, the gym was being cleared to serve as a morgue, and teams were organized for litter-carrying duties.

When a blizzard blew up, the search of the Erebus area was temporarily halted. It was decided to search the Minna Bluff area just south of Ross Island. Beginning at around 10 P.M., Blackburn searched there in a C130 but the visibility was poor. The weather started improving over Ross Island, so he headed north for a look at the region between Erebus and Mt. Bird.

"Around midnight we were over the northern slope of Erebus," he said. "It was about eleven hours since Mac Center had last heard from Five Zero. Worst thing that could have happened would have been a forced landing. With a breakdown in communications. You would all have frozen to death—within an hour. Kindest thing that could have happened was a crash. Everybody dying immediately.

"We were trying to guess where Five Zero was. Had it gone down in the Sound? Lewis Bay? Exploded? Sunk? Shot over to the east and crashed on the ice shelf beyond Crozier? At times I was pissed. The Kiwis went into this tourist business against our advice. And warnings. Now we had to bail them out. Risk our lives. Use up scarce fuel. Foul up our science programs.

"You know Harry Cantrell, my copilot? He said, 'I'm thinking of Doc. I can't stop thinking of him.' The other pilots in the SAR felt it too. It was unfair to get worked up over one person. There were so many on board. But I couldn't stop thinking about you.

"Then Harry said, 'I see a visual disturbance on a lower slope.'

"I thought, 'What kind of talk is that?' We made two passes. It was thc DC10. All that was left of that Kiwi bird was a long gray smear. Running upslope. In a bunch of blizzarding snow. I remembered warning you against taking that flight. I blamed myself for not having insisted more. In a way, I felt responsible for your death.

"I said, 'What in hell's he doing over *here*? Why didn't he let down over the Sound?'

"No sign of life. But we couldn't get close enough to be sure. Too much turbulence. And too great a downdraft. Whirlwinds and eddies of snow—long lines of snow—spirals pouring down the mountain. Judging by what was left of the plane, the crash didn't look survivable. Those winds would rob your body heat in minutes. It must have been forty or fifty below down there, with the chill factor.

"I reported to Mac Center. I told them the site's on a slope on the back side of Erebus. About one mile from the seacliffs overlooking Lewis Bay. That the place has downdrafts but helos should be able to land there in good weather. I remained on station at 1,500 feet over the bay. Orbiting. Acting as a communications and observation platform. While Mac Center was preparing to send Larry Goodhart, the flight surgeon, and a small field party to the site by helo.

"Larry left McMurdo about 1 A.M. He arrived about twenty-five minutes later. The helo made several low passes. Severe turbulence. Blowing snow. It couldn't land. Larry told me he found it hard to believe the blackened wreckage was all that was left of the DC10.

He made out one body. He saw no movement except for parts of the wreckage flapping in the wind.

"He told me he thought, 'Where has all the life gone?'

"He thought he saw some skuas poking around. He decided the uncertain light and the blowing snow were playing tricks. He thought skuas wouldn't be dumb enough to forage in such weather. It's a nasty spot. About the only place worse for a crash would be higher up. Near the summit. Where you'd be hit by altitude. Lower temperatures. Stronger winds.

"At the time, orbiting, I was an expensive, programmed machine. Doing a job. Later, when I was alone in my room, with pictures of my family around me, it got to me. Although you're not Navy, it really hurt to have you gone. I felt as if I had a bad hangover. I finally went to the head and threw up."

"Billy, I'm sorry."

"*You're* sorry. You go to sleep now, you hear? I've stayed too long and talked too much. I need some shut-eye myself."

He left soon afterwards. I tried to imagine the crash site: the wreckage, the blizzard, the iceslope. Although I had looked at it, I was sorry now I had not actually seen the site. I shut my eyes, intending to drift off.

10

I was stretched out on my back, trying to digest what had happened on that Erebus slope. When I heard footsteps I opened my eyes. It was the blond-bearded mountaineer with the long blond hair, standing at the foot of my bed. The room was empty except for us.

"You said you have something urgent to tell me," I said. "I've been puzzling over it."

"I guess I should have explained. It's not urgent for you, only for me."

"Then how does it involve me?"

"It doesn't. I need to talk to you about me."

"I hardly know you."

"The point is, I think I know *you*."

"Are you in some kind of trouble?"

"May I just tell you about it? You can judge for yourself."

"All right. But I don't understand why you want to talk to me rather than to somebody at Scott Base. I'm much older than you and I'm an American. I'm sure your own people will understand your problem much better."

"Hear me out. Okay?"

"Shoot. Draw up a chair."

He brought over a metal chair and sat near the foot of the bed.

"It's about our going up to search the wreckage. My name is Keith Thompson. I'm twenty-five," he began. "We went in to see if anybody was alive. It was supposed to be just in and right out. Before the weather changed again. The weather—unbelievable. If somebody had told me about weather like this I would have said. . . . It's now this, now that. Seems to get worse just when you're praying it'll get better. This crazy stuff of local weather. Fine over there, terrible here. Then suddenly vice versa. The weather down here—the only pattern is madness.

"We're just mountain climbers. That's all. We just happened to be down here. We know something about climbing mountains. We wanted to do our duty. But it was like falling off a mountain. We went in there without thinking too much. I was trembling when I boarded the helo at Scott Base. Lucky nobody can see that—through all the clothes. I was shivering when I got off it. And I have lots of body heat. The guys kid me about it. You try not to act scared. You're a man, right? But for anything you do well, you need training. What training did we have?

"When that helo left us—disappeared—the wind howling—that rough terrain—and our job to do. I was almost paralyzed for a few minutes. You understand? We're only young mountain climbers. That's all. We're not what people think we are—tough guys. We know about survival—the techniques. But we haven't really been up against it—God help us, not in that way. I wanted to do my duty to my countrymen. Those who got killed. And to any who might still be alive. To those who sent us up there. To anybody else who could use me. But I hated that helo for leaving us there, even knowing it couldn't land. I hated it. I hated Scott Base. Still—*some*body had to do the job. They better be mountaineers. Or else there'll be more dead people up there.

"Why am I telling you all this? You have your own story. Guess I'd better tell somebody. Who better than you? When I think, all those bodies that'll have to be brought down off there. God have mercy.

"We stayed two hours. Helo couldn't land. Too windy. No level place. Hovered close to the ground. Pilot wasn't happy doing that. But we were desperate in case there were survivors. We jumped out one at a time, and then they threw our gear out to us. We had a camera. Our photos will be the first to go to the outside world. Let the world have a good look at what happened to that plane, those tourists. What the world sent down here. What it did to that mountainside. Talk about pollution. I suppose in time the snows will bury it all. And the snows will turn to ice. And the ice will move seaward. And will calve off that icecliff, and drift out to sea. And bury that wreckage on the sea's bottom.

"We checked through the wreckage. Altitude about 1,500 feet. Ice there slopes about thirteen degrees. The slope is hard. Solid ice with a cover of powder snow. Snow four to six inches thick. Lots of air turbulence. Temperature around fifteen degrees Fahrenheit. Winds gusting to thirty-five knots. The chill factor must have been about thirty below. We saw a large piece of the tail section. The largest intact pieces were part of the fuselage, parts of the wheel assembly, and the tail.

"It was a much bigger job than we expected. The wreckage is all spread out. The wreckage trail is some 1,800 feet long. 300 feet wide. That's what happened to the plane you were on. Boggles the mind. The place is crevassed. Many of the crevasses are pretty small. But they're still dangerous. Two large ones cross the wreckage trail at right angles. About eight feet wide. Thirty long. The snowbridged crevasses are the bad ones. If you're not careful you find them by falling in.

"What a kerosene stench—aviation fuel. Gave me a terrible headache. I felt like throwing up. Some of the fuel—it's icicles down the sides of one of the bigger crevasses. But there was no smell of death. No rotting flesh. All the blood has turned brown. Except I knew what it was. It wasn't paint. But it wasn't what I was afraid it would look like—a place painted red with a big brush.

"We didn't look for the two black boxes. Actually they're orange. Didn't have time. And it wasn't part of our job. We just checked to see if anybody was alive. I prayed somebody was alive. I just found myself praying for it. That place felt like a fresh cemetery. Only nobody was buried yet. I thought, 'Come on. Please, God, let somebody be alive. I can't handle so much death. I haven't been prepared.'

"We saw lots of bodies. Many of them burned. Some are partly snow-covered. Others may be completely covered. It'll be a problem finding these. Longer we have to wait to recover the bodies, the more we're going to miss. But you can't rush that weather. The world can send the plane down here. But then the world has got to wait, like everybody else. You can rush things in New Zealand. But you better not try to rush them down here. We saw sixty to seventy bodies. We didn't take an actual count. Most were naked. Some near the left front of the wreckage had their clothes on. Blowing snow has also started to cover some of the debris. And some of the debris is blowing down the slope.

"I got a terrible shock. I saw just a woman's hand. With a wedding band. Oldfashioned band—on a young hand. No age spots. No wrinkles. A beautiful hand. Reminded me of my girl friend's hand. I started to cry. We all cried. We couldn't help it. We had no training for that stuff. We're mountain climbers. That's all. All the bodies were frozen. I touched one. Cold as the iceslope. I guess they'd stay like that, unspoiled, for hundreds of years if we let them.

"No survivors. Nobody alive. No life. Just the three of us. It was bloody bad. Then we spotted you. Or you spotted us. You were like manna from heaven. At least *some*body was spared! You were mighty good to look at. My eyes never felt younger. They felt they'd last forever. All that death. And there *you* were! I don't know who did more for whom—you for us or we for you."

He had come to the end of his story. There were tears in his eyes.

"I'm glad you got it off your chest," I said. "You'll feel better for it. Where do you live in Christchurch?"

"On Peterborough Street."

"Ah, I know the street. I once stayed in a motel on it."

"Which one?"

"Town Hall Motel."

"Sure, I know the place."

There was a pause.

"We were debriefed at the Chalet," he said. "If the weather

lets us, we're going back to the crash site this evening. We'll build a base camp for the investigators. They're on their way from Christchurch. A lot of people are on their way down here. We'll set up eight polar tents. Two radios. Sleeping bags. Food for twenty people for four days. But I'll be okay—I think. I know better what to expect. And talking to you has been very good for me."

"I'll be thinking of you."

"I'm mighty glad you came through it," he said as he left.

There were tears in my eyes as I saw him disappear beyond the white inner doorway.

11

Those sixty or seventy bodies were strangers to him, whereas I had probably spoken with some of them. And one of them might be Pamela Mansfield.

Again I sensed two voices arguing inside me.

"You should have gone over to her in the dining room and warned her about the flight's irregularities. You owed her at least that after the way you treated her at Warner's. You humiliated her at Warner's, and now she lies stone dead on the iceslope."

"Why do you persist in pressing the guilt button?"

"Because you're guiltier than you think. And far guiltier than you admit."

"How was I to know she was taking the flight?"

"You knew she wanted to see the ice. Why else do you think she was dining at the airport?"

"She could have been heading for Outer Mongolia, Mesopotamia, or hell itself. How should I know?"

I suddenly saw her on top of me, reaching behind her to pull down her bikini underpants so she could take me inside her.

"Come on, let's *do* it! I want to do it *now*!" she cried in anguish.

"You think I'm duhty!" she cried.

But let me describe what led up to this remembered scene, which will show you how uptight I was sexually shortly before I left Charlottesville for Antarctica.

This was around mid-September, when I met a woman named Sarah Preakness. She was strikingly attractive—tall, slim, golden-haired with a touch of auburn. It was about a fortnight later, in her studio in a quiet street in town, that we found the opportunity to be lovers. I had gathered through a friend that she was rather free sexually and I was worried. I wanted her badly but I had no condoms. I hated the things and rarely carried them. They denied the very thing that made intercourse so wonderful: the utmost physical closeness.

And I never liked the jelly that usually went with diaphragms. Sometimes you'd slip around so much you'd feel almost nothing, and the stuff certainly wasn't conducive to the marvels of oral sex. Also, occasionally I would meet a woman who grew furious with me because the device would slip out of her hands as she tried to insert it while I lay blissful on the bed. As for IUD's, I remembered a brief relationship in which I had pain every time I hit the tail of one. I confess that, like many men, I had been spoiled by the pill.

I decided to be honest with Sarah—and that had devastating results. I explained I would soon be leaving for the Antarctic and that I couldn't afford to risk getting VD.

"I'm sensitive to penicillin, which would complicate treatment for me," I said. "And as you know, there are new, resistant strains of gonorrhea. In Antarctica I'll be camping on remote capes and in remote, strange valleys. Being a non-scientist, I'm peripheral to the American Antarctic program. If I were to find myself with VD in the field, I'd have to radio for help. I'd probably be helicoptered back to McMurdo Station and cashiered out of the continent for irresponsibility, with great damage to my Antarctic project."

She was very silent. I loved her long silences. I loved them when we drove in the wooded countryside at night, heading for an evening with friends, she visible only in the soft illumination of the dashboard and in the reflection of the headlights. They gave me a great deal of pleasurable space.

Now in her studio with the smell of paint and turpentine she stood tall, beautiful, and cried without a sound, large tears running down her golden-downy cheeks and over her sensitive mouth as she stared at me. I hated myself for my compulsive honesty.

"I'm so sorry. I'm very stupid," I whispered.

I felt that a dramatic gesture was needed to save the day. I must burst out of the image of distinguished professor, author of books, mentor of graduate students. I must do something Dostoyevskian. Just the knowledge that I would soon be in Antarctica, far from the humdrum world of billions of striving humans, gave me a marvelous optimism, a druglike high.

Remembering scenes in Dostoyevsky, and the ancient Greek habit as described in the *Odyssey* of begging for succor or mercy by clasping a powerful person's knees, I dropped to my knees, sending a piercing pain through my right one by banging it against an unseen nail head in her rough, uncarpeted floor. I was beside myself with confusion and shame. I had thought it all right to speak frankly with a liberated woman. Now *that* was a piece of brilliance worthy of a professor of American history.

Clasping her knees, I said very intensely, startling the studio's silence, "Forgive me! Let's not destroy it before it begins! Trust me, Sarah! I'll make it right, dear Sarah! Oh, Sarah!"

There was a minute of silence during which I awaited my fate while hearing the ticking of her clock and the breathy, almost human hiss of her toilet tank. Then I felt a long, cool hand on my hot nape, tentative, possibly frightened, but also willing, courageous (how I admire courage in a woman!), and I knew all would be well. I sensed I was falling in love with her, I who for years had been unable to love, who had been locked away from it in a dessicated psychic cubicle somewhere.

Her studio cot was littered with books about Giotto, Goya, Piero della Francesca, Castagno, Orcagna, Masolino, detective stories, science fiction, and books about European travel. She was teaching oil painting at the university but was primarily based in SoHo in New York. She was very talented in the super-realist mode and could do wonders, in oil and pastel, with natural light reflected off fruit and bottles.

Silently, methodically, I moved the books to a work-table as she watched. It was as if I was preparing the cot for surgery. Then I led her by the hand to it and began to make love to her. Slowly, very slowly, she warmed to me. She had pale, opalescent, pink, very delicate skin, and her pubic hair was golden.

"Oh!" she cried softly each time I thrust, and often this was followed by "Harder!"

She walked blithely naked to the bathroom, with wonderful dignity, her long golden hair waving like triumphant flags around her creamy shoulders. I never liked her more than during those times when I lay abed, watching her move about naked, fresh from showering. She had an aura, a charisma, about her.

12

Although we didn't have an exclusive relationship, I felt guilty toward her a couple of weeks later in Christchurch, New Zealand when I met a woman named Pamela Mansfield. This was in Warner's bar, downtown. Albert Muddiman and I were drinking warm beer. He was a Marine Corps major and a C130 pilot. A three-piece middle-aged combo was playing songs of the Twenties nostalgically. Three or four middle-aged couples were dancing. There were several old men at the bar. The two young bartenders had long red sideburns, long red hair and yellow suspenders.

Spotting two women drinking at a table, we went over, said hello and bought them bottles of Bavarian beer. The older woman worked on the Christchurch-Wellington overnight ferry. The other, Pamela Mansfield, worked in Petticoat Lane on High Street. It was hard for me to understand the Kiwi accent at times. The women said imprissive for impressive and licey for lacy and seemed to grit their teeth while speaking, which contrasted with their friendly manner. Muddiman and the older woman looked interested in each other. After a while they went off somewhere.

Pamela Mansfield talked at length about her life. She was in her early thirties, pretty, with deepset gray-blue eyes, jet black hair, strong high cheekbones, and teeth which protruded a little. She had lovely, long, muscular legs and what seemed to me a muscular body. She wore a short summer dress. Occasionally, when she crossed her legs, I thought how attractive her thighs must be. I discovered very soon that she was an interesting, sympathetic person. She made an ee sound for an open e, as in remeember.

She said her maternal grandmother was an authentic gypsy. She, Pamela, had divorced her American husband. She had two daughters, ten and twelve. She was on a government pension, which she supplemented by working as a saleswoman in a clothing stall in an arcade. On Fridays she worked from nine to nine and was so tired afterwards that she didn't go home but just danced and partied till three in the morning.

"I live after work hours," she said. "The rest of the time I exist."

She said New Zealanders lived only for today and for partying, and quoted a popular saying to prove it—"She'll be all right, mate, there's always tomorrow."

She talked about life and its hardships. She wanted to swing, swing. She liked to drink fast so she could get high fast. She said she teased Americans because they nursed their drinks. She held her liquor well.

Her one great desire was to see "the ice," the Kiwi term for Antarctica. She had known many Americans who had been there. Would she ever see it herself, she wondered.

As the bar began to close, she said if I hurried I could buy a bottle of Bacardi for her from the manager in the back room, that normally he would refuse to sell one but that he might accommodate me because I was an American. I bought the Bacardi and a bottle of scotch and we went to my room upstairs.

It was nothing like the rooms at the White Heron near the airport but I liked precisely its oldness, the feeling that people had lived in it. And I took pleasure in the lift's creaking sounds, the corridor's smells, and the friendliness of the bar downstairs. The room overlooked the back of Cathedral Square and was close to the *Press* building and was terrifically noisy at night. Sounds of trucks, cars, motorcycles, the slamming of vehicle doors. But I liked all that, I preferred to be in the middle of things, not out in left field at the glossy White Heron.

We sat drinking and chatting, and after awhile she said she

was hungry, that she was always hungry, and that sometimes she woke up in the middle of the night and made herself a big meal. She said there was a little fish and chips place around the corner which stayed open late, and that she was feeling cozy and didn't want to stir out. I said I'd be glad to fetch the food.

A Maori young woman was standing in the doorway of the tiny, strong-smelling place, and some six or seven Maori young men were inside. I paused, waiting for her to notice me and let me pass.

"Let the old man in," one of the Maoris said coldly.

I was startled by the hostility in his voice.

When I entered, another Maori showed me a large dark bottle he withdrew from his jacket pocket. Then he thrust it at me. Accepting it, I tried politely to examine it.

"Don't touch it!" he said sharply, snatching it back.

I couldn't tell if they were drunk. The young male Caucasian clerk, silent, kept his eyes averted.

After Pamela Mansfield had eaten the fish and chips, we sat on the bed and continued drinking and chatting, and soon we were in each other's arms, kissing passionately and feeling each other. She was in a hurry. She took her clothes off and started taking off mine. She had a beautiful, muscular body. It was deeply tanned except for her breasts and the bikini area. I was dizzy with excitement. But now I started doing what I should have done earlier: worrying. She hadn't mentioned birth control, so I assumed she was on the pill.

The red flag of VD danger was waving at me, and I was without a condom. One thing I knew with certainty: I wouldn't go inside her without protection. It was too late for the drugstore on the Square to be open.

You probably won't believe what happened but it's true. What it amounted to was that I switched sexual roles on her.

"What we may have between us is much too good and important for us to rush it," I said, hoping I sounded sincere. "We should get to know each other better before sleeping with each other."

She looked surprised. After all, I was this older gentleman with a Southern accent, and all during the evening I had taken the romantic side of any conversation, as I usually do, so she was puzzled. Her instincts failed her, she bought my line for a while. And when she started up again, saying she needed to be hugged, I came up with an idea.

"Let's cuddle, but let's wear our underpants for protection against premature sexuality. Okay?"

"I guess," she replied vaguely, looking disturbed.

"Ah, I think you don't believe me," I said. "When I return from the ice we'll have a wonderful affair, a real love affair, with all the time such an affair deserves. See my point?"

"I suppose," she said.

I could sense her casting about in her mind for what might be ailing me. Poor Mansfield, she thought her life was painfully plain and that she had every right to brighten it in any way she could, so she asked her friends to call her April. I too called her April at times. Previously she had called herself Sahara but that hadn't stuck though her friends had accepted it. It was too exotic even for her own taste. She needed above all to be accepted, even by a middle-aged gentleman like me. And I needed above all to have peace of mind in the Antarctic.

We cuddled, and then I said, "Let's sleep awhile. It will be beautiful and comforting to sleep in each other's arms."

By now she was so confused and crestfallen that she accepted even this suggestion. Or at least so I thought as I drifted off to sleep.

And then I awoke with a sense of danger, and she was on her knees above me, her right arm behind her, her right hand pulling her bikini underpants off, and I was erect and showing through my boxer fly. What had wakened me? What had made me erect? Had she only pretended to be asleep, waiting for the chance to make my arguments a dead letter?

It occurred to me how funny it would sound if I said, "Please don't rape me." I doubted she would appreciate humor at this moment. She was out for fun, normalcy and non-rejection. How to explain the discrepancy of our needs? But it was too late for words even if I could find them. Her vulnerability made me feel like a bully.

"Please. Please don't," I begged.

She spread her thighs and took hold of me to direct me. I covered her pubic hair with my hand. The more she tried to move my hand the more firmly I cupped her.

"Come on, let's *do* it. I don't want to wait. I want to do it *now*!" she cried.

"Please don't," I said.

Sex had become a contest, a trial, a place of judgment. We struggled on the single bed, with the motorcycle noises outside, with only the dim desk lamp giving us some light, her saffron underpants hanging pathetically around her thighs, her breasts pendulating above me, she writhing to free her crotch from my hand. We were left with two aching bodies instead of a double fulfilled one, the beast with two backs.

Suddenly she changed position and sat on the edge of the bed, breathing heavily and looking tormented.

"You think I'm duhty!" she cried.

"No I don't," I lied. "I'm sure you're not dirty."

"Yes, yes, you think I'm duhty!"

Her Kiwi accent penetrated me like a needle. I felt claustrophobic, ashamed, messy.

"I'm very tired," I said. "I'd like to take you home and turn in."

I was flying to McMurdo in the morning.

We dressed. I got a cab on the Square and took her to her house in an outlying district of the city. When I returned to the hotel I found the large brown door locked. I pushed the bell button. No response. I knocked. Still nothing.

Four or five Maori young men were standing in the gutter.

"Captain! Hey captain!" one of them called angrily to me.

"Yes?"

"Are you through with the cab?"

"Yes."

"Why didn't you *say* so?"

They got into it and rode off. An elderly charwoman finally let me in. The Maoris felt demeaned by the Kiwis. I felt demeaned by the Maoris. And Pamela Mansfield felt demeaned by me. Time to leave civilization and head for the simple Antarctic air.

In the Dispensary I kept thinking of her looking so alive in the Gateway Lodge restaurant and in the DC10 cabin toward the very end of the flight. Now she was one of the frozen dead in the Erebus charnel house. I felt freshly ashamed for having ignored her in the cabin, and awful that I had survived and she hadn't. Then I had a crazy, frightening desire: to see where she was lying and in what condition, to see what she looked like now, and to set things right by visiting her.

To set things right. Is it a pathetic illusion among us humans to imagine we can do it? Or is it the noblest thread of our humanity?

13

I finally fell asleep at about four in the afternoon. I judged the time by the position of the sun, in the northwest. If I hadn't known where northwest was, I might easily have thought it was four in the morning, for the sun shone brilliantly at both times, and my time sense now was disoriented. Normally I had no sleep problems down here, my diurnal sense was good.

I slept several hours, deeply, and awoke to find myself running around the room in my hospital gown and shouting as hard as I could, "Grab your ankles! Grab your ankles! Grab your ankles!"

But where were the passengers?

Then it seemed to me I was in the tail section whereas they were in the main cabin.

I rushed into the front office, where a corpsman in his mid-twenties was on duty, reading *Playboy,* shouted "Grab your ankles!" at him a couple of times and, when he jumped up from his desk and looked startled, tried to force him into the pre-crash body position. We struggled. I gripped him around the waist. He broke loose.

"What's happening? What's the matter?" he asked, slamming into the desk behind him as he drew back from me.

We were both breathing heavily.

"What? What'd you say? Don't you realize we're crashing?" I mumbled, then ran to my bed, sat on the edge of it, grabbed my ankles and waited for the crash.

I was greatly surprised when it didn't come.

The corpsman was standing near the door, observing me.

Straightening up, I recalled that while running around I had seen a tall man in civilian clothes standing outside, staring up at the Dispensary windows and frowning. I hurried to a window now but saw no one—until I noticed a man walking long-legged away from me in the general direction of the Chalet.

Could it be Dave Breslin? Had Breslin heard me shouting? Had he seen me racing around? Breslin, the USARP rep, was tall. I remembered Westcott saying, "Dave here thinks maybe we should ship you out to the States so you can get some professional counselling," and my saying it would be very hard on my project if I were shipped out prematurely, and Breslin saying "Let's think about it" and frowning. If it was Breslin and if he knew what had happened, he'd ship me out pronto without a qualm. If it wasn't Breslin, who was it? Somebody, anybody, hurrying to report my true condition to him?

I was in worse shape than I had thought. The shouts had spewed out of me. Where had they erupted from?

"You can relax. I'm okay now," I said to the corpsman.

He stared at me.

"Please don't tell anybody."

"I can't do that," he said.

"At least don't tell Breslin."

"Who's Breslin? Navy?"

"Never mind," I said and got into bed.

He returned to the front office.

"Oh God," I thought, "don't let me be shipped out. I must keep this a secret from everybody. But he's going to tell Kate Waterhouse."

I recalled another secret I had had. In Christchurch on my way to the ice at the beginning of the Antarctic season before the present one, I had checked into a room in a motel downtown, with only one thing in mind: a shower to wash away the long flight from California, with its refueling stops in Hawaii and Samoa (it was in a C141, the so-called Starlifter). I had jet lag, I was on my usual high when heading for Antarctica, and I needed sleep badly.

I had my shower and it was heavenly. It was my habit to finish with cold water, so I twisted one of the handles. Instead of turning off the hot water I stopped the cold. My reaction to the stream of scalding water was slow. I even tried to reach for the handle through it—when I realized I was being burned. I jumped out of the stall. The stall was thick with steam. I reached in, shut off the water and went to the room to study myself in a large mirror. Reddening skin on my chest and right thigh. The burned places throbbed as in sunburn. I applied the first aid cream I carried with me.

"Should I see a doctor?" I wondered. "But he might report me to USARP or the Navy. Suppose my trip to Antarctica is cancelled. No, I'll hide this stupidity from everybody."

I kept doctoring the places with cream. The purplish scald marks were vivid quite a long time. Eventually they grew brown and papery, then peeled off.

I went back to the front office. The corpsman was reading *Playboy* again or studying the pinups. Such pinups played a large role in the Antarctic subculture. You encountered them everywhere, on the ceilings of icebreaker racks in the middle of the Southern Ocean, in wanigans on desolate capes surrounded by ice in its many exotic forms: brash, growlers, glaciers, snouts. An enlisted man, he was trained to administer first aid. But he wasn't likely to give me any, or at any rate the kind I needed. The coup de grace was what I'd probably get from him.

He stood up abruptly from his desk chair, apparently to brace himself if I tried to grab him again. The chair made a loud scraping noise.

"I'm all right," I said.

"I don't think so, sir."

"If word gets out I'll be shipped to the States before I have a chance to finish the work I came here to do. It's not my fault the plane crashed and I survived. I'd give anything to bring those people back to life. It's not my fault, I did what I could."

"You can't go wrestling people, professor. You try that on some of the other guys, you might get hurt. They might not understand. You need protection—against yourself, it looks to me.''

''Are you going to tell Doctor Waterhouse?''

''Yes sir.''

''I wish you wouldn't.''

''It's my duty sir.''

''Son, it'll cook my goose, don't you see that?''

''No sir.''

''Can you get me a bite to eat? I'm hungry.''

''Sir, I can't leave my post.''

''You don't trust me.''

''No sir, it's not that.''

''I apologize again for grabbing you.''

''No problem, sir. I'm sorry you're having a rough time. You've really had it, haven't you?''

''No, I'm the lucky one. It was pure luck that got me through.''

I went to my bed and got in.

''So he's gonna tell Kate Waterhouse,'' I thought. ''What's she gonna do about it? Breslin probably already knows. So he's gonna tell Kate Waterhouse. What's she gonna do about it? Breslin probably already knows.''

I kept repeating these sentences until I fell asleep.

14

Still sleeping, or maybe I was half-awake, I sensed that someone was observing me. Opening my eyes, I saw Catherine Waterhouse beside my bed. I sat upright, feeling apologetic for some reason.

"How do you feel?" she asked.

"Hungry."

"How about some hot cereal?"

"Just cereal?"

"Eat lightly for a little while. Still feel sore?"

"Yes."

"Where?"

"Back, legs."

"Mike, will you bring some aspirin, please?" she called.

When the corpsman brought a bottle of aspirin and a glass of water, she said, "Mike, get Professor Stevenson some hot cereal, will you? Cream of wheat, if they have any. And then take a break of about an hour. What time is it? Come back at ten."

"Yes ma'am."

He went off for the chow hall.

I have told you very little about her—that she was thirty-three, a doctor, single, intelligent and pretty. Let me remind you of what else I said: this was her first season in Antarctica, I had known her some six weeks, we were formal with each other, and she and Billy Blackburn were fond of each other.

She was a large, muscular woman of about my height, on the plump side. She had strong legs, strong arms, capable strong hands and a strong neck. She was stocky, solid. Usually she wore

Navy greens. Occasionally I had seen her in skirts and noticed she had a powerful, long stride, with muscular, heavy calves. I had heard her talk about exercise and well-being. Swimming, spas, workouts, massages, riding, yoga and karate were subjects she obviously liked. She lived in Santa Barbara and owned two horses, Arabians. She glowed when she spoke of them.

She looked flushed with health, as if almost bursting with it through her fine skin with its tint of rosy apricot, and appeared to be very self-assured in her personal habits and hygiene. At times I thought she seemed excessively wholesome, as if she emphasized the point too much. Her face was fair, or florid when she blushed and giggled, which she did easily. Her eyes were clear blue, with small pupils. They glanced directly, unwaveringly, piercingly at you in an almost aggressive way, as if probing you or staring you down. Her small teeth were strong, giving her a gleaming smile.

Her hair was long, rich, golden. She varied the way she wore it: in a pony tail, or parted in the middle and pinned up in back, or parted on a side. When off duty in the wardroom or at a McMurdo party, she liked to wear an artificial rose on the right side of her head, and a gold cross on a gold chain around her full neck.

"Need something to sedate you?" she asked me now.

"No. Why?"

"Mike told me what happened. Do you remember grabbing him?"

"Yes."

"Feel like going home for some psychotherapy?"

"No! Look, Kate, it's just one small episode, and I've got work to do here."

"Billy Blackburn tells me Breslin is thinking of shipping you out."

"I think he may have seen me running around, shouting. There was a guy studying the Dispensary from outside. I have a hunch it may have been Breslin."

"I reminded Mike—his name is Beauregard—that whatever happens with a patient in this Dispensary is privileged information. Which he's to keep strictly to himself."

"If word gets out, I'm done for, Breslin will get rid of me to cover himself. What about you? Are you going to tell anybody?"

"I don't know. Would you like me to massage your back? I have strong hands."

"I'd love it."

"I'll get some baby oil."

She started for the oil, then turned around and said, "I'm going to work at the crash site."

"Why?"

"New Zealand inquest purposes. New Zealand has no legal jurisdiction down here. They need a doctor to attest that all the victims are dead. Otherwise their estates can't be probated, life insurance can't be paid, people can't remarry. No mass pronouncements of death. I'm to examine each body individually."

"Why you? Why not Goodhart?"

"He's needed at the Pole for some metabolism experiments."

"When are you going?"

"Tuesday evening."

"May I go with you?"

"In *your* condition?"

"The crash is one of the important events in the history of Antarctica. I have an opportunity to describe it at first hand. That seldom comes to a historian."

"But you're a Usarp, you'll have to convince Breslin, not me."

(Usarp meant a member of USARP.)

"Can I count on your support?"

"All right. . . . Although who knows what seeing the crash site might do to you."

"Then you'll keep quiet about what happened between Mike and me?"

"Well . . . for a while, anyway."

"Thank you, Kate."

She went to the supply room and brought back a large bottle of oil. I turned over and lay face down. She uncovered my back. The oil was cold. Her hands were indeed strong.

"Like it?"

"Yes," I whispered.

"Then why don't you say something?"

"I love it."

"That's better. I need feedback if I'm to do a good job."

"It's marvelous. Best thing that's happened to me since I came to the ice."

She interrupted the massage so I could eat the cream of wheat Mike brought. The aspirin was beginning to have its effect. She resumed the massage.

"I'm very intuitive," she said. Her tone made it sound like a simple, unqualifiable fact.

"We all are . . . to a degree . . . aren't we?"

"But I can read minds. Even yours."

"Oh I'm an easy book to read. Sure enough!"

"I'm very instinctive, alert to emotions, intuitions, psychic things," she said.

"Catherine, you're a right interesting person!"

"You're making fun of me."

When she finished, she wiped the baby oil off with a harsh-grained towel.

"I have to go now," she said. "Get as much rest as you can. Tomorrow will be a busy day for you. The crash investigators will be interviewing you. And the media people too, if it's okay with you. Dr. Gould wanted to visit you this evening but I persuaded him you've had enough visitors for today. He's leaving for Christchurch tomorrow. He said he'll drop by to see you in the morning."

"Thanks," I said. "For everything."

I got out of bed and adjusted my hospital gown.

We gazed at each other silently, gently smiling. Then we hugged—suddenly, affectionately, as if it were a goodby. As we separated, she rested her fingers lightly but familiarly on my hips and studied me at arm's length. I thought I detected a possible sexual interest in me.

Suddenly we hugged again, this time lingeringly, hauntingly. It was as if I were about to go far away, perhaps never to return, and that consequently the usual social restrictions between us had vanished. But where was I going? And why did I feel like this? I had been physically attracted to her many times. When she bent over for something, say in the dim, overheated wardroom with its huge pinup of the girl with the red pubic hair, my mouth would water at the sight of her buttocks swelling the seat of her trousers. I had put that down to Antarctic horniness, nothing more. Then why did I experience a strange euphoria after even a brief meeting with her? Was it because I had been speaking with a *woman*: woman in all her richness, complexity, mystery? *Woman*: that extraordinary Antarctic rarity?

I was unprepared for the complex emotion which resulted now: elusive, very sweet, painful, haunting, mercurial, evanescent, impalpable. The essential loneliness of people—was that what it spoke of? Which, translated, meant the loneliness of Joel? The nomadic condition of American life—was that what it was based on? Which, decoded, read: leaving tendrils of myself unwinding behind me until I felt like a blind organism sucked dry by a force far beyond my comprehension?

I turned my face away because, to my astonishment, tears were threatening my eyes. She hadn't been important to me. She had been reserved with me. It wasn't at all the way she was with Billy Blackburn, laughing with him, teasing him. I had envied him that kind of intimacy with her.

"What's the matter?" she asked.

"These hugs have affected me more than I expected."

"Me too. I feel we're not strangers. It's as if we knew each other intimately in another life. Do you realize I have a crush on you?"

"Sure enough? I'm bowled over. But aren't you engaged?"

"Yes, but I've been thinking of breaking it."

"Why?"

"Because I've begun to find him not as interesting as he

was. And . . . we're incompatible in some ways. They didn't seem to matter too much before, but they've begun to worry me more and more."

"Are you thinking of breaking it when you get back?"

"No, from here. I'll call him. I've never told a man I had a crush on him—before he told me first. But this time I feel it's too important. I must tell you how I feel about you, how special you are. When I heard you're married, I thought, 'Damn him!' "

I laughed.

"Actually, I'm married only technically," I said. "I'm legally separated."

"Good!" she cried, laughing.

She left a little later—quite abruptly. No Russian goodbyes for her. I listened to the inner echoes of our voices. Getting into bed, I told myself to fall asleep promptly but it took a while for it to happen. Meanwhile I asked myself, as in a wonderful dream, if I was falling in love.

I awoke again and went to the head, where, seeing myself in the mirror, I fell to pondering who I was and what I looked like. I had last studied my face a universe ago: back at the Gateway Lodge outside Auckland, with its swimming pool, black sky, odor of chlorine, persistent tang of jet fuel, and moist, soft air perfumed by jasmine. Gateway to what? The attractive, older woman hadn't told me as I registered at the Lodge. Where had I come? To what was I going?

I had sweated heavily at times on the DC10. I thought I smelled myself stinking now, but in the extremely dry air of McMurdo (the Dispensary was not humidified) it was hard to be sure. You rarely stank when camping out, even if you didn't change clothes for days. Partly it was because you didn't sweat much but mostly it was due to the very low humidity. What had happened to the deodorant stick? I had last showered the morning of the flight. That was yesterday, Thursday, 29 November, Thanksgiving Day here and in the States.

My stomach growled. I was hungry but I had better not risk

going to the chow hall. Catherine would take a dim view of my doing that on my own. And what if I had another eruption there, started shouting "Grab your ankles!" and tried to force people to do it? Breslin would rush me out of Antarctica and he would be praised for doing it. He lacked the Antarctic desperation, the Antarctic stubbornness, the Antarctic addiction, that I had.

There was a stoniness in my face that shocked me, and the lines were all downward despite what had just occurred between Catherine and me. My face looked grimmer, sadder, and my lips were tighter, thinner. Had they been tightly sealed, hoping to keep my perfect upper teeth from cracking, when I huddled unconscious on the iceslope, nourished not by my mother's womb but by a windblown snow hummock? My eyes stared back at me, ice blue, clean, outlined by black lashes, and asked me to be friendly toward them, suggesting by their muteness that they had done their utmost in my service. I felt guilty toward them. I felt the need to reassure them that I would do nothing to harm them. Had I suffered an ice change, then?

I went to the chair near my bed where my clothes were piled, and smelled the clothes to see if they were tainted by aviation fuel. I was relieved that they smelled only of fresh air. Nothing in the pile suggested where they had lain. I checked trouser pockets for the deodorant stick. It was gone. What had happened to it? What job of deodorizing was it doing? The dead smelled of ice on Erebus. No rotting there, as there had been no rotting in Scott's tent, containing himself and Bowers and Wilson, when it was discovered in November 1912.

15

At about 1 A.M. Saturday, 1 December, while I was asleep in the Dispensary, the three Kiwi mountaineers who had rescued me were removed from the crash site after having set up a small camp to shelter those who would soon construct a larger one. This was the camp the blond mountaineer, Keith Thompson, had told me he would help build.

At around 3 A.M. a party of Kiwi DV's (distinguished visitors; at McMurdo we never referred to important visitors as VIP's) arrived at Willy Field. It consisted of several members of the New Zealand accident investigation team, some from the New Zealand DSIR (Department of Scientific and Industrial Research, in charge of Kiwi Antarctic operations), a party of mountaineers, and a three-member press pool which would file reports for the world press. Some of the visitors were housed at Scott Base but most were put up at McMurdo.

Enroute to Antarctica to help in the investigation were Americans representing the National Transportation Safety Board, the Federal Aviation Agency, the McDonnell Douglas Corporation and the General Electric Corporation.

At 8:30 A.M. a briefing was held in the Chalet, and at around 11 A.M. a number of the DV's made an aerial reconnaissance of the Site by helo. (At McMurdo the crash site was spelled with a capital S: Site.) Meanwhile preparations were under way at McMurdo and Williams Field for helo operations between McMurdo and the Site as well as at the Site itself.

At about ten that morning Larry Gould dropped by to visit

me briefly before leaving for Christchurch, Gould that wonderful friend and loyal supporter, who had been science leader and second in command of Byrd's first Antarctic expedition and who had explored in Antarctica in the year of my birth. Then Billy Blackburn came by to see how I was doing, and sat on my bed while we chatted. A half-hour later (he was still with me, which was lucky for me, as it turned out) two Kiwi crash investigators came to interview me, accompanied by a Kiwi male stenographer. During the interview I sat in bed, wearing the hospital gown. Blackburn sat at the foot of it. The others used the metal chairs.

One of the investigators began by asking what I knew about the crash. I described what had happened on the flight deck. He asked me to tell about my survival. I complied gladly, eager to help them understand what happened. Of this mild investigator I have only the vaguest memory. The other left his mark on me. He was of middle height and his posture suggested physical softness. He had thin reddish hair, and blue eyes which refused to meet mine although he wasn't shy in questioning me.

"Did you notice anything unusual about the aircraft's behavior?" he asked.

"No."

"Any special vibration? Noise? Loss of cabin pressure? Lurching? Anything that might have sounded like an explosion?"

"No."

"Any unusual behavior among the passengers?"

"Not that I was aware of."

"Cabin crew? Flight deck crew?"

"No."

"By the way, why were *you* chosen as flight commentator?"

"You'd better ask Kiwi Airways. They're likely to be less biased than I in answering that."

"Professor, let me say this frankly. One of our thoughts is that there may have been some malfunction of the DC10. The American manufacturer, McDonnell Douglas, has had considerable embarrassment this year with the DC10. I refer to the crashes in Chicago and Mexico City. Naturally we'd like to give McDonnell Douglas a clean bill of health on this one. But we won't be able to until we find and decode the DFDR. The digital flight data recorder, one of the black boxes. But even then we may not be absolutely certain. Now. Where on the plane was your survival gear?''

''In the tail section, port side.''

''And why did you bring it along?''

''Because I knew the flight wouldn't have any.''

''And how did you know that?''

''None of the Kiwi Airways Antarctic flights had them. It was a form of Russian roulette, in my opinion. The Aussie flights do have them.''

''So you thought it advisable to carry your own?''

''Yes. Especially when I heard about the flight's irregularities.''

''Who did you hear about those from?''

''Commander Blackburn here.''

''I see. Now. When did you leave the flight deck to suit up?''

''As we were rushing toward Mt. Erebus.''

''And when was that?''

''Two or three minutes before the crash. As far as I can judge.''

''So you believed the crash was inevitable?''

''Yes. Given the captain's refusal to heed my warnings.''

''And you rushed to your gear and suited up?''

''No. I didn't rush.''

''But surely you must have run. Didn't this create panic among the passengers?''

''I walked as naturally as I could . . . under the circumstances.''

''Precisely. And wouldn't it be normal to run then?''

''I suppose so.''

''You suppose so?''

''But I didn't.''

''Then you certainly must have hurried. Wouldn't it be natural to hurry . . . under the circumstances?''

''Yes. I suppose I hurried.''

''And that created a certain excitement?''

''If it did, it wasn't my intention. I did my best to act as if nothing unusual was happening.''

''And did many see you suiting up?''

''No. Almost all were in the main cabin.''

''Almost all?''

''A boy and a woman came out of the two rear lavatories on the port side.''

''And what did they see you doing?''

''I was putting on my parka, hat and gloves.''

''And did they panic?''

''Not the boy. He seemed amused by me. But the woman looked shocked. That must have been just a second before the crash, because her shocked look is the last I remember of the flight.''

''Now, is there a door between the main cabin and the tail section?''

''No.''

''It's one continuous space?''

''Yes.''

''So it was possible for passengers in the main cabin to see you suiting up?''

''Yes. But I don't remember seeing anyone observing me from there.''

''You don't remember?''

''No.''

''But you had an episode of amnesia after the crash?''

''Yes.''

''So it's possible your memory may still be faulty?''

''Possible, but I doubt it. It feels intact.''

''Intact but not complete?''

''Intact and complete.''

''Now. Did you ask for permission to bring your survival gear aboard?''

''No.''

''Why not?''

"Because I didn't consider that my agreement to be flight commentator meant that I couldn't have survival gear in Antarctica."

"Yet you knew that the flights carried no such gear. And that therefore bringing your gear aboard was very unusual?"

"Yes."

"Did the crew notice your gear?"

"I don't think so."

"Did they notice you storing it in the tail section?"

"I doubt it."

"But you're not sure."

"No."

"Did any of the passengers notice you storing it?"

"I boarded before they did."

"Did you tell the captain you had survival gear aboard?"

"No."

"Why not?"

"It would have served little if any purpose."

"Yet you knew you were the only one on the craft with such gear—in case of a forced landing."

"Yes. But it wasn't I who decided the craft shouldn't carry such gear on its Antarctic flights."

"Did you tell any of the crew about your gear?"

"No."

"Let's consider your survival. You say you remember nothing about the crash itself."

"Nothing."

"Or about how you left the plane."

"Right."

"No recollection of being thrown from it? Or crawling away?"

"No."

"Do you recall any sounds of the crash?"

"No."

"Any smell of raw fuel?"

"No."

"But you remember thinking you were part of a party caught in a blizzard."

"Yes."

"Doesn't that strike you as odd?"

"What?"

"Having that kind of hallucination immediately after the crash. Wouldn't you expect to be unconscious?"

"I suppose so."

"But you did have this hallucination?"

"Yes."

"You believed you were on an iceslope in very thick weather."

"Yes."

"And you remember heading for a large sastrugus and lying down in the lee of it?"

"I think so."

"And that's all you remember before waking up?"

"Yes."

"But you say your hands were gloved?"

"Yes."

"And inside your parka sleeves?"

"Yes."

"But you don't remember being thrown from the plane. Or crawling. Or falling asleep on the slope?"

"No."

"Then how come your hands were inside the sleeves?"

"What do you mean?"

"Isn't that a bit convenient?"

"I don't understand."

"Doesn't that strike you as a deliberate, intelligent effort to protect them? Or are you suggesting you protected them in your sleep?"

"I don't know."

"You say that on coming to on the slope, you found the opening of your parka hood was closed?"

"Yes."

"Doesn't that also suggest deliberately taking steps to protect yourself?"

"I don't get your drift."

"But I do!" Blackburn broke in. "Look," he said to the investigator, "my buddy here can't defend himself. He's had a hell of an experience. So I'll do a little defending for him. He's had enough. Don't you think? Apparently not. Apparently you think he deserves to put up with your hostile line of questioning. As if he had something to do with the crash."

"What do you want me to do?" I asked the investigator. "Admit my guilt? Yes, I feel terrible guilt about their death and my survival. I feel I didn't do enough to save them. That somehow I could have done *some*thing. I had some knowledge. And a sixth sense. I had a sixth or seventh sense. Even before I boarded the plane. I feel I didn't do my utmost. That I should have done more than my utmost. That no matter what I do, I can't ever recover my innocence. I lost it in being a witness to their death. And in being spared—partly through my own efforts but mostly by fate."

"See what I mean?" Blackburn said vigorously to the investigator, leaning forward toward him. "He's in a hell of a condition to deal with your hostility. I was in New Zealand several days before the crash. And I know there were some serious irregularities with Flight Five Zero. I got them from Sam Ogilvie, the captain, himself. Not a single member of the flight crew had been to the ice. There were only one captain and two first officers on that flight. The rules call for two captains on an Antarctic flight. At the route qualification briefing none of the pilots were shown their nav track on a topographical map. And why is there no survival gear on those flights? And why do you Kiwis assume we Americans are going to pick up the pieces for you? And risk our necks? When the reason for the flight is profit? That crash should be marked 'Made in New Zealand.' "

"That's not fair."

"What? You talk about fairness?"

"Look, commander, for all anybody knows, the crash may

be due to the aircraft itself. And the craft was made in the U.S. of A. I'm sorry I've upset you. And I apologize to the professor. It's not easy to investigate *any* large crash. But this is one of the largest in the history of aviation. And we carry a grave responsibility. We realize the Americans are sending their own investigators. We aren't alone in this bloody thing. But we're first on the scene. And it's our aircraft. Our flight crew. And most of the victims are our nationals. It's a messy thin business, from any point of view. There are pressures. People demanding to know what happened, and expecting us to produce results *fast*. There's immense pressure to *know*. Everybody wants to *know*. And we're in the midst of the murkiness which always crowds the start of any crash investigation. *Know?* For a long time you have to tolerate the pain of knowing little—or nothing. And in that kind of pressure cooker we ourselves crack. Investigating a crash like this—the whole world watching you—it's a complex messy business—but the professor complicated it by surviving. We have to factor him into the final equation—one way or another. His surviving has created a lot of emotions. And an added burden for us. It's a very mixed bag. So much for this interview. Thanks, professor.''

''Wait a minute!'' I said excitedly. ''Why aren't you addressing the essential thing? The nav track had us going down over the Sound. Was there something wrong with the track? With our inertial nav system? The captain assured me it was the best. Was he wrong? The crucial question, it seems to me, is why were we off course. Why couldn't we contact the Ice Tower? And why aren't you addressing yourself to the radar? How can a radar screen show nothing when you're hurtling toward a mountain? What does it mean? *Both* the captain and the copilot couldn't have hallucinated, seen an empty screen when there was something on it. I suspect we were heading directly for Erebus from the time we pased Cape Hallett, our next-to-the-last waypoint. But why? Why weren't we to the west of the mountain? Safely to the west of it. Over the Sound where we should have been?''

''Calm yourself, professor. It will all be dealt with in due course. It takes time to handle these things,'' the investigator said.

The interview ended soon afterwards, and Blackburn left too.

The investigator's questions had suggested I had behaved badly by bringing along my survival gear, but above all by using it (as if there was a mystical point in bringing it just for symbolic reasons); had suggested I had done something nasty, was in some way responsible for all those wasted deaths.

''In short,'' a voice in me said, ''you let everybody down by surviving. You should have joined the victims, or at least been badly crippled or burned. Yet here you are, scot-free, as far as anybody can tell.''

But I *was* injured, I told myself, for although a weighty part of me knew I had nothing to be ashamed of, that I had done all I could to persuade Ogilvie of our mortal danger, my conscience kept bugging me (and this proved I was injured), insisting it would have been best for all concerned if I had died—''Because by all the laws of nature you *should* have died,'' it said.

''Why weren't you crushed?'' it asked. ''You weren't alone in the tail section—there were the woman and the boy. Dead. Why not *you*? People—good citizens, with everything to live for—were impaled by sharp objects, were exploded against the iceslope, were mashed like ants by the tumbling fuselage. But *you*?''

''I'm a Presbyterian by rearing,'' I thought. ''I should believe in the notion of the elect. Yet when it applies to me now I resist it fiercely. Why? Because I sense that death is a more natural state than life in my present situation? And that I was unnatural in clinging to life, both during the crash and after it? Yet part of me is delighted to be alive, eager to go on loving, working, teaching, writing, exploring. Why is everything murky? What does it all mean?''

He had kept hammering at me, and I had felt he was able to look into my soul and read its essence despite what I might have been trying to hide from him. But instead of resisting him, I had wanted to help him build up his case against me, whatever it was.

I had been all for saying, "Right! I confess! My presence on that craft caused it to be drawn inexorably toward Erebus and to splay itself over the mountainside, and with it those who had come for a glimpse of the ice over cocktails and who have left their frozen selves as a memorial to Byrd's historic flight."

It was an odd interview, but perhaps, I thought, appropriate to the mysteries surrounding the crash, and appropriate to the site: the exotic volcano, and the universe of ice crowding the lost, wandering continent, the landmass that suggested it had floated away from the planet itself.

16

A couple of hours later, after examining me again, Catherine said she could discharge me, and added that the Kiwi media people were coming to interview me in the Dispensary, accompanied by Westcott and Breslin, and suggested I get dressed to receive them, for they would want to photograph me.

"What have Breslin and Westcott to do with it?" I asked.

"You're too big now to leave unwatched. And you're going to get bigger. You're not a team member, can't be controlled too well. I've got to go. Talk to you later."

It turned out to be a simple interview, with the usual questions, and photos taken with still cameras, movie camera and video camera, with available light as well as with lights the media trio brought. The man with the still cameras kept addressing me as "Sir" as if we were both in the military, and his motor-drive cameras clunked disconcertingly as I did my best to answer questions.

Breslin and Westcott had come in with the trio and now stood near the windows, observing us closely. I gave Breslin several searching glances and concluded he knew nothing of the "Grab your ankles!" episode—yet. Meanwhile I trusted I wasn't giving him and Westcott anything to fear in the way I replied to the questions.

From the outset the Kiwis let me know they were angry. They were being kept from reporting directly from the Site. Perhaps they spoke up because they hoped Captain Westcott would help them with their own police and own Antarctic people, who, they said, were preventing them from doing their job because they feared that the trio might invade the privacy of victims and the feelings of mourners by photographing gruesome details.

"What have your police to do with it?" I asked.

"Sir, it's a police operation, essentially," the still cameraman said.

"Have your police arrived, then?"

"Oh yes, sir. The DVI people—that's Disaster Victim Identification—are mostly our police, and the police are overstepping their authority."

"What about your Antarctic people? Won't they help you?"

"Hell no, sir, they're obstructing us as much as the cops are. They and the cops don't trust us to have the simplest good taste. They set themselves up as moral guardians and see us as potential barbarians. We have no way of complaining to their superiors quickly enough before the recovery operation is finished."

The TV cameraman in particular was incensed. A tall, thin man with bushy dark hair, horn-rimmed glasses and a killer mustache—his name was Katzufraikis, unusual for a Kiwi—he said that in having been refused permission to overfly the Site, he was sure he wasn't trusted enough to photograph the wreckage even from the air, although in New Zealand it was agreed he could photograph it from the ground.

In a sense I benefited by their frustration. They compensated by showering me with tenderness: the motordrive cameras, the array of lenses and lights, the slow film, the fast. I don't mean to be snide. They treated me gently and with respect. People need heroes. If they lack real ones, they invent substitutes. They need myths and work compulsively to produce them. To the media trio I seemed to be the Great Survivor, as if there was some special virtue in having survived. What was it? Some assumption that if I had been spared by Fate, I must be loved by the gods, as it were?

All of which caused me to wonder as I observed Breslin and Westcott with sidelong glances. They seemed to be upset by the attention I was receiving, this propulsion toward instant celebrity. How to control me, who might unwittingly catch Washington's attention? How to ship me out before my time, without a hue and cry that might engulf them? The world's sympathy was with me—or would be soon.

After the interview I went directly to my quarters, and was grateful for the smiles of recognition on the way, which at the same time left me the comfort of anonymity. I lived in a USARP personnel building which I had dubbed the Lodge, a long, blue, two-story prefab metal structure with soaring buff stripes, set on heavy timbers so that snow drift, instead of piling against it and turning to ice, would blow under and past it. It was faster and cheaper to build in this way than to drill into the volcanic permafrost and blast it. Also, if the building were set directly on the ground, the heat produced inside it would thaw the upper layer of permafrost and unsettle the foundation.

I worked a while, then thought a visit to the wardroom might refresh me. I hoped I'd run into Kate there. Instead, I joined Billy Blackburn at the bar. Again my privacy was respected. At around nine o'clock, after drinking with him and feeling the need to stretch my legs, I walked to a point close to Scott Base.

The evening was extraordinarily warm. I removed my cap and left my parka unzipped. The road through the Gap, gravelly, gray, in spots soft, looked well-traveled. It was the main way to Willy Field: over the Gap; a brief distance northward of Scott Base; east past pressure ice and onto the ice shelf; and several miles east on the shelf to the field.

A truck coming downhill toward McMurdo stirred a cloud of volcanic dust resembling steam. On my left the southern slope of Crater Heights still held much snow. Pools of meltwater marked the road shoulders. Those in the shadow of Observation Hill had ice skim forming on them. In the sun my ungloved hands were warm. In the shadow of the hill they turned painfully cold. A rivulet was scurrying across the road on its way to the Sound. The road was pockmarked as if by small explosives. Each hole contained milky water.

I reached the Gap's crest. Pressure ice on the left of silhouetted Cape Armitage rose in jagged masses, its crevices showing cobalt blue. On my right the lower portion of Ob Hill swooped down in a black plane. Beyond the hill lay the mottled, pale-blue annual or sea ice, which in the evening sun had a faint, lilac, pearly cast. Directly ahead of me, some miles away on the ice shelf, the gray of White Island's cliffs and hilltops showed through embayments of creamy snow. The little island, rising gently out of the shelf, looked idyllic.

I made out a faint, ribbon-like white line on the icescape, running roughly north and south. This was where shelf and sea ice met. At this point the shelf was barely ten feet higher than the Sound. The low-hanging sun illumined hills, ice and snow in a subtly dramatic, at times beautifully nostalgic way with a gentle ivory light. The sky was smoky except at the zenith, where it was azure.

I heard hillside snow and ice melting, and occasionally a metallic tinkle as a piece of ice skittered down. The sun was lower at night, so there was more glare then, and it was painful to observe the Royal Society Range (which Scott had sometimes called the Western Mountains) without sunglasses. My hands were atingle with warmth, but just yesterday, on the iceslope as I was being rescued, they had felt like frozen claws when I briefly removed my gloves, and the nails had been dead white.

I spotted the Kiwi base below me, with its handful of pale green huts on Pram Point. I had lived at the station, yet now it seemed strange to find a human settlement there. The sudden green, suggesting young grass or spring leaves, struck me as extraordinary, for I was surrounded by a land that seemed to have been blasted into infertility—all around me were porous volcanic rocks, most of them black but some with a reddish hue. Still, I was aware of visual beauty: the great contrasts of the sweeping black shapes with the faintly blue ice, or of the rose-tinted powder-puff clouds with the sky's intense blue verging on purple.

In the south Mt. Discovery was tall, large, majestic, its cone suggesting a bald white head. In the north, beyond the great white stretch of Windless Bay, Mt. Terror, a contemplative-looking mountain sweeping eastward into a cape, its bayside edge resembling chalk cliffs in the lowlying light, its luminous shadows the palest blue-grays, was thrillingly opalescent, a fairy world of watery blues, dappled grays and gleaming, glowing nacres.

In the bay itself—this was the bay well-known to Wilson, Bowers and Cherry-Garrard from their midwinter traverse between Capes Evans and Crozier, vividly described by Cherry-Garrard in *The Worst Journey in the World*—the shelf ice looked subdued, a twilight blue. But nothing was flat or dead there, everything was textured, even if only faintly, and was therefore alive.

But above all there was Mt. Erebus. It was to the left of Mt. Terror, looking deceptively low in its gently rising great mass, a plume of smoke and steam thrusting from its crater like a thunderhead and sailing away northwestward, driven by the prevailing southeasterly. Just then it looked little more than an innocent white hill, oblivious of man (hardly the place of evil I would soon be convinced it was), and all its serene beauty only made more poignant for me the terrible knowledge of what lay sprawled on the other side: 248 broken, frozen human bodies. I found it hard to accept the fact that whereas they were dead, I was still capable of enjoying this wonderful walk.

When I turned my head I experienced a tremendous sweep of space, and within the framework of this relatively monochromatic world there was the excitement of color: the sweet blue of the zenith, the lime above the horizon, the lavender, lilac and prune in the ice shelf, the slate blues of islands and mountains. The sea ice was a fiery mirror. The water rushing down the hillside gleamed like a stream of mercury. The unspoiled silence, the uncluttered views, the aloofness of the Western Mountains, the scene's incredible expanse worked profoundly on me.

I felt in love with something or someone. Also, I felt loved, blessed, graced. And I knew now that I was in love with Kate.

17

Next morning, Sunday, helicopter operations began when three crash investigators, three policemen, three mountaineers and two surveyors, all Kiwis, were flown to the Site, which had to be surveyed. A grid pattern was to be made and a helo landing pad built. The digital flight data recorder, which had been installed in the wall of the cargo hold at the rear of the DC10, was found at about 3:30 P.M. It was intact. So was the cockpit voice recorder, located eight hours later.

While I was lunching with Catherine in the officers' section of the mess hall that day (I had officer status while I was in the Antarctic), Breslin came over.

"Doc, there's going to be a memorial service for the crash victims at Scott Base at four," he said, not sitting down. "Brian Edwards has asked that you be there. Can you make it?"

Edwards was the Scott Base leader.

"Of course."

"Bill Murphy will drive you there and back."

Murphy was a young field assistant I had camped with and was fond of.

"Thanks, I'll walk. I need the exercise."

"No problem for you?"

"I'm in good shape. Ask Kate."

"He certainly is," she said. "He's a medical phenomenon."

"Great," he said.

After he left I said, "If he suspects anything, he's keeping cool about it. You think the corpsman has said anything to anybody?"

''Mike knows I'd roast him if he did. May I go with you?''

''Marvelous!'' I said.

''I've never had a good look at Scott Base. You lived there awhile, I hear.''

''Last season.''

''Like it?'' she asked.

''They were wonderful.''

''Will you show me around a bit?''

''You bet. But in that case let's go a bit early.''

It was wonderful walking toward the Kiwi base with her. But at one point she startled me by saying almost casually that she had broken her engagement to her fiance.

''When did you do that?'' I asked.

''A couple of hours ago.''

''By phone patch?''

''Yes.''

''How did he take it?''

''Not well. He begged me to reconsider. He said it's unfair to do it at such a great distance, with no warning. I said I had to end it just the same. He asked if his shrink might try to reach me, if I'd be willing to talk with his shrink. I said the matter is closed.''

''Weren't you rather abrupt?''

''Yes, but I think I did the right thing for us both. I've begun to realize we're incompatible in some important respects—but I've already told you this. Also, he has a sexual problem which I don't want to talk about but which I recently decided is too much for me to handle.''

''Did you break the engagement because of us?''

''No, you affected only the timing. I'm sure I wouldn't have been able to go through with a marriage.''

''I'm sorry for him.''

''I feel bad too. Let's change the subject. I'm sorry I mentioned it.''

''No, I'm glad you told me.''

There were such powerful feelings of grief and anxiety at the now crowded little base that I was barely noticed. A couple of men, one of them Brian Edwards (soft-spoken Brian, who had a way of whispering into a phone, velvet-voiced, ''Edwards here''), came over and embraced me silently.

I showed Catherine around, lingering in the tiny hospital room which had been my quarters. It had a speckled green linoleum floor and two small square windows that were opened and closed by a screw arrangement. It felt like a freighter cabin and was cold even though I had worn waffleweaves and a heavy wool shirt while working in it. Overhead was a bright electric bulb called a ''glim'' by Edwards, who liked to use Maori words, such as potai (poe-tie) for head covering and smoko (smoe-koe) for tea break. The walls and shelves were painted enamel white. On the shelves were medicines, dressings, first-aid kits and splints.

In a corner, to the left of the door as you entered, was an old-style, high, wheeled, white metal bed, above the head of which was a ventilator. To the wall opposite the bed was attached a little plywood table that could be folded out of the way. It had served as my desk.

To save on laundry (water at Scott was made by melting ice cut and transported from the ice shelf's pressure ridges), Edwards had asked me to use a sleeping bag instead of sheets. To my amusement, the thin, zipperless khaki bag on the bed was narrower than a mummy bag. It had a pale blue liner and was provided with a pillow in a fresh case. It was tricky to slip into it. You mounted the bed, braced your behind against the wall, set your feet into the bag and slowly snaked your way down. Once you were inside, it was difficult to move about, but I had no trouble sleeping in it. Billy Blackburn compared it to a body bag, the kind used to contain a battlefield corpse.

On the whole the regulars at the base were a youngish lot, friendly and attractive, and looking as if they had spent much of their lives outdoors in clean air. They had keen eyes alert for humor and they smelled good in their heavy beards and rough, tweedy clothes.

''Professor, did you ride with Osman when you lived here?'' someone asked.

He was a young man with a tense, humorless gaze and a very red nose shaped like a triangle. I didn't know him.

Osman was a lead dog.

"Yes, I did. Why?"

"He died last night after vomiting and excreting blood."

"Oh, that's too bad. What did he die of?"

"Probably deterioration of the intestinal walls, caused by bacteria. He was nine. It's not uncommon for working huskies to die by that age."

I remembered sledging on the ice shelf with Osman, racing madly while leaving a trail of blood because of a general fight that had occurred while the huskies were being harnessed, and flying over narrow crevasses (called slots by the Kiwis), and I recalled the Siberians and Greenlanders with their eyes suggestive of an oriental look, and the dog driver's virtuosity in swearing at the animals. I had never heard four-letter words used with such art before, even if they seemed to have little effect.

"Ready, dogs! Ready, dogs! Ready ready ready *ready,* dogs!"

"Osman, you dirty bastard!"

"Tighten the traces, you bloody fuckers!"

"Look at the bloody fuckers! They're too used to roads! Koo-woo-woo! Koo-woo-woo-*woo*!"

And I remembered that an Osman was also a leader on Scott's last expedition.

While I was showing Kate around the garage, Osman was carried in on a stretcher. He looked fast asleep. Large, heavy paws, gray fur. Somebody said he would be opened up in an effort to understand the cause of his death. Three five-month-old pups, dark-coated and weighing about fifty-five pounds each, were moaning and howling outside the doorway. We went over and patted them. Their thick coats felt greasy, as if they had been treated with a water repellent. They had delightful faces.

The service was simple and brief. Some thirty of us stood bareheaded at the guy-wired flagpole with its New Zealand flag at half-mast, our backs to the pressure ice thrusting skyward, and to the bluish sea ice, and to icemantled White Island rising from the ice shelf beyond. Catherine was the sole woman present. No sign of Breslin or Westcott or any other McMurdo high-muck-a-muck. A priest from Christchurch and the chaplain from McMurdo, facing black, gaunt Cape Armitage in their robes. A media guy looking extraterrestrial with his shouldered video camera. Red plaid wool shirts, a red Ford pickup, a red Chevy van—making me think of the blood spilled on Erebus, which the blond mountaineer had described as having mercifully turned brown. I imagined it gushing on impact, as if flesh-colored balloons filled with red water suddenly burst. I was grateful to have Kate with me, but standing beside her didn't prevent me from remembering Pamela Mansfield vividly, and the beautiful woman in the plane's tail section, and wondering if they were intact, and feeling guilty about their deaths.

We headed back toward McMurdo. Seeing an orange bus going our way, we hailed it, mounted it by the middle door and found ourselves among green-clad enlisted men with green survival bags. This was the Willy Field-McMurdo bus. Above the driver's head a sign read PLEASE TALK TO THE DRIVER. We got off in the vicinity of the Lodge and went to my room to chat and to be alone.

After a while we were sitting in the armchairs, drinking beer. She set her glass down on the coffee table and suddenly closed the space between us, joining me in my chair, pressing against me. I put my arm around her. She buried her face in my chest. I stroked her back gently. Soon we were kissing, at first tentatively, then with increasing passion. And soon we were making love.

18

On Monday, 3 December, four days after the crash, bad weather over Ross Island and its environs shut down helo operations at the Site. I continued debriefing myself about the crash, and I still had not caught up on my journal. Next morning the first movement of DVI people (Disaster Victim Identification, as I mentioned earlier) to the Site began. That afternoon I met with Dave Breslin in his office in the Chalet. The Lodge was situated on the station's eastern extremity, and the Chalet, the USARP administration building, was a little way south of it, on a hill above the helo pads and hangar. As you approached the Chalet from the Lodge you saw beyond it the sea ice of McMurdo Sound and the beautiful white cone of Mt. Discovery. The Chalet was a rare building on the continent because it had a bit of style, even though imitation-Swiss.

Breslin was dark-bearded, tall, thin, with a tendency to be dour. He had long, loose limbs, long fingers, and even a long, thin, straight nose. I had seen him smile but I couldn't recall him laughing. Do I sound as if I disliked him? Actually I admired him. He played no political games, he wasn't manipulative, he had a strong sense of justice and duty, he was intelligent, and he respected Antarctica.

I told him I wanted to visit the crash site before the recovery operation was completed, and I gave him my reason: the crash was an important event in Antarctica and important for my book, and it was particularly important for me not to lose the opportunity of dealing with it at first-hand.

"I know, I know," he said, nodding. "Larry Gould spoke to me about it after he saw you in the Dispensary. He recommended I send you there. Larry's opinions are pure gold with us. But helo space is at a premium now, as you know. All our helos are being used for the crash ops. And camping space at the Site is even rarer. Anyhow, it's primarily a Kiwi show. I'll have to get Brian Edwards's approval."

"What about you? You approve?"

"I'm still not entirely sure—no, I guess I'm with you. Look, Doc, I'm swamped by this mess. Our scientists are frustrated. They're stuck in the field or here, without helo support. I have to go to the Pole this afternoon for a day or two. Be patient."

"When can I expect to hear, then?"

"As soon as I get back I'll give your request my attention. Okay?"

I saw that that was the best I could accomplish for now. At least he hadn't turned me down cold. I also saw, to my relief, that he suspected nothing of my mental state.

I dined with Catherine in the chow hall and accompanied her to the helo pad. She took off for the Site at 7:30. I envied her going there.

Cranky as a result of working long and hard, frustrated about the Site, and missing her more than I had expected, I turned in disgruntled and slept uneasily.

I awoke and began running around and around my room, shouting violently, "Grab your ankles! Grab your ankles!"

Then I sat on my bed and grabbed mine as hard as I could, waiting for the crash.

There were sounds of people stirring, culminating in a knock on my door and a deep voice asking, "You all right?"

"I'm okay," I said, breathing heavily. "I had a nightmare."

The house settled down. It was 3:20.

There were two items on my program that I had postponed doing because they seemed boring. One was to wander around the station in the dead of night to get a feel for it when it was asleep. The other was to climb Observation Hill by day. It suddenly occurred to me I could kill two birds by observing the station from the hill. I dressed hurriedly and went outside.

The Penguin Power and Light Company was thrumming with the never-pausing sound of generators. There was no one to be seen. The shadows were very long. The sun was drawing close to the hill, which is some 750 feet high. On its summit stands a great cross, made of Australian jarrah wood, in memory of Scott and his four companions, who, as you know, never returned from their trek to the Pole. It was erected by members of Scott's last expedition, who took two days to carry it to the hill's crest. Apsley Cherry-Garrard, a young member of the expedition, wrote of the Polar Party Cross:

> "There was some discussion as to the inscription, it being urged that there should be some quotation from the Bible because 'the women think a lot of these things.' But I was glad to see the concluding line of Tennyson's 'Ulysses' adopted: 'To strive, to seek, to find, and not to yield.' . . . We went up Observation Hill and have found a good spot right on the top, and have already dug a hole which will, with the rock alongside, give us three feet. . . . Observation Hill was clearly the place for it, it knew them all so well. Three of them were Discovery men who lived three years under its shadow: they had seen it time after time as they came back from hard journeys on the Barrier [the original name for the Ross Ice Shelf]: Observation Hill and Castle Rock were the two which always welcomed them in. It commanded McMurdo Sound on one side, where they had lived: and the Barrier on the other, where they had died. No more fitting pedestal, a pedestal which in itself is nearly 1000 feet high, could have been found.
>
> "*Tuesday, January 22*. Rousing out at 6 A.M. we got the large piece of the cross up Observation Hill by 11 A.M. It was a heavy job, and the ice was looking very bad all round, and I for one was glad when we had got it up by 5 o'clock or so. It is really magnificent, and will be a permanent memorial which could be seen from the ship nine miles off with a naked eye. It stands nine feet out of the rocks, and many feet into the ground, and I do not believe it will ever move. When it was up, facing out over the Barrier, we gave three cheers and one more."

I walked the long way from the Lodge half-way up the hill by the road to the former nuclear plant, Nooky Poo as it had been called, a nest of green buildings snuggled against the brown earth and rock. Then I started up the trail etched into the volcanic gravel, soil and shards. The way was steep. For me at fifty, it wasn't easy. I told myself to take my time, to rest often, that there was no one to help me in case I got into trouble. I was probably already beyond shouting range, and anyway the wind from the ice shelf would carry my voice out over the Sound rather than down to the station. And even if somebody heard me, which was unlikely, I'd be invisible in a sitting or prone position.

Several times I felt like quitting, it seemed an unnecessary punishment, and foolish to have come alone and without telling anyone where I was going. If I sprained an ankle or had even a mild heart attack I'd be in bad trouble. I remembered my daughter, Morgan, urging me to be careful in Antarctica, and my promising her I would be, and I felt guilty because I was being stupid, and untrue to her. My heart beat madly and I was covered with sweat but I was determined to reach the top come what may, for I believed that to chicken out would set a precedent that would surely snowball.

Whenever I grew unhappy I turned my attention to work—with my camera, or my small tape recorder, both of which I carried under my parka to keep them warm—and at once I calmed down. Getting my mind off the goal was clearly a good thing. To look up or down raised questions best not asked.

When I reached the point where I could see everything to the east—Scott Base and the great ice shelf—I caught the full blast of the noisy southeasterly, that prevailing polar wind in this region, a regular local character, which I introduced earlier when I described myself waiting in the little bus shelter the night I flew to Christchurch on my way to join Flight Five Zero, and that other time, when I hiked to Scott Base with the faulty parka hood strap. I began now to chill rapidly, and I recalled that wet skin conducts heat twenty times more efficiently than dry. But I knew I mustn't stop to rest, for the sweat, instead of evaporating, might turn to an ice casing, with its moist layer next to the skin, a fine invitation to frostbite.

From the summit, beside the Polar Party Cross, I had a view in all directions: the vast ice shelf in the east, Mt. Discovery in the south (the poleward route that Scott and Shackleton had taken), the mountains and glaciers of Victoria Land in the west and northwest, and Erebus in the north. Directly below me were gray, brownish and umber volcanic chunks, sharp, flinty, lying on a series of dead hillsides that were part of the hill. The buildings of the former nuclear plant seemed far below me. I remembered that, seeing the hill from McMurdo, at times I wanted to spread something over its embarrassing, ugly nakedness.

McMurdo, dark, its background hills dark also despite their patchy mantle of snow, was much uglier than it was in winter, when it had a benign covering of snow and ice. Littered as it was with much equipment, some of it on pallets (crates, cases, gas cylinders, sledges, huge fuel tires, generators, bulldozers, trucks, reels of heavy wire), it suggested a wartime supply dump.

At first the way down was so steep and slippery with loose gravel and rock and dirt I had to almost sit to descend. I made my way bit by bit, usually standing, one foot down sideways to brace with, the ice-cap and ice-shelf wind buffeting me. Let me note that I bring this icy, heavy southeasterly to your attention not merely for authenticity's sake but because it becomes a life-and-death matter later in my story.

But I must not overlook that other local character, Erebus, not visible from McMurdo but in full view of me now, sending up steam puffs like smoke signals and leading me to think, how I don't know, that it was winking at me and that I was being trailed by someone—until I saw the DC10's captain, Sam Ogilvie, standing behind me, looking pale, frightened, bewildered and apologetic all at once.

"Grab your ankles!" I shouted, and tried to force him to grab his.

Luckily for me he vanished, and I managed to steady myself and not go flying down the hill as I wanted to.

Next morning I slept later than usual. My knees and thighs were very sore.

I felt pressured by chores. I had many to do if I was to keep on top of things. Cameras and tape recorders needed attention, as did clothes, my person, my room. My person received a minimum. As usual, my fingers were in bad shape: I had hangnails, deep cracks, nails separated from flesh, cuts. My flesh was too dry, and I was constantly thirsty. It wasn't smart to cut your nails short if you went camping, for then flesh tended to separate from them, and the dirt under them was difficult and painful to remove.

I put in a solid day's work. I was pushing myself. Yet part of me wasn't really in it. I was waiting for the day to end, for Catherine to return from the Site so I could see her again and hear what her visit had been like.

19

I was heading for the chow hall when I saw a helo land near the Chalet and Catherine emerge from it. I hurried to the pad, where she waited for me. I was shocked to see how tired and subdued she looked, and how her gaze was out of focus. Her Navy greens showed dried blood in places, and soot, and smelled of aviation fuel, kerosene.

"Bad?" I asked, my heart beating heavily with empathy.

"Well . . ." she said vaguely, looking at the ground. "Come to my room. Will you?"

In her room I learned she had examined bodies from 7:30 yesterday afternoon to 2:30 this morning; had slept four hours; had worked from 6:30 this morning until 5:30 this afternoon. She had taken three hours for rest and meals. She had had four U.S. Navy photographers and a Kiwi field assistant to help her.

She said ten Kiwi cops, a dozen Kiwi mountaineers and the four photographers were working at the Site under great pressure to get the job done as quickly as possible. The mountaineers were necessary to keep the others from hurting themselves in crevasses, or with frostbite, or from moving about on the slippery iceslope. All were pushing themselves despite increasing fatigue and depression. Some were on the verge of tears much of the time. Usually after a shift the men's first thought was to get some sleep, but they managed to play cards, have a drink, read magazines and paperbacks flown up there. They needed diversion badly. Some built igloos, others raced each other down the slope, riding plastic bags.

"I had to give the body recovery people bodies to work with and prepare for the first load out this morning," she said. "Bodies had to be identified temporarily—by grid number, position in the grid, by tags, by being photographed. They're scattered over a wide area. It's a nightmare. Much of the time I moved as if in a trance."

Some of the bodies in the clear plastic bags had begun to thaw, attracting skuas, which ripped through the bags to get at the flesh, so the men had to cover the bags with snow mounds until they were ready to be airlifted out. The men swore at the skuas, aimed smoke flares at them, but nothing scared them.

For a while there was a limited amount of water for washing oneself, so all the food and water tasted of kerosene until fresh water was flown in from Willy Field and the two cooks were ordered to stay away from the wreckage. Hot stews were flown in from Scott Base to supplement the camp cooking, and McMurdo sent fruit juice, so much that the camp felt swamped by it.

Some things had miraculously survived the crash—a hot food container from a galley, and a food trolley. And a number of bar containers were intact, with bottles of red wine, white, sparkling wine, many bottles of beer, some brandy.

She paused and took a long breath.

"Now about you," she said. "If you still want to go there I won't stand in your way. But I'll be worried for you, it's a terrible place."

She said she needed to take a shower and turn in. I touched her cheek gently, kissed her and went to my room, where all I could do was lie on my bed, feel the heavy beating of my heart and realize how much I loved her.

There was a knock at my door. It was Breslin. He poked his dark-bearded head into the room and said, "You're going to the Site tomorrow afternoon. Come by the Chalet in the morning, Murphy will give you the details. Right?"

"Okay."

"Doc, don't try to be macho. If it's too much for you, ask them to fly you out on the first available helo. I hope you don't get socked in by the weather. Well, I hope you find what you're looking for. Good luck. Let me know how you make out."

"Thanks."

"You okay?"

"Yes."

"You don't look too good. What's the matter?"

"Something I ate, I think."

At two o'clock the next day I took off for the Site. The visibility was good. As we swung across the saddle between Mt. Erebus and Mt. Bird and overflew Lewis Bay I saw Beaufort Island in the north. I imagined the DC10, which weighed some two hundred tons, approaching the iceslope blindly at close to five miles a minute. I remembered seeing a racing car at Indianapolis go out of control and hit the retaining wall. The car had disintegrated as if it had been full of explosives.

What had happened on the flight deck during the last seconds? Had Ogilvie realized he was about to be killed? Had he tried to take over from automatic and pull up? Or was he unaware of the danger?

If you approached the Site from the bay at around 1,500 feet it looked like a grainy, sooty alpine slope. The DC10's impact mark suggested a skua in flight. Unlike the rest of the wreckage, the mark wasn't darkened by fire, so it had a kind of angelic look by comparison. Farthest inland was the largest piece of wreckage, part of the fuselage. It seemed like a killer whale's snout rising black from an icy inlet and pointing westward while eyeing the terrain for a victim.

We swung over the Site, and there, on the eastern extremity of the wreckage trail and near its highest point, was the tail engine pod and the vertical fin to which it was attached. Seeing them recalled for me those moments in which I had put on my Antarctic clothes. Why was the tail to the left of the wreckage instead of in its middle? The plane must have tumbled wildly after the first impact, smashing itself as it went. Some fifty yards to the west was the camp, about a dozen conical polar tents (blue, yellow, red) in a row parallel to the icecliff. Above the massive iceslope loomed the bare, ribbed, barren, black hulk of the Fang, rising to over 10,000 feet. Erebus's active crater wasn't visible from a low altitude here.

We landed on the helo pad, just west of the camp, which the Kiwis had built out of six by six beams borrowed from McMurdo. I was greeted by a Kiwi inspector of police who was in charge of the body recovery operations—Jim Barker, the hearty, booming-voiced, sunburned, bright-toothed man, who informed me we would be tentmates. He was surprisingly young, probably still in his mid-thirties, and tall, rangy and strong looking. He wore an orange unzipped parka over a heavy, plaid woolen shirt, and dark woolen trousers the cuffs of which were encased by high mukluks.

I gathered he had been working hard, for although it was cold, he was hatless and gloveless. However, he kept both hands deep in his parka pockets after shaking hands with me. He had a dark mop of hair which fell over his brow, and he wore large, circular, dark mountaineer goggles which gave him a sporting look and which reminded me of photos of Edmund Hillary, the Kiwi who had been the first to climb Mt. Everest and who later selected the site of Scott Base and made the first overland journey to the Pole since Scott's ill-fated one in 1912.

"What would you like to do for a start?" he asked me.

"May I wander around and get a general perspective?"

"Good idea. Let me know if I can be of help," he said, and went off somewhere.

I could see Beaufort clearly, a slateblue rock sitting hunched and mute on the icy horizon. To its left was the Cape Bird icecliffed shore and the rounded bluewhite mass of Mt. Bird. Closer to me was pockmarked Lewis Bay, jammed with pack ice. Looking eastward, I saw the iceslope descending to the bay on the left, its shoreline sinuous as it raced away from me. Clouded blue sky, blue ice, and in the foreground the blackened wreckage.

A hovering helo, resembling a long fish, was lifting a net-load of bodies for delivery to Willy Field. Its rotors created a snowstorm that made me think of steam rising from icy fissures.

The red twin-engine Huey, which had only one set of rotors, looked light, sleek, streamlined and rather small beneath its long main rotor.

I made a tour of the Site, going downhill at first, then crisscrossing the wreckage as I moved slowly upward. The snow and ice had been so thoroughly walked on that it wasn't necessary for me to wear crampons. Occasionally I was aware of people stopping what they were doing in order to stare at me. I didn't blame them. It must have been strange for them to consider that, but for the grace of God or destiny or luck or whatever, I would have been one of the frozen bodies they were recovering.

Some of the men wore round wool caps of various designs and colors and others wore lilac balaclavas, for it was cold despite the sun. Almost all the men were bearded. Most, like myself, wore mukluks but a number wore huge white bunny boots, which kept your feet warm despite very low temperatures even if they did prevent moisture from escaping, so that you'd sometimes find yourself working with moist feet and wet socks, yet without danger of frostbite.

Everywhere I went I kept looking for Pamela Mansfield, hoping to find her so that by the pain of looking at her I might set things right between us. But my guilt toward her spread like a blot until it included everyone on the plane—passengers and crew alike—toward all of whom I felt I had behaved very badly, and I found myself looking for other people as well: for Ogilvie, for Duncan the copilot, for the lovely woman in the plane's tail section who had sparked a feeling of love in me, and for the handsome boy I had presumed was her son, who had stared at me as if I were a circus performer. Curiously, whenever I thought of her I also thought of Sarah Preakness, that beautiful, charismatic woman. I had begun to blend the two in my memory.

All the while I was aware of Erebus's activity. The volcano coughed, gargled, belched, grunted, growled, and now and then shuddered, causing the iceslope to shudder too, as if with a small earthquake. The thought of a quake reminded me that, so far as was known, there hadn't been one in Antarctica, perhaps because the immense weight of the icecap dampened such earth movements.

Standing amidst the wreckage, I had the feeling I was in an extensive, burned airplane junkyard. The largest intact piece was huge when you were close to it. I heard somebody guess it weighed some thirty tons. About eighteen feet high, it was a botch of fuselage, wing and engine pods. The inside was a mess of jagged metal, odds and ends of seats and whatnot, and patches of snow.

I was curious to see where I had managed to survive, or rather where I had survived without managing it, for no amount of Antarctic clothes could have saved me without a combination of three things: the wind, the sastrugus and the snow. The wind caused the snow to drift, the sastrugus made the snow pile up over me, and the snow gave me the thermal margins without which I would have died of hypothermia quickly. So I made my way slowly upslope, poking here and there with an ice ax. At last, investigating a small snow hummock, I broke through the crust and was startled to see a fetal shape enclosed by thinly glazed, colorless ice. The warmth of my body had made that shape.

It was an odd moment, a bit like staring into the womb which had sheltered me before giving me birth. At any rate, that was the metaphor that came to me. I was becoming aware of having been reborn on that tragic slope, and aware that my love for Catherine Waterhouse—my ability to love her deeply and to receive love from her—was part of my rebirth. I had felt the stirrings of love for Sarah Preakness. Perhaps if I had not gone away to Antarctica, that love might have developed into the real thing. But on second thought, probably not. I had needed first to come close to death, it now seemed to me.

I met two U.S. crash investigators, who were examining a long, uncowled jet engine which looked like a powerful, black, oily phallus. Both wore USARP clothes. The kneeling older man, parka unzipped, had horn-rimmed glasses. His companion, standing, bundled up, wore white goggles with eye slits, bulky black windpants and gray mukluks. His left hand idly held an ice ax. We got to talking and they told me, in response to questions, they had been able to reconstruct approximately what had happened to the DC10.

The two wing-mounted engines, the underside of the wings and the bottom of the rear fuselage bore the main impact of the crash. The left engine stopped immediately. The right one provided power for a little while. Leaving a clear impression of its fuselage, wing engines and flap hinges in the ice, as well as parts of itself in the impact crater (such as part of a wing, the bulk cargo door, a door frame, a rear toilet drain access panel), the craft lofted over the mound of displaced ice and flew up the slope, dropping a turbine disc, a tailcone lower access door, an outboard aileron, the left stabilizer, an outboard elevator, the left outboard flap, an engine low pressure turbine, the left wing tip, the upper tailcone platform, the tail cone, an inboard elevator, a fan rotor, a right horizontal stabilizer, a fan case, the top half of the fuselage, and the number one and number two doors.

The two wing engines landed far up the iceslope. Farthest upslope were the nose gear and the flight deck. The air pressure differential of about a pound per square inch between the inside and the outside of the fuselage helped the destruction.

An intense fire broke out in the middle of the fuselage aft of the front galley. The largest part of the plane remaining as recognizable was the damaged portion of the cabin attached to the wing's center and inboard sections. It burned fiercely. The front galley and the flight deck were untouched by the fire. The number two engine, mounted in the tail fin and now sitting all alone on the iceslope, roughly midway between the two wing engines, continued to deliver power for some seconds before dying.

I saw men searching the crevasses and wreckage for bodies, and hauling bodies and parts of bodies to pick-up points. A number of bodies, impaled by pieces of the plane, had been frozen into the iceslope and had to be freed with ice axes, ice picks and other tools. Some of the work, such as probing the large crevasses, was clearly dangerous. Other work was hazardous without being obviously so. The huge, still inflated tires could explode, or one of the generators of the emergency oxygen system might be activated accidentally and give a nasty burn. There were many oxygen cylinders around, and some, in a damaged state, might explode. But the greatest danger, the men believed, was the general insecurity of the wreckage, which might suddenly shift in a gust of wind and inflict cuts or crushing injuries.

The Site had been surveyed by two men brought from New Zealand, and a grid of ninety-six thirty-meter squares had been made. Black flags marked the perimeter of the grid and all the squares. Red flags warned where the holes and crevasses were. The two main crevasses, at a right angle to the line of wreckage, were deep. In places they looked bottomless. Large icicles hung down the sides of both.

Green flags indicated where the bodies and parts of bodies were. Each whole body was placed into a separate, clear plastic bag. Any property found on a body was put into the bag with the victim. There was a great variety of such property—cameras, binoculars, watches, handbags, purses, coins, banknotes, rings, wallets, bracelets, earrings, necklaces, spectacles. I was told that one bag contained about $60,000 in yen. The bodies in their plastic bags were removed in cargo nets suspended from helos. Each netload consisted of eleven bodies or the approximate equivalent of them.

Near the top of the wreckage trail, a couple of hundred feet from the flight deck controls, I came upon the bodies of Ogilvie and Kelly Duncan. Easily recognizable, they were fully clothed and reasonably intact, although it was plain, from the odd contortions of the limbs, that these had been broken. Ogilvie's face was caked with blood. Aside from its pale blueness, Duncan's was free of any unusual mark.

I studied Sam Ogilvie's face, with its wispy, boyish sideburns and very light beard. I stared at his dark, straight hair and recalled his strange, brittle laugh, uttered in small explosions. His eyes were closed.

"Are you a radio expert too, professor?"

"Not to worry. I *know* where we are."

"I'll arm the nav again."

"There's absolutely nothing ahead of us."

"I assure you we're absolutely on course."

"The radar screen is empty."

"Then why did you smash into this slope?" I wondered. "You never lived to be fifty, my age. You had never been to Antarctica. And now look what's happened."

"But why *me*? Why was *I* spared?" I kept wondering, and feeling guilty because I was alive.

Duncan's aquiline nose and poor occlusion looked quite calm.

20

"Professor?"

It was Jim Barker.

"Ah yes, we've seen them," he said when I pointed at the two bodies. "You know them? So do we."

Studying me intently, he began speaking in an intimate tone. He said it was his country's worst tragedy, worse even than the 1931 Napier earthquake. His country had three million people. Mine had—how many? 225 million? There were about 200 New Zealand crash victims here, including the crew. That would come to about 15,000 Americans.

"Good God," I said.

There was a long pause.

"I first saw all this from a chopper," he said. "I was surprised so many bodies were intact. Then, when I was on the ground, I realized they had been thrown clear. The worst is around the wreckage, under it, inside it. Bodies just torsos. Some without heads. Some scorched. Others charred."

Another long pause.

"We're having trouble sleeping. Last night I dreamed it was raining. It poured—warm rain. Flooded all the bodies down the mountain and out to sea. Some of the men have become withdrawn. They wander off alone. Stare out over the bay, toward home. Or clown around. We clown around a lot, I guess because we work practically nonstop. We're a strange bunch. Some of us are in our twenties, some in our fifties. Some never stepped on snow before."

A pause.

"The Antarctic boys are iron men. An example to our police troops."

He said you handled the greasy, grimy, sooty bodies—and wished you were anywhere but here. All you could think of was a shower, clean clothes, a day at McMurdo. But you *were* here—huddling in the tents, waiting for a blizzard to stop, a whiteout to clear, a chopper to bring cigarettes, something to read—contact with a world uncontaminated by this place.

"But I don't want to leave you with a false impression," he added. He said when he had suggested replacing some of the troops with new boys, they had balked. "Their team spirit is remarkable." He had concluded that an attempt to replace any would damage the morale of all.

That evening he decided to concentrate on the DC10's tail section, which he assumed weighed about a thousand pounds. It was the engine pod and vertical fin I have mentioned. Painted on the fin was a kiwi silhouette, silver on a purple ground. The fin lay on its side and looked as if it had been peppered by shotgun blasts. About a dozen of us managed to move the section. Pinned beneath it were the bodies of an elderly man and a middle-aged woman.

Later a contact search was made of all the grid squares—a line of men walking abreast and picking up any property of value or anything which might help in identifying the bodies. The search took nine hours and turned up many items, including anonymous limbs.

I joined three men working on a section of the flight deck. We cut it up with saws and an acetylene torch to recover instruments. I helped the attempts made to shift it. It was entangled by wires, and parts were frozen to the iceslope. When we finally moved it we discovered a woman wedged behind a mass of wiring. She lay on her left side, her back to us. She was unburned, unbloody, undisfigured—as far as we could see. Her hair, cut short, was almost black. She wore a sheer blouse—robin's egg blue—and a blue skirt of a light material. The skirt, drawn up to her hips, revealed brown, muscular, unstockinged, shoeless legs.

Using metal clippers, the men freed her of the wires and turned her over. Her blue-gray eyes stared. Her mouth was open, the teeth protruding a little. It was Pamela Mansfield.

I remembered seeing her in the dining room of the Gateway Lodge. I recalled the taste of the tua tua, crayfish, lemonfish chowder. I saw again the gray-haired stout man dining with her.

"Come on, let's *do* it. I want to do it *now*!"

She was always hungry, she said. She had ordered fish and chips, and the Maoris had behaved badly. So had I.

"Let the old man in."

"Don't *touch* it!"

She liked to drink fast so she could get high fast.

"She'll be all right, mate, there's always tomorrow."

She had once called herself Sahara. *Remeember me*. She looked like a gypsy, took after her grandmother. A passionate woman. Had wanted to sleep with me but I had refused her.

"Handle her gently," I said. "I knew her."

The men looked surprised, almost shocked.

The chance of finding her at all was slim. Some of the bodies had already been moved to Willy Field. Some would never be found, having been pinned beneath the largest piece of wreckage. Some had been hurled into the main crevasses. And some had been mutilated beyond recognition. And so to find her in such clean, recognizable condition seemed too great a coincidence. The men said they hadn't seen another body in such good shape.

"Why *she*?" I asked myself. "And how did she get from the cabin to the cockpit?"

Then I heard Erebus growl and felt the slope shudder. It was at that moment I began to believe the mountain had preserved her so well. I thought of how it had gotten its name, and what the name meant.

I left the wreckage, went to my tent, crawled into my bag. I hoped to find some solace in sleep.

An inner voice said, "Joel, consider how lucky you are. What if you hadn't found her? Or if she had been mutilated? You'd feel even more guilty than you do. She survived, just as you did, even if in a different way. Now, from this moment, you're released from your guilt."

"You must be kidding," I thought. "I'm too old for fairy tales. Or not old enough. Spare me the nonsense."

I awoke during the night, feeling restless, disturbed. Barker's breathing was steady, with a thin, high whistle. I went outside and stared at the icescape. There was a heavy overcast now. A gusty wind blew snow around like deep mist.

Back in my bag, hearing Erebus's belches and grunts, I thought of the fact that Erebus, in ancient Greek religion, was the western region in which the sun never shone and which contained the House of Hades, that mighty house of the dead. And that James Clark Ross of the Royal Navy, the discoverer of the Ross Sea, Ross Island and the Ross Ice Shelf, had named the volcano after his flagship, the *Erebus,* the same ship that had disappeared without a trace in the Arctic while serving with the lost Franklin Expedition.

I fell asleep again. When I awoke I heard the sounds of a plane crashing: the rending of metal, the screams of engines gone wild, the shouts and screams of people.

I rushed out of the tent and ran around and around it, shouting, "Grab your ankles! Grab your ankles!"

Barker caught up with me and tried to calm me.

I tried to force him to grab his ankles. Then I let go and grabbed mine. I waited for the crash. It didn't come. Men poured out of tents to see what was happening.

I returned to my sleeping bag. For awhile I was convinced I was armless and legless, a crash victim myself. And I was afraid if I died in Antarctica, God wouldn't be able to find me.

21

Within a half hour of my return to McMurdo the afternoon of Friday, 7 December, I received a phone call from Breslin asking me to meet with him immediately in the Chalet. He had all the details: my running around the tent, shouting "Grab your ankles!", trying to force Barker to grab his, grabbing my own. His reaction was forthright and simple: he was manifesting me on a flight to Christchurch tomorrow morning, and doing it in my best interest—I needed professional counselling not available in Antarctica.

I had already concluded I mustn't remain on the continent in my present condition. I told him I would leave without any objection but that I hoped he would let me camp the week at Cape Bird which had already been scheduled so I could observe the predation activities of leopard seals and killer whales and learn more about the cape and the Kiwis working there.

He said no, that was impossible now. I said I would start packing at once.

But when the next day came it turned out that flights between McMurdo and Christchurch were grounded because of sunspot activity. I have already discussed the effect of sunspots on the shape of the ionosphere and have noted that they disrupt and sometimes black out high frequency radio communications. I was told to stand by for an early departure.

In the meantime I busied myself, studying McMurdo and taping two interviews with scientists, the first on the relationship between Antarctica and the rest of Gondwanaland, together with the effect of recent paleontological finds in Antarctica on the theory of continental drift (I was told they had nailed down the theory from the paleontological point of view and made the position of the anti-drifters shakier than ever); the second on the natural mechanism of the gathering together of Antarctic meteorites in blue ice abutting nunataks (a nunatak is land projecting through the icecap), and the strong suspicion that two recently found meteorites came from the moon and Mars respectively.

The flights, grounded for four days, resumed late in the afternoon of 11 December, a Tuesday. When I wasn't notified by Breslin of a departure time from McMurdo, I went to the Chalet to inquire, and learned that the tables were turned; now he wanted something from *me*.

It seemed the relatives of four of the crash victims wished to have two of the victims' ashes scattered at the Site, and they requested that I be the one to scatter them. I'll spare you the chain of communications as Breslin described it except to say it included the American ambassador to New Zealand, and National Science Foundation headquarters in Washington. Everybody wanted to please the Kiwis in their time of national tragedy. The ashes were already at Scott Base, and two letters addressed to me had arrived from relatives.

Breslin said Captain Westcott wasn't happy with the idea of my scattering the ashes instead of the chaplain's doing it but he recognized he lacked authority in the matter. He urged that the chaplain go along to witness the ceremony for the Navy. Breslin agreed and thought Kate Waterhouse should go to keep an eye on me in case I reacted badly to visiting the Site again. How did I feel about going there?

Not good—not after what had happened Thursday night.

He lifted a long arm and stroked his long face with long fingers. He handed me the two letters.

"Will you read them? And will you please let me have your decision within two hours?" he said.

I went to the chapel, where Chaplain Don Lynn (Protestant), a lieutenant commander, was practicing hymns on a little organ.

He was the McMurdo custodian of the Discovery Hut key. (The Scott Base leader had the other key.) The Discovery Hut was Scott's hut on his first Antarctic expedition. I borrowed the key and headed for the road that swung down and around the bend of Winter Quarters Bay. The dry streets of the station looked particularly ugly, and the black hills felt ominous. Occasionally a huge truck or bulldozer raised a cloud of volcanic dust that gritted between my teeth.

As I descended the bend I saw equipment stacked on the shore below: large vehicles, fuel lines, a Jamesway hut, a roaring generator making electricity for a welding arc. Seabees were bulldozing and grading, preparing the offloading area for the resupply ships that would be coming soon. A skua circled above me and swooped at me several times before flying away. The gray-green tidal crack was now some six feet wide. The rotten sea ice along the shore had been shoved up by pressure.

The hut was about thirty-six feet square. It had a pyramidal roof and overhanging eaves. Its old, bleached wood was unrotted. I removed my gloves and struggled to unlock the small padlock that secured the lockless, latchless door. The southeasterly made my hands cry out in pain.

After I entered, it seemed demonically intent on destroying the door, which kept exploding open so violently I feared it would fly off its hinges. I could pull the door shut by a rawhide thong but couldn't fasten it. I found a bit of ancient rope near the blubber stove, tied one end to the thong and knotted the other to a rusty nail above the door frame. This partly managed to hold the door shut. Rattling of padlock against dry wood. Banging. Howling.

It was dark inside. (The few windows were small.) Black slabs of gleaming seal meat in a pile against a wall. Splotches of milky ice on the floor. Acrid odors like those of a stable. Sticky blubber in the blubber pot near the stove, the skin black, the blubber orange. Long wooden arcs that had probably been used in gravity experiments. On the shelves were boxes of oatmeal, cans of marmalade, cans of sardines, jars of damson jam, boxes of biscuits—all from the Scott days. I poked my flashlight beam into the rafter corners in the absentminded expectation of finding spider webs. Then I remembered. "No webs down here. No spiders. No insects. This is Antarctica."

I stepped outside to glance at the sky, then climbed the black hill to Vince's Cross nearby, placed to commemorate the loss of young George Vince during Scott's first expedition at the turn of the century, when the hut was erected. On the station side the hill sloped gently, on the western it fell like a cliff to the sea. The southeasterly was strong enough to blow me off the soft ridge, so I avoided the edge and leaned into the wind as I moved upward. At the cross I observed the Sound, the tidal cracks, the skuas skimming over the sea ice.

The Western Mountains were under cloud cover but I could see the slateblue planes of the craggy foothills, and the glinting cradles of small glaciers, and Hobbs Peak (the northernmost part of the range), and Hobbs Glacier, and the broad outlet of the Blue Glacier. The combination of overcast in the west, together with the spotlighted, white-cradled glaciers among blue hills that seemed to be in motion, was dramatic. In the foreground the subdued sea ice with its unevenly glowing textured surface seemed to heave subtly.

I returned to the hut, went inside, opened one of the letters and read by flashlight.

> Dear Professor Stevenson,
>
> My parents were Mark and Josephine Partridge of Auckland. My Dad was a retired pediatrician. The day of the tragic flight was their golden wedding anniversary. They were married the very day Admiral Byrd flew over the South Pole. My Dad was in his seventy-sixth year. My Mum was three years younger. They have two daughters and a son. I'm Michele, the youngest, in my early forties. I have a son and a daughter.
>
> I admire the kind of marriage they had, old-fashioned, lasting, not the current kind that seems to wither so rapidly. They were very close, they had many interests in common. They took quite long walks together right to the end. They were both lean. My Dad's abdominal muscles were amazingly youthful, as you could see at the beach.

There was always harmony in our house, and even when we were kids our rebelliousness was never out of bounds, and although our parents were very happy together, they weren't perfect, so we did have something to rebel against. Maybe they were *too* close, which tended to exclude us at times, but this turned out to be all right on the whole, I think. It was a civilized household, and we were taught that it's a privilege to be an adult.

I was close to my Dad, we had a good relationship. Professor Stevenson, may I tell you some things about him? For me he's still very much alive. He was an inspiration to me, and to many others as well. Although he wasn't actually tall, he gave the impression of being so, he stood so straight and was so lean, so fit. He walked like a young man, rapidly, with a bounce, and he wore loafers, his feet were in excellent condition, as was the rest of his body. His teeth were good and all his own, his voice was clear, his enunciation careful, precise, as if he had plenty of time left for saying what he wanted to say. He had all his hair, too, and it was gray, not white, and was parted in the middle in the old style. His mustache, though, was white. His face was lean, and even in winter suggested it was tan. He had gray, keen eyes. His grip was surprisingly strong.

He simply didn't give the impression of being in his mid-seventies. He belonged to a group in Auckland called The Old Guard, which met once a week and sometimes had a lecturer. They were all older men. You can be sure my Dad wasn't the sort you'd ever find nodding.

He wasn't jowly in the least. Like everybody else, he had touches of vanity. Sometimes when talking to you he had an absent-minded way of pinching his throat, as if to reduce the extra folds of skin. Of course, he was proud of his youthfulness, but I think he had a right to be. He gave you the feeling that it was fun to get older, and that if you followed his example you too might enjoy life to a ripe age.

But sometimes, talking to a friend, he would say, "Well, Phil, I'd better enjoy myself *now,* do the things I want to do, read the books, take the walks, hear the music. I don't have much time left, you know. I've been very lucky in my health. So has Josie."

No doubt much of his luck was genetic but much of it was also something he made. He worked at staying in good shape, didn't do all the things that people so often do to abuse themselves. He had been a pediatrician—did I mention that? I'm rattling along so, I'm surprised at myself and a bit ashamed, I know you're a busy man. But I think retirement did change him, he didn't seem to take as strong an intellectual interest in the world after that, mostly he was physical. But I still had a solid respect for him. He had earned the right to be mostly physical if that's what gave him happiness. I don't think anybody could help but respect his vitality, curiosity, interest in people, in new friendships, as if he had a long future to look forward to.

Professor Stevenson, they went away together, but only *he* (his poor body) returned. What a shock it was for us to lose them both at one blow. To us they seemed still in the prime of life. It's wrong to say it but I sort of felt they were immortal. They were taken from us in the fullness of their health and vigor and happiness, in a celebratory mood. Thank God for it, they did not die decrepit. But our lives are so impoverished as a result. I can no longer go to the phone in happy anticipation and call them in Auckland (I live in Christchurch) and draw comfort from them and comfort them in turn. We can no longer look forward in the old way to family holiday reunions. I'm apprehensive about Christmas this year, I fear it will be very empty.

But our sorrow is ours to bear privately, we're only a small part of a great tragedy. Professor Stevenson, I hope you don't think I'm complaining too much. I'd be so ashamed if you think I'm whining. I just feel a strong need to reach out to you. I believe you'll understand because I sense you have a broadly understanding and tolerant nature. So many of us admire you and are amazed by your ability to survive your terrible ordeal. It seems unfair to ask *you* for help, yet in a way it seems right, as if fated. You of all people on this harassed globe know our parents' final resting place. We beg you to reunite them and to give them a last farewell. Will you kindly scatter our Dad's ashes near our Mum? We humbly trust you'll be able to oblige.

We send you our warm good wishes. Thank you and may God bless you.

Yours truly,
Michele Partridge Gordon

22

The door was slamming insanely. The smell of blubber burned my nostrils. I opened the second letter.

Dear Dr. Stevenson,

I am writing on behalf of my sister and myself. Our dear sisters, Joanna and Helen, died in the crash. Helen's body wasn't recovered. Joanna's was. Some of us think it was a mistake to bring the bodies home, a terrible addition to the family's grief. It would have been better to leave them there and to erect some kind of memorial on the site. As only a proportion of the bodies were recoverable, surely it would have been kinder to us all to leave them all there than to make us face the ordeal of identification.

Bits and pieces—that's what was brought back in many instances. The police called and asked us, "What color were her eyes? What was her blood type? Did she wear false teeth? Did she ever have her fingerprints taken? What was she wearing?" Couldn't we have been spared such calls?

We lack words to properly express our sorrow over this whole great tragedy, and the loss of our sisters in particular. We were always very close, we four sisters, and we sometimes wonder how we can manage to go on with our daily life, knowing that they're gone forever from us. We saw them off at the airport here in Wellington. It was such a beautiful day. It was like the end of May in your country. They were going to have the time of their life, were actually going to see the Ice. They went off so happy but only one came back to us. Dead. The other was one of the "unrecovered." A terrible word for those who must hear it whether they want to or not. God in His infinite wisdom has struck this small poor country an awful blow. May He forgive us for resenting Him and doubting His wisdom at times. We're merely his handiwork. We New Zealanders have a new realization of shared tragedy. It darkens our hearts, cuts short our days. We mourn as a nation but we also have our intimate grief, untellable.

Oh, Dr. Stevenson, you were flight commentator on that ill-fated flight, you may even have spoken with them. It's true we could have an official of the airline scatter the ashes for us, or someone else, but we feel we know you personally, we've read so much about you and we've heard you're a sympathetic and generous person, and we feel you are somehow very close to our departed ones.

Dr. Stevenson, you have been spared by a divine miracle. You would honor our poor deceased sisters if you were to scatter Joanna's ashes in the neighborhood of Helen's body. It would be a large good deed. But whatever you decide, we send you our sincerest wishes for your health and happiness.

Sincerely yours,
Jill Watson

I felt I had no choice. Afraid though I was to revisit the Site, how could I turn the requests down?

I headed uphill toward the chapel. Seeing some flag markers moving in the wind, I had the illusion of ducks or chickens before remembering that there were no domestic animals here, no sound of a cat or dog.

Two enlisted men were on their knees in the chapel corridor, scraping old wax off the linoleum with razor blades. I returned the key to Don Lynn. He pocketed it, dropped to his knees and scraped away too.

"For Christmas," he explained to me, then added, "My wife always makes me scrape off old wax whenever we move."

Like the enlisted men, he wore a white T-shirt. He was a weight lifter, in terrific shape. I watched his great back, shoulder and arm muscles ripple. He worked out at the little gym near the hangar. I had heard he was a strong swimmer, with a powerful butterfly.

I gave Breslin my decision. He looked pleased and somewhat surprised. Then it was my turn to be surprised—he said I could have three days at Cape Bird. I would have my main meals with the Kiwis there and be under their general supervision. He said the Kiwis at Bird had been increasingly touchy with McMurdo of late because our helos had been dropping in on them unexpectedly and disrupting their scientific work. He asked me to bring them some fresh vegetables, fruit, also some protein stuff like frozen steaks, and to do what I could to soothe them. As for the ashes, I would scatter them tomorrow if the weather was okay. There was a lot of cloud cover in the north and west. He would have somebody call air ops. I was to get myself ready for early afternoon tomorrow. And the chaplain was going along for the Navy, and Kate Waterhouse was going along to keep an eye on me—Westcott insisted on it.

That evening I spent two or three hours alone in my room, thinking and reading. I had brought the *Odyssey* with me from home. Now I found myself visiting the House of Hades with Odysseus, and meeting the ghosts of Odysseus's mother and of Agamemnon and of Elpenor, the young follower of Odysseus who broke his neck when, drunk, he fell off Circe's roof. It moved me again to hear Agamemnon tell how he had been killed by his best friend, Aigisthos, and by his own wife, Klytaimestra, who had become Aigisthos's lover. The ghosts seemed to need to justify their life and death to Odysseus.

I mention his visit to Hades because soon I was to experience a powerful echo of it—in the form of my own ghosts.

23

I was scheduled to meet Kate and Don Lynn at the helo pads at 1 P.M. next day. At about a quarter to one I headed for the helo hangar, leaving a GFA (general field assistant), Jim Shepherd, at one of the lower helo pads to handle my gear, which he was offloading from a truck and which he had gathered for me, for I was greatly pressed for time. Twenty, from Arizona, he was tallish, lean, reticent and always quietly eager to help. From the way he carried himself I took him to be a strong hiker. I rarely ran into him except when I visited the Field Center.

I had turned over to him the key to my Field Center cage, in which my camping gear was stored, with verbal and written instructions regarding my needs, including the special foods I planned to give to the cape Kiwis, which Shepherd had garnered from the Navy commissary: frozen rock lobsters, frozen steaks, dehydrated shrimp, lettuce, cabbage, apples, oranges, bread, chocolate.

I wasn't carrying a radio on this trip. The cape Kiwi radio contacts with Scott Base would keep McMurdo informed of my whereabouts. But I was taking an ice ax and two cot mattresses, one of them to be used under my sleeping bag, the other as a work surface on the tent floor. As for the tent, I had selected an Air Force survival tent because, never having used this type, I wanted to familiarize myself with it. It wasn't a tent one person could easily load gear into. It had two entrances, tubelike, wormlike, double-layered. You crawled to reach the interior. Such entrances helped keep wind out and body heat in, but because they created a potential trap it was a good idea to have a sheath knife on you; in case of fire you would need to cut your way out fast. I was counting on Kate and Don Lynn to help me haul my considerable gear from the beach at Cape Bird to the cliffside plateau where I would camp and to help me set up housekeeping in the tent.

My friend the Navy helo pilot, Biggie (Ron Biggerstaff), flight officer of the day, emerged from the hangar.

"Doc, there's too much cloud cover over the route," he said. "Some of your flight would have to be under the cover. The cover is massive. Both high and low. At times the flight would be over water instead of ice. I guess you know the sea ice is breaking up fast north of Royds. If a Huey has to ditch in the water it'll sink. Certain death for all on board because of the temperature."

The Huey was the helo used by the Navy in Antarctica. It had a rudimentary landing gear. The water's temperature was around 30° Fahrenheit. The McMurdo-Site route, like the McMurdo-Bird route, fringed the island's western coast. By contrast, flying in a helo over the island's interior was considered to be very dangerous because Erebus, with its iceslopeḍ, icefalled and crevassed sides, occupied so much of the island's mass, making a forced landing very hazardous. Not that the coastal route was viewed as safe by the Navy pilots. They referred to it only half-jokingly as "the suicide route."

"What are you telling me?" I asked.

"The Hueys are grounded today."

"Do I have an option?"

"Well. . . . A Coast Guard helo, the H52A, with its hull and pontoons, can fly over water with some safety. Unless it hits the deck too hard it'll stay afloat. At least long enough for a rescue attempt. So if you insist on flying today, the Coast Guard helo on the upper pad can take you. Doc, it's a hell of a day for flying. Maybe you should postpone."

"Biggie, I'm fast running out of time."

"Okay. The pilot is Bob McIver of the *South Wind*. He's in the hangar having a coffee. I've briefed him on your flight. Tell him I said you'll go."

"Right. See you later."

I entered the hangar, greeted McIver and informed him I'd fly with him to the DC10 Site, then to Cape Bird. He delayed the flight some ten or fifteen minutes while he had a leisurely cup of coffee. It wasn't unlike him to keep people waiting while he paid close attention to himself. It was obvious he liked himself a lot. I couldn't recall flying with him but I knew him from both the *South Wind* and the McMurdo wardrooms. I had bought him a drink or two in the McMurdo wardroom last evening.

He was a quiet man of thirty-three or thirty-four, of medium height, with straight brown hair, a wispy mustache, a soft-skinned face that gave me the impression he had the lightest of beards, a soft-voiced drawl (he hailed from Georgia) and dark eyes lidded like an owl's. I never felt a desire to lessen the distance between us, probably because I sensed a dark side in him that I didn't feel in the other pilots. He was remote not only with me and other civilians but with military men as well. He often sat alone in the McMurdo wardroom, aloof from the singing or hilarity. I sensed he might be soft physically, that he felt much more comfortable in semi-tropical places, and that he disliked being in Antarctica. I sometimes even wondered if he hated the continent.

We walked to the upper pad, where I found that my gear was already on board. Kate looked trim, muscular, in her Navy greens. Don Lynn was also in greens. His huge muscles seemed to bulge in them. The crewman went to the front of the craft while Kate, Lynn and I climbed aboard and strapped ourselves in.

McIver, boarding, said he had to fuel up at Willy. In the H52A the pilot entered the cockpit via the cabin. Cabin and cockpit were on the same level.

McIver surprised me by asking, "Doc, would you like to sit in the cockpit?"

"Yes *sir*!" I replied in delight.

Although I had often flown in Huey cockpits, I hadn't expected to be invited to share a Coast Guard one. I went to the copilot's seat on the port side, harnessed myself, squeezed the spherical helmet onto my head and plugged it into the intercom. The helmet was so tight I wondered if I'd be able to endure it all the way to the Site.

Departing McMurdo, we flew southeast. The sky was blue but in the north some lowlying clouds hugged the horizon: moisture cast up out of the pack ice and open water of the Ross Sea. The slopes of Mt. Terror billowed and cascaded like clouds. The ice shelf was flat, immense. Willy Field was a speckled cigar-ash smudge afloat on a whipped-cream ocean.

I made out a row of dashes like a comb's teeth, gray, and the field took on a businesslike air as it rose to embrace us. We banked to port. The ice shelf glared. The field began to suggest an army camped on a salt plain, with heavy artillery, and the enemy was in the white mountains in the northwest, where the plain shone bitterly. As we banked toward the sun I sensed the enormity of the polar light.

Touching down, we shut off the engine. Only the crewman left the craft as we fueled up on the chaotic, flaring ice. Castle Rock was jet black, an old volcanic throat, beyond the khaki fuel bladder. I wondered if the crewman, who couldn't have been more than twenty, had remembered to ground us. The Antarctic was notorious for its static electricity.

And then I thought of where we were heading—the Site—and I felt repugnance at the idea of handling the ashes. I felt a tap on my shoulder. It was Kate. I removed my helmet so I could hear her. Neither she nor Don Lynn wore helmets.

"Thanks for not making a fuss about my coming along," she said.

"Fuss! I'm relieved!" I said.

24

We flew briefly over the shelf to Scott Base, where we were on deck just long enough for my friend Paul, with the blond beard, who managed the Kiwi post office and who was standing by for our arrival, to run out, duck under the spinning rotors and hand me a sealed cardboard box through my open hatch. I passed it to the crewman. We lifted off and proceeded toward the Site.

Castle Rock was on the right, looking exquisitely jet, and near rock outcrops which suggested Japanese brush strokes, touches of a master. Just ahead of us was a massive iceslope with partly snowbridged crevasses showing muscular slashes. But why were we moving northward while still inland? Why hadn't we swung back around Cape Armitage, then hugged the island's western coast, the safety-prescribed route? What was McIver thinking of?

We looked out over the Sound. In the middle distance were four black dashes: the Dellbridge Islands just west of Ross Island. Then we were north of Castle Rock and the sky was heavier with clouds and we were still edging inland. Why wasn't McIver heading for the Sound and relative safety? I assumed he knew his business, and I was grateful to him for having invited me to share the cockpit.

I saw more of the Sound now, and more jet rocks thrusting from the low white mass of Hut Point Peninsula. The sea ice of the Sound, an extensive plain of whites, lilacs and pale blues, was speckled with cloud shadows. Bits of the coast of Victoria Land on the extreme left horizon. A busyness of light, the joyousness in seeing such an expanse, and sensing the pure air, and knowing the bristling light was out there if you wanted it. There was still plenty of blue sky—no immediate sense of a bad cloud cover. Why had Biggie worried about our flying today?

We had been gaining altitude. Looking across the Sound, I could see some of the Western Mountains. And that was the Bowers Piedmont Glacier, named after tough, plucky little Birdie Bowers with the beaked nose, who had died with Scott. And just south of it were the Dailey Islands on the western coast of the Sound. And the dark gray dot on the Sound was the *South Wind*. I was much more aware of the clouds now. Were they moving in on Ross Island from the north, or were we rushing to embrace them?

Then we were just southeast of the Dellbridges: Tent, Inaccessible, Big Razorback, Little Razorback. The first two lay like black Weddell seals on the sea ice. North of them, on the right, was the dark strip of Cape Evans, and beyond this the broad, dark mass of Cape Royds. The Barne Glacier's snout, a sheer icecliff, separated the capes. Almost beneath us was the sawtooth line of Erebus Glacier Tongue's southern shore.

Large cloud masses stretched southward toward us. Did we have a northerly, and was it blowing the cover toward Erebus and McMurdo? The cover hugging the horizon, and the clouds above the cover spreading like tentacles in our direction, made me wonder about McIver's judgment in continuing on our present course. Under the clouds the route to Cape Bird was still open. Why didn't he go straight to Bird that way? No whiteout there, I could see Royds clearly, and beyond it what I took to be the westernmost tip of Bird. We were heading toward a cloud snout threatening us with its luminous, deepening gray.

Both pilot and copilot had two altimeters, a barometric one indicating elevation above sea level, and a radar one showing elevation above the ground. 5000 feet—6000—8000. I observed my barometric altimeter with fascination.

I leaned out my hatch to avoid the dusty, streaked windshield and photographed in the direction in which we were moving. The air—thick, very cold—caused tears to splash onto my dense sunglasses. Roar of engine and rotors; heavy vibration; excitement of looming onto places like a bird; and the play of light, light, in the sky and in the spattered cloud shapes sprawling on the sea ice. Black shapes and deep-gray ones were more aggressive, electrifying the icescape and the thickening sky.

We were inland from Royds. Looking down at the cape, I made out its seaward side. Its upper slopes were covered by massive clouds resembling vast steam explosions. The western ranges across the Sound were dimming fast behind curtains of weather. In the direction of Cape Bird there was a great deal of thick, ominous looking cover. We continued to climb. I saw many crevasses—curved machete slashes, some of them snow-bridged—and many clifflike rock slopes. Beyond Erebus's large second crater—that is, north of it—hung a great cloud bank. We were hugging the precipitous slope of this crater and encountering more and more naked rock.

Now we were moving directly toward Erebus. Why? Our side of the mountain, the western one, was cloud free. So was the sky above it. But beyond Erebus I saw clouds which appeared to be almost as high as the summit. From the summit itself a wisp of smoke and steam furled—toward the southeast? Possibly toward the south? So we had a northwesterly, perhaps a northerly. Were the cover and cloud masses moving southward to engulf us?

If McIver was afraid of the cover, why didn't he head for McMurdo? What was he looking for? Why was he climbing? Did he think he could outflank that looming cloud arm, that threatening snout? Was that why he had scuttled toward the mountain? But why didn't he head north over the Sound, over sea level, by far the safer thing to do? Was he afraid of possibly having to ditch in the pack ice? Best of all, why didn't he return to McMurdo? Did he fear being called chicken if he did? I glanced at him occasionally, hoping to read him, but I never saw his features. He looked extraterrestrial in the large spherical helmet which hid them from me. My own helmet squeezed my skull. I yearned for the time when I could remove it.

McIver's gaze seemed riveted on the windshield. There was

much silence between us, and between him and his crewman. He broke it only rarely.

"Doc, you know the way to Cape Bird?"

"Yes."

"And to the DC10?"

"Yes."

"Good."

He sounded relieved. I should have wondered about that tone, and about Kate's safety. I should have worried about the safety of all of us. And about McIver's mental state, and my own. But I didn't.

The summit was crisp—ivory. The southern side was ice-sheathed, less heat came from the south, the sun dropped lower in the sky there. The northern half showed the mountain's volcanic ribs in a scattering of ice and snow. Looking straight down out my hatch, I saw we were above Erebus Glacier, the source of Erebus Glacier Tongue, with its network of huge crevasses. The cloud cover, gleaming like ice and spreading inland rapidly now, suggested steam rising from a million volcanic jets. Above it thin, shredded clouds. A mottled dark cape—Royds?—stretched leftward like dark pebbles showing through a bed of milk.

The grainy Erebus side, dark, bouldery, snow-patched, dropped away gently from the Fang. A large high cloud had moved in behind the Fang. Was it part of a cover moving in from the east? Couldn't we fly northward at a lower altitude? Was McIver intent on seeing how high we could go? Was he using the cover as an excuse to change the mission, leave the prescribed course? Was he overestimating the craft's altitude capability and his skill as a pilot?

The craft's rated maximum altitude capability was some 10,000 feet. The turbo-powered engine would air-starve if he wasn't careful. What perversity was making me refuse to ask about his intentions or to complain? If I didn't care about my own life, what about Kate's?

We seemed to be heading straight for a ledge just to the left of the crater, a ledge higher than the Fang. The western side of the mountain was still free of cover. Dark, ribbed, grainy, it fell majestically away from the Fang. The arm of cover, thin in the vanguard but followed by thick, high clouds, had advanced down the Fang Glacier. The cover's elevation was midway between the Fang and the summit, or about 12,000 feet. Everything on the right of the mountain and southward of it was still free of cloud or cover. *Then why didn't McIver escape by running southward?* Did he know about the downdraft? Was he aware of the downdraft? Had he forgotten about the downdraft?

I recalled the night I waited in the tiny bus booth near Mac Center the last time I flew to Christchurch, and the prevailing southeasterly buffeting the booth, and I remembered the southeasterly battering the door of Scott's Discovery Hut. I thought of the time I had camped in a wanigan on Cape Evans near Scott's last hut, the Terra Nova one. I had wondered if the southeasterly would rip the structure from its guywire moorings. And I thought of how the wind—cold, heavy, dense—improves helo engine and rotor efficiency, and of the fact that my buddy Jim Brandywine flew an H34 helo, with a rated maximum altitude capability of only 6,000 feet, to the crest of Erebus by shuttling back and forth in the airstream—the wind that climbs the southeastern Erebus slopes, pours some of itself into the crater, and roars as a downdraft on the northwestern side.

But the downdraft was McIver's business. Mine was to observe everything carefully and to take good photos. I was not about to cry chicken.

"I don't think we can make it. What a shame," he said calmly.

A little later he said, "I think it's as high as she'll go," yet he seemed to be pushing the craft to go higher.

We were higher than the Fang and we had moved around to the north. The crater ash mounds were starkly visible. There was no doubt now that the plume was furling southward. McIver headed for the summit, then north toward Bird, then toward the summit, always climbing. But the cover was steadily climbing too, climbing faster than he was. Soon it obscured all the summit except for the mounds. Was he trying to see if the Bird area was free of clouds? No sign of Beaufort now, nor of any cape. Just the snow-splashed Erebus slope, dark, volcanic. And some milky blue of the open sea to the north, with ragged clouds. And pack ice in the middle distance. And serene blue sky—far, far away.

Now we were above the cover. We were over the high ledge which was a plateau of the old second crater, higher than the Fang, and we were remarkably close to the naked, lonely ash mounds. Gray smoke pouring out of the crater furled away from us. The sky was empty, and fiercely blue at the zenith. A scattering of minor slopes: ashy hills like veined decaying leaves. Plenty of snow. Huge boulders around. We were heading directly for the mounds.

I thought of Sam Ogilvie, the DC10 captain, and of his cockiness regarding Antarctica, and, comparing McIver with him, decided that both were arrogant in a similar way, and both were green to the continent. Of course, Ogilvie had never even been here before the crash. What was I thinking of, not urging McIver to give up this insanity? I was as crazy as he and Ogilvie, probably more so, I understood the dangers better. Or if not crazy, then *possessed*. We were all possessed: Ogilvie, McIver, myself.

The craft was straining. I felt it trembling. We seemed to be on a level with the summit.

25

Suddenly we seemed to hang still. Then we descended quickly, not flying—falling. Yet it wasn't a vertical fall, it was a forward one, as if we were trying to land too rapidly.

"We're going down, *down!*" McIver cried in a brittle, bitter tone.

For a moment I thought he meant we had merely failed to clear Erebus.

"We've got a downdraft!" he cried.

The wild landscape rose up to meet us. I thought perhaps he was trying to land somewhere, anywhere, to have a look around, to think things through. A white mass of snow came up at us, magnifying with great speed and intensity. There were gray boulders and outcropped rock shoulders everywhere.

Shouting "Mayday, Mayday, Mayday! Any station! Any station!" he flipped toggle switches desperately.

The snow mass reared up and slammed us. We bumped, buckled, spun around, skidded. Feeling naked, with only Plexiglas between me and Erebus, was I finally going to be killed?

Suddenly we were motionless. A terrific stillness.

Jumping up, his face contorted, McIver shouted, "Fuck! Fuck!" and did something to some overhead switches.

I unfastened my harness and realized I was in one piece, that my two cameras, which hung from my neck, hadn't been damaged, that the engine had quit, that the rotors were still and that we weren't on fire. It was only then I grasped that our single, turbine-powered engine had air-starved in the too thin air and that in addition we had been shoved by the downdraft. I asked myself what I was doing on the slopes of Erebus at around 12,000 feet in bad and worsening weather and with absolutely no possibility of walking down.

Going to the cabin, I saw a heartbreaking scene. Don Lynn lay crumpled on his back near the cockpit, eyes closed, a small, widening pool of blood around his head. Kate was kneeling beside him, feeling for his throat pulse. In her Navy greens (like his) and dark cap she looked like a man.

"What happened?" I asked.

Looking up with eyes that seemed very tired, she said, "He unbelted himself to take some pictures. He was thrown around. He hit his head."

"Is he dead?"

"Yes."

"Fuck! Fuck!" McIver cried.

"Kate, you all right?" I asked. "What's the matter?" I cried to the crewman, who was sitting on the floor beside the hatch, clutching his head.

It turned out he too had been unbelted during the crash, had been tossed around and had hurt his head.

Looking dazed, he got to his feet, went over to Lynn and stared.

"What'll we cover him with?" he asked.

"I have a blanket," I said.

We moved Lynn to the rear of the cabin, set him down on his back and covered him with the blanket.

I remembered he was married and had two kids, a boy and a girl. Attractive, balding, blond, pink-skinned, in his mid-thirties, he had a fine stocky body, with powerful calves. I remembered his blue eyes, clean look, sunny disposition. This was his first season in Antarctica. He was well-liked. He didn't distance himself from the enlisted men and was popular with the officers. He had looked serious in his black robes as he read aloud from the Bible at a lectern.

"How are you?" Kate asked the crewman.

"Okay."

She examined the back of his head. The slight oozing had stopped.

"I'm fine, Doc," he said.

"Does it hurt?"

"Not too bad."

We went outside for a look around. The summit was remarkably close. We had landed on the second crater's great plateau, whose rugged cliff was near us. It seemed a miracle we had found a bit of level, snow-covered ground among all the rock aprons and boulders. The helo's tail pointed at the summit. In that direction a series of horizontal rock ridges rose one above the other, interspersed with boulders and patches of ice and snow. It was about the worst place for a ditching imaginable, death to walk down from past icecliffs, iceslopes, icefalls, snowbridged crevasses—unless we had plenty of special gear and plenty of time. Doubting my companions suspected what a man-killer Erebus could be, I resolved to keep this knowledge to myself as long as possible.

The helo was resting on its hull and tipping strongly to port. One of the rotor blades was hardly head-high. Luckily we hadn't come down in straightforward, tricycle fashion or we would have had sufficient momentum to pile up on boulders and burst into flames. Coming down on one side had caused us to swivel around and skid sideways. That had given us enough traction to brake us short of disaster. If we had hit down on ice or flat rock we would have pancaked.

An examination of the craft revealed we had struck the ground on the port side. The port tire had blown, the port wheel had been slammed out of position on its axle, the port pontoon was almost vertical instead of horizontal. The main strut connecting it with the fuselage had been telescoped and its covering shredded, and the strut had broken loose from its mounting. The small tail wheel had been rammed upward.

Studying the damage, once again McIver cried "Fuck!" in despair, his face in anguish. The crewman's lips trembled. He said ''Fuck'' in a low voice, bit his nether lip and swung his head from side to side. Kate was silent, pale.

''I'm going to be shipped out,'' McIver muttered.

He walked around the craft a couple of times.

''We're lucky a rotor didn't hit the snow. If it had, we'd have flipped over,'' he said.

He went to the cockpit and tried to start the engine. The crewman stood by with a fire extinguisher.

''We have plenty of battery power but the engine isn't grabbing hold,'' the crewman said to Kate.

I recalled a story about a Coast Guard helo going too high on Erebus, landing, shutting down its engine and being unable to start it without help from other helos and special equipment. And that had been at a lower altitude than ours.

''Look for a fire! I have a red warning light!'' McIver shouted.

''There's just some smoke pouring out the exhaust,'' the crewman said.

But the smell of fire in the cabin was too strong to be ignored. I asked Kate to help me remove my survival tent and survival gear from the craft. We set the tent up on the helo's starboard at a sufficient distance from the craft to protect the tent if the craft burned. Whether the helo burned or not, we would need the tent if the temperature kept dropping. Then we lugged cartons of food out of the craft and set them on the snow midway between the helo and the tent. The effects of the altitude, which became apparent as soon as I moved about and particularly when I worked, were unpleasant now: breathlessness, a pounding of my heart, quick fatigue, the possibility of blacking out.

The smoke and the smell of fire stopped. We were still warm from the craft's heating system. Things could be worse. They could also be better: for example if the HF radio was working. But the radio required a lot of juice, which we had lost with the engine's failure.

McIver fetched a hand radio and walked around the helo,

calling, "Mayday, Mayday, Mayday! McMurdo, McMurdo! Any station! Any station! This is copter one three zero three down on the northern slope of Mount Erebus!"

Frowning heavily, he said, "I've got a killing headache."

"Me too," the crewman said.

"And me," Kate said.

"Here, Doc, keep calling while I try to start the engine," McIver said, handing me the small black gadget, which had a flexible, tubelike antenna.

I pressed the transmission button and walked around and said over and over, "McMurdo Station, McMurdo Station. Mayday, Mayday, Mayday! This is helo one three zero three down on the northern slope of Mount Erebus!"

But I was dubious, for the radio was limited to line-of-sight, and Erebus was between us and McMurdo and Scott Base.

Again McIver got a fire warning. He came outside.

"We'll have to walk to a ridge overlooking McMurdo and use the hand radio from there," he said. "Doc, you know Ross Island best. Can we walk to the top?"

"We have no crampons. No rope. Only one ice ax. And there's the altitude. And very poor visibility. And iceslopes. And possibly crevasses."

"Hell, let's walk down the mountain and get away from this altitude," he said.

"We're close to a huge cliff. And there are icefalls and iceslopes," I said. "We have no belaying equipment. No knowledge of the safest way down. The best way down I know about is above Royds. We're too far north of that. There are snowbridged crevasses. If we fell into one, even if we survived the fall we'd have no rope for a rescue. And there'd be little time. Down there, below the surface, we'd be at mean temperature. Maybe fifty, sixty below."

He looked startled.

"We're trapped," I said. "Our best chance of being spotted is to stay close to the helo."

I wanted to say more. I wanted to ask, "Why don't you drain

the helo's fuel and lubricant while they're still warm, so we can use them for heat and for smudge pots?'' It was standard polar survival procedure to drain lubricant and fuel immediately after a crash. But I sensed he still hadn't accepted the fact the helo was here to stay. He was still hoping the engine would somehow catch hold and rescue us from this predicament.

Had McMurdo heard our HF Mayday signal? But even if it had, that was before we gave our identity and location. Was the hand radio working?

McIver walked around examining the craft, muttered a few more ''Fucks,'' then turned to Kate and said, ''Kate, I'm sorry I got you into this place.''

''Forget it, Bob,'' she said.

''We'll *have* to get to a ridge. If not up there, then a lower one, maybe lower than here,'' he said. ''Kate and I will look for a ridge.''

''Why Kate? Why not me?'' I asked.

''She's a lot younger than you.''

''I'm in fine shape,'' I argued.

''Joel, I'm going,'' she said firmly.

''All right. I suggest you stay on rock whenever possible. And probe with the ice ax when you're on snow,'' I said.

She and McIver headed southwestward, she probing with the ice ax and he still looking unearthly in his large, spherical white helmet. Soon they disappeared beyond a nearby ridge, leaving me alone with the crewman and Don Lynn.

I felt spooked. One crash might be an accident. Two had to be by design. Was I being pursued by something malevolent?

26

I walked to an outcrop to view the crash scene from a distance. A white, gleaming wasteland; a metallic white that had tarnished into a dull, pale gray. A rare, tiny oasis of snow-ice among fields of volcanic boulders. In the direction of the summit a line of boulders reminded me of New England stone walls. The snow cover was shallow. The helo's hull had barely dented it.

"But that snow saved us," I thought. "The tanks are in the hull. They would have exploded if we had hit rock."

The helo suggested an exotic, injured, tropical bug resting at a desperate altitude. The hull's red front, resembling a boat seen head-on, gleamed dully. A spot near the single headlight (one-eyed monster) glowed like phosphorescence. Most of the craft was white. The pontoons were black and white. The three main rotors, black with orange tips, curving downward slightly, formed an umbrella that extended far beyond the craft.

"That new helo cost half a million," I thought. "They'll never salvage it at this altitude."

The crewman, dressed in a dark green flight suit and white communication helmet, was standing on the damaged port pontoon, which pointed at the ground instead of straight ahead, and on a little step that could be flipped out from the helo's side. He was aiming the long hoselike end of a fire extinguisher at the engine intake.

"Doesn't he know it's useless?" I thought. "But how tremendous if the engine suddenly grabbed hold, *roared*! Time we got acquainted."

I went to him and asked his name.

"Derek VanDyke. They call me Van," he replied.

He was gracefully tall, with a pleasant, easy-smiling, longish face and little brown hairs that sprouted from his bony chin in what, with a bit of hope, was the beginning of a beard. He wore flight gloves and beat-up desert boots. I told him my name.

"I know, Doc."

"How old are you?"

"Twenty. You?"

"Fifty. Will you help me stake down the tent?"

"In a few minutes. I think it would start if we had some sunlight to warm it and a head wind to blow air into the turbine intake. There's still plenty of battery power."

He went to the cockpit. I stood near the starboard cockpit hatch. The engine spewed smoke out of the exhaust and emitted a strong smell of fire.

"The red warning light's flashing," he said.

Leaving the helo, he murmured, "Christ, Christ, we're fucked," his face showing despair.

"Take it easy," I said.

"Doc, *you* spray the extinguisher into the intake. I'll turn the engine over. The carbon dioxide's gone. There's only some air coming out. But maybe the air will help the engine catch."

I climbed onto the port pontoon and did what he asked. It was useless. Without a thicker air mixture the engine was dead.

"Let's stake the tent down," I said.

"I'll get the small fire extinguisher. We can use it as a hammer."

We worked together, he at the ropes and poles while I hammered at the pegs with the extinguisher. We had thin cylindrical metal pegs, meant for earth or rock, instead of square wooden ones. In snow and ice in a steady wind the metal pegs, providing less friction, work loose more easily. The sound of metal on metal echoed around us. The temperature was steadily dropping. Occasionally he looked on the verge of panic.

Once he said harshly to himself, "Fuck! What am I *doing* here?" and his hands trembled.

"We'll be all right," I said.

Glancing up, he asked hopefully, "Think so, Doc?"

"I wouldn't miss this for anything."

He laughed. He seemed more relaxed after that.

He broke out smoke bombs, flares, a Very pistol.

"Van, shoot the pistol overhead. Let's see how high it'll reach," I said.

The flare rocketed up, burst, divided into two brilliant red mushrooms and fell, dying. It came nowhere near reaching the cover.

He drew out his sheath knife and said, "Doc, I've always wanted to stick this into a helo and now I can," and went over to the tail section and stabbed it a number of times. Soon he stabbed harder, harder. He seemed unable to stop.

"Is it the blow to his head?" I wondered. "What if he decides to stick it into *me*? I shouldn't be witnessing the destruction of government property. I don't want to have to testify against him at a hearing."

I went to a distant outcrop to take photos of boulders showing in the cloud cover. Jagged boulders, a battle terrain, the earth in fits. And miniature mountain ranges with ice rivers.

Studying the helo's skid marks, I saw we were heading north when we landed and that we had swung around until we faced west. The site sloped portward as we were heading north. If we were in level flight just before impact, the starboard wheel would have been closer to the ground than the port and we would have crashed on the starboard and swiveled to the right instead of the left, as we had. Had McIver deliberately hit down on the port (my) side, figuring better me than him?

"He was too low for autorotation, he would need an elevation of at least 500 feet," I thought. "Did he have that much control over the craft?"

We were on an exposed ridge near a cliff, with snow, rock, ice and dark boulders around us. Just to the north, quite close to the cockpit, which was pointing that way, were two large ice formations among gray boulders and outcrop. I knew from my reading of Shackleton that they were ice fumaroles, dangerous to approach closely. A fumarole is a subsidiary vent in a volcano. It gives off gases and water vapor. On Erebus the vapor freezes, making ice fumaroles.

The one on the left looked solid, a sturdy bullet-shaped snow sculpture, roughly hewn. The other had a large cowl tilted toward me. The two structures were apparently at the cliff edge, for nothing showed behind them except the dark, threatening sky.

I went over to Van. He said his feet were numb. His boots could be called boots only by extravagant courtesy.

"Try standing on rock," I suggested. "The rock is dark, so it's warmer than snow."

We made our way across hard, squeaky snow to the outcrop near the fumaroles, going on the path we had probed earlier with the ice ax. He said his feet felt better on the rock. We chatted idly, with many silences. Occasionally we glanced up to see if the cover was thinning. The cover was engulfing us like a fog. It made the largest, darkest boulders appear to be faint gray shadows in a vast milky stuff. Soon visibility was perhaps a hundred feet. Beyond that range, in every direction, was a potentially murderous white wall.

"Who would have dreamed it would climb so high?" I thought. "It's malevolent. How will Kate and McIver make their way back in this stuff?"

"Doc, you know what those things are?" Van asked about the fumaroles.

I explained what they were and warned him to stay on rock when going near them.

"There are soft conduits like snowbridged crevasses leading up to them. You can fall through. I've read about two guys barely saving themselves with ice axes."

"I'll be right back," he said, and he went to the helo and returned with two flares.

"Doc, watch this. I'm going to lob a flare into that mouth."

The extensive outcrop, veined and creased like elephant hide, looked severe with its snow mantle. The fumaroles resembled huge snowmen. A dark figure except for his white helmet, Van made his way closer to them and tossed a flare. Its red, fiery glow was startling in that world of grays and whites.

Hunched over, he ran leftward, apparently afraid of an explosion. I too ducked. We were ignorant: after all, what gases might ignite in the mouth? But the flare had fallen short of its mark. It lay behind a boulder, red smoke ascending from it, its glow reflected by the tops of the fumaroles. The maw looked mysterious.

Standing on rock, he contemplated the glow. There was an end-of-the-world feeling about the scene.

Beside him was a wide boulder as high as his chest. Another, to the right of him, was much higher than he. Both of these were small compared to the fumaroles. He tossed the second flare toward the mouth but it too fell short.

The rock on which we stood grew bitter cold. Soon whether we stood on rock or snow made little difference to our feet. I judged the temperature to be about five below.

When Van again tried to start the engine I wandered off in the direction Kate and McIver had taken, going farther from the helo than before, intending to photograph the crash scene so I would be able to convince myself, if we were rescued, that the weather had been as bad as it now looked. I crossed narrow, long, green crevasses. The mostly white craft wouldn't be easily visible from the air.

Glancing by chance into a deep fissure in some rock, I saw a patch of pink lichen.

"How wonderful. The tenacity of life—beyond belief," I thought.

"Doc?" Van called.

I went to see what he wanted. Again he was aiming the long extinguisher at the turbine intake.

"We'd better not get separated," he said and handed me a khaki plastic whistle with a black braided cord.

Kate and McIver had been gone too long.

"We crashed at about 2:30. It's now a quarter to four," I

thought. "Will they be able to see their tracks? They're lightly dressed. They must be very cold."

I myself was lightly dressed for this temperature. I wore waffleweaves, a wool shirt, threadbare cords, a parka, a cap, double gloves and my beat-up hiking boots. I had begun to experience fits of shivering, as had Van. The cold was penetrating my body and sending alarm signals to my brain, crying as if in panic, "Look *out*! Parts of you are in danger of freezing!" Adrenalin flowed accordingly, whether I liked it or not.

"We should have decided how long they'd be away," I thought. "How stupid of me not to have formed a plan. We had no right to improvise so casually. How could I have agreed to let her go? If she dies. . . ."

Warning Van I intended to use the whistle, I walked southwestward and blew a long blast, hoping I would hear a cry in return. It wasn't easy to blow hard at this altitude. For a moment I thought I was blacking out. I blew half a dozen times at intervals of about five minutes but heard nothing. I became increasingly alarmed. Our best chance for survival was to stick together, stay near the helo and keep up our morale.

27

I was in the helo, staring at Don Lynn's body covered by the brown blanket (I recalled how powerful it was; how still youthful; that his 35mm single lens reflex camera still hung around his neck), when I heard McIver and Kate talking to Van outside. They were safe. I rushed out to greet them.

Kate was still carrying the ice ax. Her head was covered by her parka hood. Her face was red, drawn. She looked unhappy. McIver, shivering, didn't look at all well. He was silent, his glances were averted.

"Did you find a ridge?" I asked them.

After a pause Kate replied, "Yes . . . but there was always another."

She had waited for McIver to answer.

"Did you have trouble finding your way back?"

"No. We followed our tracks."

"Were you on rock a lot?"

"No. We stayed on snow so we'd have our tracks to guide us."

"How was the visibility?"

"Fair."

"No whiteout threatening?"

"No."

"Did you hear me blowing a whistle?"

"We heard only our footsteps and the wind. We got very cold. And the altitude gave us splitting headaches. My feet got wet. They're numb. And Bob took three falls. His legs flew out from under him. He landed on his back and head. It's a wonder he didn't break anything. Good thing he was wearing the helmet."

"This radio's useless, the battery's too cold," McIver said.

His gaze didn't meet mine.

"Did the falls happen on your way out?" I asked him.

"As we were heading back," she replied, again after waiting to see if McIver would answer.

"Were you walking behind her?" I asked.

"No," she said.

"Did you notice any change in the look of the snow?"

"Why?"

"When certain patches are a grayer shade it's best to avoid them. They may be a thinner layer over blue ice. Treacherous without crampons."

A strong northerly came up, whipping the tent flaps. It had a permanent feel to it. Using the ice ax, I pounded at the tent stakes and checked poles and ropes.

"Prepare for a long stay," I thought. "And prepare the others."

We gathered in the tilted helo cabin, which still felt warmer than the outside, and slid the hatch door shut. As we sat in silence we felt the heat leaving us. Soon we were very cold.

"Bob, let's move to the tent," I said. "This fuselage is a heat sink. Perfect for sending body heat into space. An aluminum-magnesium alloy is no place to try to survive in."

"It's a good place, roomy and comfortable," he said.

"Too roomy to warm with our bodies. We'd have a better chance in a snow trench."

"Check the thermometer," he said.

I reported that the windshield thermometer read minus twenty-five Centigrade, or about minus fifteen Fahrenheit. We had expected it to be cold so high up on Erebus, possibly zero, but minus fifteen shocked us. Each of us knew then that it would take some doing—not to mention a great deal of luck—to survive without irreversible damage.

McIver continued to be silent.

"Does he suspect he may have said too much by saying, 'I'm going to be shipped out?' " I wondered. "Or is it because of the falls? But I mustn't be critical. His mental state is important to our safety. He's the leader, he'll pull us through."

Why wasn't he draining lubricant and fuel? Only slowly did it become clear to me that there would be no leadership from him. He was unwilling or unable to take command. As he turned more and more inward, Kate and Van looked to me for suggestions, even orders. I found myself forced to assume his role.

"What's bothering him?" I wondered. "Does he sense he's dying? I hope he doesn't die. If he does, I hope it happens quickly so we don't have to nurse him. Our thermal margins are almost non-existent."

And now certain facts came abruptly to light.

Suddenly, on an intuition, I asked McIver, "Where are the helo's survival packs?"

He didn't reply and he didn't meet my gaze.

"They're not on board," Van said slowly.

"Why not?"

"They were removed for the shuttle flights between the ship and Willy."

"All four?"

"Yes sir."

Each of the packs weighed about fifty pounds.

"Doc, I forgot to bring my survival bag," Van said in a small voice. "Bob didn't bring his either. Nor did the chaplain."

"Kate, what about you?" I asked.

"I forgot mine too," she said, frowning.

Our survival depended on what I had brought along: survival bag, sleeping bag, tent, two cot mattresses and the food for the Kiwis.

McIver, staring at the floor, remained silent, remote.

The history of Antarctica was sprinkled with people who took the continent for granted, sometimes to their sorrow. Now my companions' sorrow was mine also, for I would have to share my survival gear with them.

They had been lulled by the security suggested by all the aircraft, technology, heavy equipment, all the men. I was by far the oldest of the group, with the least chance of coming through despite my good physical condition. My ability to survive would be greatly lessened by having to spread my gear thin. A bitterness rose to my palate as the facts of our situation began to take hold of me.

Van, looking pale, said, "Doc, I forgot to tell you something. As we were taking off, Jim Shepherd shouted that he forgot to pack matches for you. He didn't think it was too important—you could get them from the Kiwis."

"Are there matches on board?"

"No sir."

"Anybody got matches?" I asked.

No reply.

We were losing moisture rapidly. When we spoke, clouds of steam escaped us. The continent was notoriously dry, the driest on earth, its air was like a sponge. Now we had the added complication of the special dryness of high altitude. I thought our lives would probably first be threatened by dehydration, loss of blood pressure, collapse of certain organs. Somehow we would have to make a fire, heat snow to make water. The snow was already too cold to put in our mouths safely. And the temperature was steadily falling.

The lubricant had no doubt congealed and couldn't be drained. It should have been drained within a half to three quarters of an hour after the crash. With the lubricant and using wicks we could have made smudge pots. But the fuel was probably still fluid, we could drain it, using a section of the canopy or some other thing as a container. We could improvise a stove out of a large can or whatever else was handy and, using bits of gravel or small rocks as a base, pour fuel on them and burn the fuel for heat, for making water, for thawing food, cooking. The fuel, if carefully conserved, could last us quite a while.

I thought that if the sun came out and we had a magnifying glass—maybe one of my camera lenses could be used as one—we might make a fire, for the sun was strong in this dry air. I wondered if the helo's battery could be used to make sparks. How long would the battery hold up at this temperature? Possibly it was already dead.

Van's feet were the first to go. I was shocked to see them, they looked like marble. I pulled my mukluks out of my orange seabag—they were rated to forty below—and gave them to him. He had had the least chance among us to live his life. He had no headgear aside from his helmet, and only his flight suit and flight gloves. I gave him my woolen balaclava and a pair of heavy gray mittens. To Kate I handed fresh wool socks to replace her wet ones, a double pair of gloves, a scarf, and a pair of bear paws if she needed them. I had no headgear to give McIver. I handed him a double pair of gloves to be used in addition to his flight gloves. Luckily he was wearing sturdy boots, as was Kate.

My own boots were inadequate. The soles had been ripped by my climbing around the volcanic terrain of Royds and Evans. My feet felt frozen, especially the left one, and my legs were turning numb in the threadbare corduroys. After considering the matter a moment I asked if it was all right if I put on my windpants, explaining that I was losing feeling in my legs.

"Hell yes!" McIver said loudly out of his silence.

I said, "This gear belongs to all of us."

Then—I hated myself for doing it, for I had only one pair of windpants—I pulled them out of the survival bag, removed my boots, laboriously donned the black, very baggy pants, and put the boots on again, my head spinning with the effort of bending over, my hands thick, clumsy, my thoughts murky. I felt guilty, nasty, for wearing the windpants when no one else had windpants. On the other hand, I thought, only Van had mukluks, and he was delighted to have them and to know he wasn't going to risk the loss of his feet.

And then I thought, after all, the pants were mine, and I was the oldest of the group and presumably the least able to take the thing that might be coming: a tremendous test of our ability to cling to life. A second thought came forcefully: at what price was it worth hanging on?

''If we had all brought our survival gear and the helo's four survival packs we wouldn't be in a bad way unless a long-lasting blizzard blew up,'' I thought. ''We could set up a couple of tents and be comfortable in our sleeping bags. We could rest and sleep the time away until we were found, even if it took a couple of weeks.''

I was convinced we must move to the tent. I could say simply, ''I'm moving into the tent'' and let whoever wanted to follow me follow. But that would humiliate McIver and lower his morale even further. If it continued to decline, his will to survive would fall with it. With a weak will his chances of survival would greatly diminish and he might do something to decrease them further—he might take a deadly fall. If one of us suffered, the rest would have to minister to him. In the process we would lose our narrow margin of safety and we might all go down into irreversible damage or death. So I refrained from saying ''I'm moving into the tent'' not out of altruism but out of self-interest. The clear fact was that our lives depended on each other.

It was now 4:45, two and a quarter hours after the crash. The cold had begun to feel savage. When I repeated that we would freeze in the cabin, McIver at last said, ''Maybe we'd better move to the tent.''

In preparation for the move he and Kate stripped the helo of everything that looked useful, including the seats, and they took the blanket off Lynn. I carried the stuff to the tent about twenty-five feet away and gave it piecemeal to Van through the complicated, wormlike entrance. All I saw of him during this operation was his long hands. I also passed to him the two cot mattresses, the canteen (the water had frozen) and the sleeping bag.

When I crawled in to examine his handiwork I made my way through a billowing red tube of light material, then through some white, gauzelike stuff that served as a curtain-door, and fouled myself at times as though in a shroud (I felt like a crawling blind man), and even the extra little exertion of getting down on all fours made itself felt by a wild beating of my heart. I was surprised to see how neatly he had arranged things. He had spread the helo insulation on the tent floor, the mattresses side by side on top of the insulation, and had made a blanket of the sleeping bag by unzipping it. It all looked unexpectedly cozy.

"What a fine boy he is!" I thought.

But not McIver. He was not at all a fine boy. I realized I had to contend with my irritation with him, had to shove it down inside me, muffle it, hush it, throttle it. I thought of Sam Ogilvie, tall, wiry, with his straight brown hair, blue eyes, oval face, wispy sideburns, very light beard like a boy's. I remembered his strange, brittle laugh. He looked intelligent and self-confident, and in general had impressed me more than McIver did. I couldn't help comparing them, both had played a large role in my life.

However, I liked McIver for apologizing to Kate. A little later, when I was briefly alone with her, I said, "Kate, listen. It's not true *he* got you into this mess. *I* did. I could have tried to stop him. Could have asked him to turn back. I don't know what got into me. I hope you'll forgive me."

"There's nothing to forgive," she said, and gave me a secret kiss.

28

I sensed that the altitude was like an animal, lurking to assail me. It would work on me suddenly—when I was walking, working, even standing still, talking. It made my speech fuzzy, disarranged my thoughts. My words came out too slowly, or mixed up. It was easy to do something stupid or dangerous. I couldn't warm up by jogging in place: to try jogging was to invite vomiting or blacking out. My companions, Van especially, were plagued by headaches which I took to be as bad as migraines. I wondered how much of Van's headache was due to his injury.

In addition to the altitude, I sensed the immense, threatening personality of Erebus. This domineering, mysterious volcano, once remote to me, now had an intimate place in my mind, my life, possibly my death, and it menaced the woman I loved. Glancing at her and at the others, I wondered who would outlast whom. Again I thought of my age. Fifty. How long would my heart, which pounded rapidly even when I didn't exert myself, endure the demands being put on it? But I mustn't think about my age. I must put all negative thoughts aside if I meant to survive. I must keep up my morale and the morale of the others.

And I must behave well. This, in the end, was what it was about, my having come to Antarctica. It was what had intrigued me long and intensely: getting at the heart of this wild continent.

When I thought of my daughter and what my death would mean to her I tried to put her quickly out of mind. I couldn't let myself be softened by feelings. Anyhow, I felt that my truest loyalty was to my present companions, two of whom were strangers to me. It was for them I must behave well. But primarily it was for myself.

Then there was the cold, that thief of my life's warmth. We kept glancing hopefully at the sky. When the scud showed thinner patches, our hearts sang, we grinned, cracked jokes. If the sun were to come out we might be *warm*. My left foot was worrying me, it had begun to lose all feeling.

"I don't feel too good," McIver said. "I'm gonna lie down. I may be getting pneumonia."

"What do you feel?" Kate asked.

"My chest is congested."

He crawled into the tent.

I thought, "Please, McIver, we've got enough to cope with."

When I was alone with Kate a moment I asked, "Can you get pneumonia so fast? Or is it pulmonary edema?"

"It may be the beginning of edema."

"What can we do?"

"Nothing—except get him off this altitude."

"I'll see if I can get some rocks to secure the tent flaps. We've got to cut down the wind in the tent."

I took the ice ax to some boulders but the volcanic stuff was too hard. What I needed was a pickax or a sledge hammer.

Van, emerging from the helo, said, "Doc, how about inflating the one-man life rafts? Stick them up against the tent. They'd be better than nothing."

"Great idea."

We inflated the five rafts but to little effect. Later, when we were huddling in the tent, we would feel minutely the variations in the wind's strength. When the wind subsided, the tent grew warmer. When it rose, we felt threatened, alarm signals would go off in our bodies, appendages cried out, "*Do* something! We're dying!"

I walked to a distant outcrop to take some photos. Returning to the helo, I found Van in front of the cabin hatch, munching on a chunk of lettuce. He held a whole head, from which he had cut a hunk with his sheath knife. He had thrown the outer leaves onto the snow. Picking them up and tossing them into the cabin, I said, "Don't throw *anything* away. Our lives may depend on these. There's no telling how long we may have to hang on."

He stopped eating.

I thought, "McIver has made no move to inventory the food. Or to prepare to ration it. What's he thinking of? Is he sure we'll be rescued? Doesn't he realize this cover can hang on for days? And that fatigue will worsen, causing irritation, illness, accidents? But first will come the hypothermia, then the dehydration. Does he have pneumonia? Edema? What?"

"Can we eat snow, Doc?" Van asked.

"No. It's now probably twenty or twenty-five below. It would injure your lips, tongue, palate."

"We've got fruit," he said.

"Which will be like billiard balls soon."

"Good Christ, what am I doing here?" he said in anguish.

"We'll be okay."

"Think so?"

"I know so," I lied.

I went to the cockpit to read the thermometer. It registered minus thirty-five Centigrade, the equivalent of minus thirty-one Fahrenheit. The wind was blowing steadily. What was the effective temperature? Fifty, sixty below?

Van and Kate crawled into the tent, and I followed. We lay on our backs under the sleeping bag at a right angle to the entrance. Any motion by one of us disturbed the others and robbed them of body heat. I was nearest the entrance. Farthest from me was McIver, lying parallel to me. Next to him was Van, lying opposite him. And next to Van was Kate, lying opposite me. The unzipped sleeping bag wasn't large enough to cover us adequately. We had to shift the brown blanket from time to time. My right side and thigh, only partly covered, grew very cold.

"Kate, how are your feet?" I asked.

"Losing feeling."

"Put them under my parka and shirt."

I felt like crying about her. She had come on a turnaround flight to witness the scattering of the ashes and to watch over me. Now she might die.

And Don Lynn, turning to ice. . . .

What in God's name was the point in having him dead?

And what was the flight for?

To scatter ashes.

Who would scatter them?

I.

Who decided to fly despite the cloud cover?

I.

Who refused to cry chicken in the cockpit?

I.

Who was responsible for Lynn's death?

I.

For Van's head injury?

I.

For McIver's possible edema?

I.

The possibility that Kate would die?

I.

My feet were a problem, especially the left one, which had been run over by a car many years ago. For awhile I hoped it would recover under the blanket (we had removed our boots) but I realized it wasn't responding. I tried wiggling the toes. I rubbed it against my right foot. I curled the right foot over it. Finally I handed Kate my two left gloves (leather shell and woolen liner) and asked her to put them on my left foot. The foot came around. Then my right foot started to go.

I felt sleepy. I wanted to sleep to conserve strength. But if I slept I would fail to stay on guard for my foot's sake. How would it be to return footless to the world? I resolved not to sleep unless my whole body was secured. Meanwhile it was becoming plain that it wasn't just my right foot that was in trouble but my right side from the hip down.

"I'm not going to make it if my left leg doesn't get more cover," McIver said.

Van rearranged himself, unavoidably disturbing Kate and me, and the brown blanket was passed to McIver temporarily. We huddled close together, shivering fitfully. It was remarkable how small our thermal margins were.

We were struck by what the red tent did to colors. The green sleeping bag had become a deep navy blue, my red parka a pale yellow-orange. Van kept commenting on this transmutation.

"Look! It's magic!" he would say.

He seemed more relaxed now, although once I overheard him say to Kate, "Every once in a while I feel panicky." He cracked jokes, revealed a comic, mugging side.

We heard C130 engines in the north, the south, the west. The search was on! We wanted to shout, "Here we are!" and to send up flares.

We took turns crawling out of the tent to see if there was a break in the cover. Each exhausting effort dissipated some of our body heat. Each shivering returning person brought in more cold. Invariably the report was, "It's the same."

I thought, "If only there were a tiny Plexiglas window in the top of the tent, so that we could see the weather. What a lot of body heat it would save."

For awhile all we wanted was for the cover to break up. That would signify *the next step,* without which there could be no help for us. Long hours passed.

Then, to my astonishment, McIver asked casually, "Would anybody mind if I smoked?" and broke out a small lighter.

And Van, asking the same question, withdrew from a pocket an identical lighter.

"Great Christ!" I thought. "I'm dealing with children!"

One charitable explanation I could put on their having failed to reveal the lighters was that they didn't know we were in a genuine survival situation. They had to have assumed we were sure to be rescued.

But then why had they shown signs of panic? Were their minds dissonant with their bodies?

Another charitable explanation was that they had misunderstood, or failed to grasp, or disagreed with, or discounted, my warnings about the dangers of dehydration. A less charitable one was that it graveled them to be helped by a middle-aged civilian, a professor at that, somebody who typically spent much time sitting on his behind. And what about McIver's claim he was coming down with pneumonia? Would anyone with pneumonia want to smoke? Or with edema?

At any rate, we could make a fire after all!

A non-smoker, I didn't enjoy the prospect of the small tent's being filled with smoke. But if smoking was good for their morale I was for it—for the moment. I hoped they wouldn't enjoy it at this altitude and would quickly give it up. I was wrong. They seemed to find much comfort in it.

We were all sitting up now. The tent felt most crowded when we were on our backs, our heads against the tent walls or helo seats, our chins thrust down, cricks developing in our napes and in our throat muscles. How long would it take before we'd become savagely irritable?

Van had begun to expand. He was greatly intrigued by the vivid, electric green of the cigarette flame.

Often, happening to glance his way, I discovered him staring intently at me. At one point he said, "Doc, make it out of this one and we'll call you a survivor. How do you rate this on a scale of one to ten?"

He and McIver finished their cigarettes. We lay down.

29

Time dragged on. I focused on Morgan, felt I was communicating with her. I imagined saying to her, "Lift the cloud cover. It's urgent. If you wish for it hard enough it may go away." Then it struck me that if there *was* anything to ESP I might alert her to my situation, which would be terrible, for it would make her aware of her inability to help me. So I quit that game.

I wondered about my heart beating so hard, so fast, so oddly. It hammered against my chest cavity, jumping, twisting, bouncing in a way I had never experienced. When I had swum hard, my lungs had worked hard in rhythm with my heart. Now they worked heavily, quietly, while my heart beat powerfully—a unique, alien entity, a small, mad bit of life which had gotten trapped inside me and was frantically trying to escape. It must have been due to the altitude. If it was due to fear, the fear was an entirely new kind for me.

I felt ready to die peacefully. I knew that freezing was a peaceful death. It didn't seem at all like a big deal to take off. At times it even felt like a pretty good moment for me to go—despite the fact that Kate was there and that I was in love with her. I was comforted by the fact I was well insured.

There were hours of silence, during which I asked myself what my resources were for hanging on. I felt that Erebus was cunning and that I must be more cunning than it to survive. If I kept my face under the blanket my face was of course warmed by my breath, and the energy saved in this way went into warming my right thigh and foot, making their temperature bearable.

Whenever I sat up I had strong abdominal cramps and felt on the verge of vomiting. To vomit would mean to leave the tent and lose body heat. I took to sitting up slowly, calming the cramps with a mental effort and not mentioning them.

McIver said, "I need to take a dump. I'll try to hold it in."

Defecation meant leaving the tent and exposing yourself to cold and wind. A trifle, perhaps, but a series of trifles by their sum could decide whether you survived.

I would try to survive—but for whom? Morgan? Kate? Myself? It seemed redundant, meaningless, self-serving to survive for myself. I felt the need to survive for Morgan. When I was tired and on the verge of not caring what happened to me, on the verge of drifting off to sleep or gangrene or death, I thought of her needing me, and my eyes opened wide beneath the blanket, and that popping open roused me with a lunge to full consciousness, or to superconsciousness, as it seemed to me. Over and over, thinking of Morgan needing me, I came wide awake and resolved I would live. If I didn't have the will to live for myself, I had it for her. Perhaps this resolve to live for someone else was also a part of being cunning.

How silent it was when the wind died down! The great Antarctic silence: a ringing of blood in my ears. It was like being in an anechoic chamber. Mostly I didn't hear the silence, for my breathing was heavy. My chest rose and fell with force to provide me with sufficient oxygen. Whenever I began to drift off toward sleep I would suddenly awaken, feeling I was choking.

Cunning. I warned my companions not to eat bread, it was gas-forming, and the expansion of gases at 12,000 feet was considerable as compared with that at sea level. My friend Dale Flint had eaten too much bread at one of his first meals at Vostok, the high-altitude Russian station deep in the Antarctic interior, and had gasped for hours on his back.

When I lay with my face exposed and opened my eyes now and then I didn't mind the pink, dappled light of the red tent. (How that light tricked us into thinking the cloud cover was lifting!) But when my face had been under the blanket and I had to uncover my eyes and look around the tent, the light was atrocious, it assaulted my eyeballs, it caused nerves to throb all the way from my eyes deep into my head. I couldn't endure many such seizures without becoming snow-blind. I developed a strategy. I covered my eyes with my fingers, opened my eyes slowly, then carefully spread my fingers until the light was bearable. It was strange that the light was so intense though the cloud cover was so thick.

Cloud cover was mostly what I thought about, wondering when it would lift and asking myself how to be patient, even if I had to wait for days. Unless you were patient Erebus would destroy you. You must be as simple-minded as a penguin. At Cape Evans in the bone-destroying southeasterly I had observed Adelies lying on their breasts on the sea ice, facing the wind, their beaks in their breast plumage, seemingly asleep, waiting for the storm to pass. That was what I too must do. And it was what we were doing: lying low, waiting for the momentous time when we would be able to use our flares and smoke bombs.

The cover was endlessly on my mind, endlessly the subject of tent conversation—when there was conversation. The silences conserved energy. They allowed me to animalize in this primitive moment, to sink somewhere inside myself to a place where I could concentrate on clinging to what strength I had. But what if the cover hung on day after day? Would there come a time when I would crack?

The hours passed. McIver and Van lit up again.

I said half-jokingly, "Easy on those lighters. Our lives may depend on them."

Neither McIver nor Van responded to the remark. I resolved that if they tried to light up a third time I would ask them to make the lighters common property.

McIver said, "I can't hold it in any longer. I'm going out to take a dump."

He crawled outside. Returning with a rueful expression, he reported, "It froze while I was wiping it."

I suggested it wasn't necessary to move our bowels in the open. We could defecate in the cabin's large metal cabinet that contained cans of lubricant.

"What about the chaplain?" Van said. "He's in the cabin. Wouldn't that be disrespectful?"

"I don't think so," Kate said. "Don wouldn't want us to add to our danger by doing it in the open. We have to conserve body heat."

I said it would be a simple matter to line the cabinet's floor with a helo seat cover. This would allow us to dispose of the feces from time to time. One could shut the hatch and keep out of the wind, and have the cabinet's side to sit on.

I removed my gloves, withdrew a Swiss army knife from a parka pocket and cut away a seat cover. Although the cover was very cold, to my surprise the foam rubber inside it was much warmer, and the styrofoam warmer still. These materials weren't as efficient heat conductors as the plastic cover. Another aspect of cunning: saving body heat by using foam rubber and styrofoam as pillows instead of whole seats.

Occasionally we heard planes. They always sounded far away. How long would they keep looking for us? McIver said they'd never quit, this was no civilian matter, the search would continue until the mystery was solved. I was privately skeptical. We might have fallen into the open sea without a trace, or into a giant crevasse. The search couldn't go on indefinitely. If it stopped, *then* what would we do?

Unlikely though it seems, at times I was glad to be in this spot. If I survived, what an episode I would be able to add to my history of Antarctica! Over and over a gear slipped in my thinking as I projected myself into the future and found myself a rare historian, one who had crashed on Erebus and lived, not once but twice. It was pleasant and perhaps necessary for me to dream like this. It lessened the burden of waiting. The dreams always ended abruptly when I faced the present and a future that might never come.

30

Several times I put on my boots and left the tent to take photographs. What a beautifully subtle, menacing scene it was! In my mind I threw my life away on each of these solitary excursions. If I died now I would have the satisfaction of knowing I had died fairly well. The glow that sustained me was the knowledge I was behaving decently, as far as I knew. This knowledge was the best gift I had, the best I could hope to bring down off Erebus.

There was now more light although the background of sky and mountain beyond the tent and helo was still a gray curtain through which dark boulders loomed. The trail in front of the craft was creamy on gray snow. Helo and tent pasted on a gray sheet. Gently burning highlights on the front of the white hull, on the turned-down port pontoon. Illuşion of an idyllic scene, a stage set. Burning cherry of the tent. Burgundy of the cockpit. Pearly gray of sky and snow. The helo looked almost graceful in its list to port.

I stared at the two ice fumaroles. Twin, squat towers. Cowls. No warm colors here. Grays, blacks, the tin-white of a small snowfield. No sign of vapor rising from the cowls, nor of conduits leading to them. The cowls looked harmless. It was well I knew they could be deadly. To make sure I hadn't been mistaken, I went to the cleft in the outcrop where I had seen the lichen. There it was. Its pink made me think of human flesh. Where did it get moisture in this frozen desert? From meltwater when the sun burned fiercely and the winds slept? What was it like up here in midwinter? Where did it find light for photosynthesis then? From moonlight? Aurora? Starlight? How did it survive the volcanic activity? Poisonous gases? Ash rain? Fall of pumice? Its existence comforted me. We had much in common if we compared ourselves with the inorganic world.

Van said his headache was killing him. He went to the helo and fetched a first-aid kit, which contained morphine but no aspirin.

"Shall I take some morphine, Doc?" he asked Kate.

"No!" she said. "You'll fall into a deep sleep and won't know if you're frostbitten. Nor will we. You have some aspirin, Joel?"

I told Van where in the cabin he could find my aspirin. He swallowed two or three tablets without water. His headache didn't respond. He sat up, broke out a bar of chocolate and ate some of it.

I turned to McIver, "Bob, I don't think we have a right to eat whenever we feel like it," I said. "We should ration everything. We may have to hold on for a long time."

"I thought it was the other way around," he said. "We eat as much as we want while we're still in good shape."

"You're still fresh from McMurdo, the ship," I said. "You're well fed. The time may come when we'll need food and water desperately to survive."

He thought a moment.

"Let's all eat a bit of chocolate and an apple to stave off hunger," he said.

He and Van each placed a small apple in an armpit, meanwhile munching chocolate.

Lying with eyes closed, I thought, "You son of a bitch. You threw our lives away."

As if reading my mind, Van asked, "Doc, are we gonna die?"

"We'll make it."

"I have this funny feeling. Like . . . something wonderful is about to happen. But something is saying I shouldn't be hurting like this. That it can't go on much longer. I sure hope they find us soon."

"You'll be fine," I said.

"Just stay away from the morphine," Kate said. "Please let me have it."

"Don't you trust me?" he asked.

"It's best I keep it."

A long pause.

"No, Doc. I don't think it's right for you to ask me to hand it over," he said. "You can't know how terrible I feel."

Again I resented McIver. I knew I must stop it. If I didn't I would soon hate him, and his sense of my hatred might lower his morale even lower than it was. Without high morale we couldn't show Erebus what human beings were capable of. In this place McIver and I were one, bound together. To hate him, or just to continue to resent him, was to threaten my own survival as well as that of Kate and Van.

The hours passed. Always, except for the wind and the sound of engines, there was silence. The engines faded away. Had the search stopped temporarily? When would it resume? If we weren't found in time when *would* we be found? *If* we were found, how would it happen? And if we *weren't* found?

The ceasing of the engines brought apathy. No longer an urgent need to check on the cloud cover. Even if the cover lifted now, what good would it do us with no planes in the vicinity? The hours passed without signposts. On eternity's edge time itself was apathetic.

During the next hour Van went out twice to vomit, taking the first-aid kit with him. Hearing him retch, imagining the smell, I worked to keep myself from imitating him.

"Is it the head injury that's doing it?" I asked Kate.

"A head injury can have strange consequences," she said. "The brain is like gelatin."

"That's no way for a body to behave," Van said when he returned the second time.

"Whose body?" she asked.

"Mine," he said in disgust.

Soon she too left to vomit. McIver and I were spared. She didn't seem herself after that. More silent. More distant. Remote.

Van went out again. This time he seemed to be gone too long.

"I'm going out to check on him," I said.

I shouted, "Van!" No response. I blew the plastic whistle. Silence. I checked the cabin, the cockpit. Remembering his fondness for the fumaroles, I went to the boulders near them. He was sitting on the ice behind one of them, propped against rock, facing the cowls. His head, arched back, showed his full throat. He looked asleep. His head was uncovered. The shaggy, saffron, frost-tinted balaclava was on the ice beside him, as was the first-aid kit.

"Van? You okay?"

I shook him by the shoulder. I felt for his throat pulse. There wasn't any. His throat felt very cold.

His hair was short, brown. He had a handsome nose, sensitive lips. His lips, slightly parted, revealed strong teeth. The faint mustache and wispy little beard had struggled to get a foothold.

"Joel?" Kate shouted from the tent entrance.

"Over here!"

"He's dead," I said.

"*No*!" she cried.

She felt for his pulse.

"Did he take the morphine?" she asked.

I opened the kit.

"I don't think so," I said. "I think it's hypothermia."

She began to weep.

"She examined all those frozen bodies, yet now she's crying," I thought.

It hurt me to see her bent over and sobbing so bitterly.

"Oh Kate. . . ." I said, putting my arm around her.

I felt a rage stirring inside me.

Staring at him, she said, "I feel I let him down."

"But you didn't," I said. "Why did you vomit? Did your head hurt too?"

"No. I feel very cold. Very strange."

McIver appeared, looking like an Indian with the brown blanket tightly over his head.

"Is he dead?" he asked, eyes wide.

"Yes," she said.

"Fuck! Fuck!" he cried in despair.

He went close to Van and stared into his face.

"Shall we try to move him into the helo?" she asked.

"I can't help," McIver said. "I'm too sick."

"It'd be hard at this altitude," I said.

"Unless something is done very soon, she's going to die," I thought. "I feel it in my bones."

Still sensing murderous intent inside me, I resolved to try for a trek to the summit for a possible line of sight with McMurdo. Saying nothing and taking the ice ax standing in the carton beside the shroud entrance, and the hand radio, which I hung under my parka to warm the batteries, I started out.

31

I reached the wall of boulders, some of them five or six feet high, which marked the southern boundary of the little snowplain on which we had crashed. Snowdrift had formed dunes around rocks. I crossed them with care, but my footing was uncertain. I floundered even with the use of the ice ax.

A wide snowfield sloped gradually upward before me. I looked around to see if I could bypass it, decided I couldn't, and proceeded over it, wondering about crevasses. It took me much longer to cross it than I had expected. As usual, distances in Antarctica were deceptive. I passed parallel rock walls: frozen waves of lava. Meanwhile, slowly ascending, I felt the altitude taking it out of me and had to stop often to catch my breath.

Abruptly, I came to the last of the walls. The terrain darkened, there was less snow, I was on a field of sloping outcrop. To moderate my rate of climb, I took to zigzagging. Although it was comforting to have something steady underfoot, I was worried. I was leaving few footprints now. Glancing back, I could spot neither tent nor helo. However, I could make out the uppermost curve of the Fang arcing across the sky, vertical snow splashes giving it the appearance of a machete whose edge has been ruined against rock. I decided to use the leftmost edge of the Fang as a landmark.

Cape Bird was hidden by weather but Beaufort Island rose like a snowcrested dark equilateral triangle out of the pack beyond the cape. I gauged that the tent was quite close to the cliff overlooking the Fang Glacier and not far from the DC10 site.

I reached a last, small snowfield. Looking up I saw, slightly to the right, a large ash mound sitting at the crest, from which rock ribs flowed, forming a long hill. Crossing the snow, I recalled that the crater is some 500 feet deep and about a third of a mile in diameter. I kept the ash heap on my right and followed a ridge to the north rim itself.

"Mayday! Mayday! Mayday! McMurdo! McMurdo! McMurdo! This is helo one three zero three on the north slope of Mount Erebus!"

I repeated the call so many times that my throat, dry to begin with, grew harsh. I had to rest it.

Presuming the hand radio was working, what were the chances for a line of sight with McMurdo? Not good. The crater's width probably barred the way. However, my call just might reach an airborne craft in the general neighborhood of Willy Field. If I were on the opposite rim I'd have no problem getting through. On a clear day I'd see the pressure ridges of Windless Bay like parallel arcs drawn by a careful draftsman; White Island rising phoenix-like from the ice shelf; the serrated blade of Erebus Glacier Tongue lying peacefully on the Sound; bald Mount Discovery in the southwest; and the white sword of Hut Point Peninsula stretching away from me as if to stab Black Island. Castle Rock would be a mere black pimple, as would Arrival Heights at the peninsula's southern end. And on a line of sight would be McMurdo's antenna towers on the heights.

But alas for such daydreams. I was on the crater's wrong side. It was out of the question to trek to the southern rim, given the weather, the treacherous way, my lack of crampons and my condition. So I called McMurdo, McMurdo, McMurdo. It was what I had come to do. Quite possibly it was like calling to the gods, for all the good it did.

I stood between the vast maw and the western edge of the Fang. If Ogilvie hadn't descended to 1,500 feet, if he had flown southward from Beaufort Island at 13,000, we would have passed precisely over the spot I now occupied. Directly below me was a vertically striated wall of light and dark layers like comb's teeth, but steam and smoke clouds kept me from seeing clearly. The east wall looked multilayered: ashes, pumice, some layers chalky. In the uncertain light it seemed to have the texture of old whalebone. Looking past smoke-steam across the great mouth, at fleeting moments I glimpsed the chalky opposite wall with its rows of vents emitting steam jets whose hiss I couldn't hear.

Then the western part cleared temporarily and I saw what looked like an earlier, now extinct inner crater, with a broad ledge. And I saw also the vague outlines of the deepest inner crater a bit to the left and in front of me. Now, without warning, I had a clear, direct view of this inmost crater and saw the red-hot lava or fire lake, which filled the crater's cylindrical pit. It looked to be about 200 feet in diameter and was winking seductively at me, red-orange dabs through steam and smoke. I felt my mind go weak as I had an urge to draw closer to the edge.

Forcing myself to look elsewhere, I saw that the best way for a descent into the crater was from the southwest rim; a series of three giant ridges led from it to the lava lake. I was astonished to note that the ridges, which suggested the semi-circular seats of an ancient Greek amphitheater, contained much snow. How could snow survive in that heat? Probably it was the crater's size which made it possible. It spun my mind to think I was in danger of freezing here, yet if I fell into the crater I would be cremated alive.

A long, loud hissing, followed by a loud whoosh, emerged from the depths, and the air around me smelled of sulphur. There was a higher, prolonged hissing below and then a giant, dull boom. Vast globular masses of steam swirled upward toward the rim. I heard a tremendous, cannon-like bang below. A dark gray ash cloud erupted high above the summit. Softish, thin, red-hot matter flew up, together with chunks of rock and blobs of lava. All of it, as far as I could tell, fell back into the main crater. I was caught in place as if hypnotized.

I sensed that my destiny was in the fire lake. I had a tremendous desire to *see* it. Peering, I had a feeling that something totally illuminating was about to be revealed. I made a mighty effort to understand, once and for all to *comprehend*. And I felt the prickling in my spine of a great premonition, a moment of omniscience. It frightened me.

Silently questions spewed out which didn't seem to come from me.

"Who am I?"

"Where am I going?"

"What must I do?"

"How can I go home, home, home. . . ."

A voice seeming not my own roared at the crater.

"Blind mouth! Cloaca! How *dare* you erupt like that? I'm the eye of the universe!"

A gurgling rose from the crater, and soon I was enveloped in a choking vapor, through which I saw blocks of lava shaped like halves of lava bombs flying upward, with bunches of long, drawn-out, hair-like shreds of black glass flowing from them. Some of them fell on the crater rim near me. The snow around me was now covered with rock and ash dust, and the air was yellow with sulphur.

Coughing heavily, sick to my stomach, tasting ash deep in my mouth and throat, I made my way down toward the tent as fast as I could, vaguely aware of much gray pumice, down which I slid as if it were a vast sandhill.

I had no trouble finding the tent. As I neared it Kate rushed out.

"You're covered with *ashes*! Where've you *been*?" she cried, staring at me, then embraced me and helped me crawl inside.

I did my best to explain to her and McIver what had happened. It took a while for my mind to settle down, and my lungs too.

Whenever Kate broke the silence to ask, "Are you all right?" I tried to reassure her. With Lynn and Van gone, she was freer with me and didn't hesitate to comfort me by stroking my leg. But I was frozen inside. I was listening to what the crater might be saying. And listening too for the sound of searching planes.

Then I had a curious experience. Imagining that I was looking down on Erebus from about 15,000 feet, I made out the two crash sites and the lava lake. They formed a triangle. When I looked northeast towards the wilds of the Southern Ocean, the apex of the triangle was the DC10 site. When I looked southeast, into the teeth of the wind roaring down from the continental plateau and over the great ice shelf, the apex was the fire lake. It all convinced me of something I had been suspecting since Van's untimely death.

The crashes were the result of magic—black, not white.

32

We lay there waiting. It was approaching midnight. I told myself that soon I would begin a log to mark the passage of days for our morale's sake. Soon there would be another dawn in this land of no dawns. A plane approached, then dimmed. I seemed to have the acutest hearing of the three of us despite my ear flaps. I could pick out a plane even when there was wind. And it seemed to me that I noted its coming before anyone else.

Another plane drew close, faded. There was a long silence. Half-conscious, I wondered if I was the only one awake. Then I heard a different engine—a chop, chop, chopping sound—for the first time since the crash. It was faint. I thought I must be imagining it. Then it sounded close and above us—how remarkable that it should be close, how extraordinary that it should be *above* us!

"I hear a helo!" I cried, sitting up.

A pause.

"I hear it too!" Kate cried.

"I'm not so sure," said McIver.

I wondered about his hearing.

Closest to the entrance, I scrambled out on all fours in my stockinged feet, fumbling with the shroud, belly cramping, head swimming. I studied the sky. Nothing. Then I spotted a Coast Guard helo between us and the summit. It was making a slow turn to head southwestward—to the right, *away* from us. It gave no sign of seeing us.

"I *see* it!" I cried, and spun around to get the Very pistol from the open carton near the shroud.

"Shoot the Very!" McIver shouted.

I aimed at the helo and fired. Rocketing up, the flare burst into two red mushrooms which descended like burning parachutes. The helo wiggled and changed course. In that twinkling everything changed for us. Erebus hadn't been cunning enough to kill us. The cloud cover hadn't frozen us. We were no longer lost. Now all the resources of McMurdo and Christchurch would be behind us.

"They *see* us!" I shouted.

"Wave him off! Don't let him land!" cried McIver.

It was good advice. We hadn't selected a landing pad, nor indicated wind direction. In his excitement the pilot might make a tragic mistake.

I crisscrossed my arms vigorously. He wiggled again, then dropped something. A moment later I realized it was a survival pack.

He departed beyond a high ridge to the right of the crater. On that side of Erebus the sky had cleared a bit, and the full ball of the sun, looking tiny, wan against the weird scape, showed through cloud cover in turmoil.

"What a haunting scene," I thought.

Black boulders advancing downward like combers. Lines of boulders suggesting trenches, embankments, the Civil War. Horizon toothed with boulders. Light boiling in a cauldron through curtains of cover. Snowsplashed ash heaps, mounds.

My watch read precisely midnight. Over there, where the full orb was, had to be due south.

Kate and McIver were out of the tent. We all shook hands. Then Kate and I hugged each other. McIver watched as if from a great distance. Tears flooded my eyes. I hugged her again. I kissed her tenderly.

A Herc arrived, made huge circles over us, appearing, disappearing in the scud, sometimes flying directly above us. We waved. He kept circling, never letting go of us. McIver, coughing heavily, selected a landing pad for a possible rescue helo—an apron of sloping, almost naked rock about a hundred feet east of the tent. I helped him mark it with my green rucksack and some food cartons.

Kate and I retrieved the survival pack. It contained no headgear and no footgear. But it had matches and fat white candles—and lots of mosquito netting. We returned to the tent. McIver, sitting under the brown blanket, warmed a stockinged foot with a lighted candle, the flame close to the blanket.

"Same poor judgment he showed when he tried to overfly Erebus," I thought. "If this tent goes up in flames, presuming we escape, all our gear will go with it. And we may well go under even though we've been found. No telling how long it will be before they come for us. Or *can* come."

"Take it easy with the candle, Bob," I said.

He ignored what I said.

He warmed his naked hand. The flame singed the elbow of Kate's parka.

"Damn it, Bob, you're too close to her parka," I said. "Get a grip on yourself."

He set the candle down on a small piece of styrofoam and stared at the flame's pure, intense green.

We wondered aloud when the rescue attempt would be made. Would Coast Guard helos hazard a rescue? Or would a Herc try to skylift us out?

"They're not gonna skylift *me*," McIver said. "You get a hell of a jerk when they do that. And you'd freeze to death before they pulled you inside. I think they'll send a couple of stripped-down helos. They can't take us out all together. We'll probably go out two at a time. We ought to decide who's going out first."

"I'll go last," I said.

"No, Joel, I will," Kate said.

"Out of the question."

"Then I'll go with you."

"No. You go soon as they come."

We waited. We heard a helo approaching. That beautiful,

familiar, chopping sound. We laced our boots and crawled outside. I saw it near the summit. The scene was unreal. We were on this ice, snow, rock. There were the red tent, well staked down, its ropes taut, and the helo leaning to port, heavy on its hull. There was McIver setting off red flares and red smoke bombs to show wind direction. There was the summit, obscured by scud, smoke, steam. And beyond it the wan sun that for months never set and which had burned me badly at Royds. Up there in that fairyland the helo was circling, feeling its way carefully.

"My God, that's hairy," I thought, and wondered if it too would air-starve.

The Herc watched over all of us.

McIver signaled the helo (1288, from the *South Wind*) to a landing. Kate and I stood by to watch it touch down. The rotor blizzard hit us full in the face. Our eyes were blasted by ice and snow particles. Blinded, we whirled to give the helo our backs.

It struck me as remarkable that the eerie, immense, marvelous silence of Erebus was being shattered by 1288's barbaric sounds. They were made by a *live* engine. I felt a new, a special intimacy with the noises a helo made in contrast with those made by a Herc like the one circling, circling above us.

When the helo was on the deck, engine idling, McIver promptly boarded it—without so much as a fare-thee-well. I was shocked to see him leave first, when every tradition required that as pilot he go last. It was a crazy thing to do, the word would surely get around, ostracism was bound to follow. I imagined the reaction at McMurdo when he, the pilot, emerged from the first rescue helo, whereas I, the passenger, the civilian, the middle-aged gent (not to forget my ordeal on the DC10), left on the second. McIver, insanely covering his ass, couldn't care less.

Without gallantry what were we? McIvers.

I thought, "All those years ago Scott had kept writing, recording, setting down the raw materials of history, while he was starving, freezing, dying alone on that vast ice shelf, afloat in outer space. But here McIver has no sense of history, he's a paraplegic of the present."

The pilot, Neil Usher, came over and said to me, "Stand by, Doc. We can only take two of you at a time. The second helo is just behind me."

"You know about Lynn and VanDyke?"

"Bob told me."

"Did anybody hear my Mayday from the crater?"

"No."

"What caused you to look this way?"

"The C130 thought he saw a break in the cover above the crater. We went to check it out. This was one of the few places we hadn't been able to check because of the weather. Kate, why don't you warm yourself in the helo?"

"I'll wait until you're ready to leave."

"Go, Kate, it's time," I said.

"You okay?" she asked.

"I'm fine."

"See you at McMurdo."

She boarded while Usher conferred with his crewman in front of the cockpit.

Shivering, I tried to warm up in the tent. But I was restless. I climbed inside the crashed helo to have a last look at Don Lynn, not covered by the brown blanket now. I stared at the once-pink face, now bluish, the once freshly shaven cheeks and chin, now stubbly, the thinning hair, and I remembered his great calves—"His wife will miss them"—and his scraping the old wax on his knees beside the two enlisted men.

I walked to the fumaroles to look at Van, no survivor, who still sat braced against the boulder, oblivious of the cold, seeming to peer through lowered lids at the fumaroles, as if to see the answer to the Mystery. Feeling the sadness of his dying so young, remembering George Vince on Danger Slope back in the days of Scott's first expedition soon after the beginning of the century, feeling the sadness of Scott, Edward Wilson (Uncle Bill), Birdie Bowers dying one by one in the blizzard-trapped tent, alone on the ice shelf in the horrible month of March, I felt heavy at heart, and heavy with all that had happened in my two crashes.

Sorrowing for all the dead, wondering again why I had been spared, hearing the idling helo engine and rotors still shattering the iceslope stillness, I checked that the cardboard box was in place where I had last seen it, then went to watch the liftoff.

33

I took the scene for granted (in the end the most extreme event seems normal), yet it was hard for me to believe what I was watching. I saw three spectacular things: the first rescue helo was *undamaged, functional* (the rotors spun, the engine growled); the men were *fresh*, full of body heat; and fiery reds riveted my gaze in this cold scape. A burning red light on the port pontoon. A red flare glowing between two men, one red-suited, the other green-clad, with a helmet that made him look megacephalic.

The red-suited man was trying to mark the contours of the rock apron in case the takeoff blizzarded the pad for the second rescue helo. The copilot, monitoring the engine, observed the proceedings from the cockpit. The overcast was still strong but no whiteout threatened at the moment.

The red-clad man, twisting, faced me. The end of his flare was a white-hot ingot. His red suit flamed. There was still no dye on the rock. Tossing the flare aside, he picked up another. Now he aimed the dye end at the rock. Red smoke spurted, hugging the ground.

Hearing a helo behind me, I turned, saw nothing, then made out a speck above the middle horizon. It was the second rescue helo, approaching the plateau from the west. The red man, having left a brilliant red line in front of the cockpit, marked the position of the tail wheel. Dense red smoke sprang from his legs.

The pilot, Neil Usher, walked to the tent, removed the

exterior rear metal pole, returned to the pad, stuck the pole in a rock crevice, stripped to the waist and tied his T-shirt to the pole as a wind flag.

"It's thirty below and he has a small, very white paunch," I thought. "He has a lot of body heat from the helo to be able to do that."

The copilot called Usher to the cockpit and said something to him. Usher came over to me.

"How you doing?" he asked, staring at me.

A pause.

"The other helo is having engine trouble," he said. "He's returning to base. I'll be back for you soon as I can. Okay?"

I nodded.

He touched my arm and asked with a glance of concern, "You okay?"

I nodded again.

"When I come back for you, bring only your cameras," he said. "We've got to get out of here fast. The weather is bad. It may close in again."

"I'm not leaving without my professional gear," I said.

He studied my eyes, shrugged, walked to the helo. I followed him part of the way.

In the cockpit he raced the rotors for liftoff. My face felt it was struck by a metal curtain. Ice pellets stung my eyes. I spun to give the helo my back, digging with my toes to hang onto the outcrop. The takeoff caused such a whiteout that for minutes I saw nothing. My double-gloved hands had been screaming for some time, saying they were being crushed by giant pincers. Wondering if reloading the cameras barehanded had anything to do with it, I tried to photograph the helo when it was just to the right of the summit. My hands refused to obey. I walked to the tent, clapping my hands. It was like clapping boards, for all the feeling there was in them.

Erebus was so still I stopped as if transfixed. The lack of any sound now, or rather the presence of a non-sound something, made the spot on which I stood feel intimately connected with everything in the surrounding region. Everything was very close, yet far away. I felt this enigmatic silence as if it menaced my sanity, even my life.

Was it George Vince approaching me out of the mist? Yes. It was. He was the young man who died in an accident near Hut Point in the early days of Scott's first expedition. He was wearing the clothes he had died in: balaclava, gabardine waterproof, dirty wool trousers, mitts, the fatal finneskoes.

I was filled with a rush of fatherly feeling.

"What happened?" I asked. "We've never known the details."

"We were caught in a blizzard, the nine of us," he said. "A southeasterly, fresh from the Pole and the ice shelf. It was so bad we were afraid it would blow our tents away. Our two primuses were broken, so we couldn't melt snow, get some heat into us. Our clothes were scanty. We were fighting frostbite, now this part, now that. We were ignorant, frightened, needed too hard the ship's comforts. So we abandoned the tents and the sledges and headed for the ship, which we took to be only a mile away. We were battered, disoriented, we had little visibility. The snow was thick, you could barely breathe, it flew up your nostrils, turned your lips to ice."

"Poor boy," I said. "And then?"

"Then we reached an iceslope. It ended in a sheer drop to the sea but we didn't know it. We were wearing soft fur boots, finneskoes, with very little grip, and were losing our footing. We changed to loose leather ski boots—all but me. They were frozen hard. The others got them on after much wrestling. They were older than I. Their greater age gave them greater fear, they fought until their feet were inside. But I, young, ignorant, impatient, irritable, gave up too soon and continued to wear my fur boots."

"And then?"

"We went forward, and when the others slid downward very fast, they saved themselves by digging their heels in. But I flew past them like a shadow, over the precipice and into the tidal crack. Professor Stevenson, I found a watery grave in all that world of ice. The water knocked all the pain and fear out of me. My body became a frozen memory of what it had been. No earth to embrace me, let me molder. No burial in freshly turned South African soil. Too far from home, from the Cape of Good Hope that had been my childhood. My cross still stands, unweathered in this worst of earth's deserts."

"I know. I've visited it on occasion."

"Remember me in your history, professor. Give me some small memorial, if only as a testament to one who was too young, too hurried, too foolish."

"You can count on it!" I said. "My word as a Virginian!"

"Thank you, thank you," he said as he faded slowly away.

Then it was my mother who approached, her eyes fixed on me. Her face and throat had turned to a fine onionskin, very wrinkled. She smiled too much, as if in shyness or self-reproach. Her dentures were patchwork. Her clothes were ill-fitting. Her wrinkled feet wore loose old slippers.

"My lovely child, what are you doing in this terrible place?" she asked. "Tell me quickly."

"Mom, I'm the sole survivor of a plane crash," I said. "But tell me about you. I heard you died of lung cancer. Did you suffer much? I wasn't able to be at your bedside. I was on an icebreaker on the remotest part of the remotest ocean, without any means of reaching you in time."

"Dear child," she said, "I died not of disease, not of an accident, not of old age, not mysteriously in my sleep, as some do. I missed your gentleness, tenderness, loving ways. It was the longing for you that robbed the sweet life from me."

Three times I tried to embrace her but she dissolved like a bit of ice fog.

"Mom, why don't you let me hold you?" I cried. "I was robbed of the comfort of being at your deathbed, your funeral!"

"I'm a shadow now," she said, "without bone or flesh or sinew. Goodby, my sweet boy."

And she dissolved into nothingness as I tried again to hug her.

And then I saw Scott himself—Robert Falcon Scott. His face had a darkened color. The skin had been blasted by polar winds and the unsetting sun. The once handsome nose was now a black button, and there was a surprisingly long space between the tip of his nose and his mouth, as if his nose had shrunk. His right eye was larger than its mate, and he was squinting, or rather barely looking, for his eyes were greatly pained by the immense amount of light they had seen. His brow was marked by two perpendicular furrows. Parentheses connected his nose with the corners of his blackened mouth. His head was encased in what seemed to be a black bonnet. An old scarf fluttered from his throat.

He wore a loose pullover gabardine which fell sheetlike to below his knees, and he had on enormous fur gauntlets secured by a harness made of white canvas tape and worn around his neck and across his chest. The harness reminded me of a child's walk harness, and there was much that was childlike, pathetic about him. He was beardless after months of marching. His harrowing experiences, the shortage of oil, and the great cold had not kept him from shaving.

"Joel," he began, "I'm being maligned in books, magazines, newspapers, common gossip. Even my widow is slandered. It's said she was unfaithful to me with Nansen at the very time I was marching toward the Pole. It's said I was a bad explorer, an impossible leader, irresponsible, too sensitive, a killer of my friends as well as myself. It's true I was sensitive, had a large female component, but I believe that was part of my strength. We died with honor. If we had wanted to survive at all costs we could have eaten Edgar Evans at the foot of the Beardmore. That would have given us the strength to wait out the blizzard. Or we could have reached One Ton Depot before the blizzard began. You know the Antarctic, know the ice shelf where we died, so judge us fairly.

"Our story is well known: how we found the signs of Amundsen's camp. It broke our hearts to know we were second. We had lost much flesh and even more spirit. We had seen too much ice, and too much light, the light that bedeviled us, hit us from everywhere. At the Pole the sun hung low like a terrible spotlight, circling the horizon in a kind of madness. Day flowed through night, there was no difference. No life to be seen around us, and no life remotely nearby. We had stepped outside the planet and now we tried to return.

"We died in March in that blizzard, particles of ice that seared us, would rip out our eyeballs if we tried to face them, only eleven miles from One Ton Depot with its life-giving food and fuel, we three tent-locked, Evans dead first at the foot of the great Beardmore, then Oates the soldier, gangrene-footed, quiet, who hobbled out into the storm to give us a fighting chance, staggered a distance, fell, was snowburied forever, we not stirring from the tent, accepting the inevitable. Birdie Bowers died first. Then came Wilson, going as he softly prayed. I, the oldest, endured the longest. We lay there unchanging though dead, the bacteria at bay, we serene as ice, drifting slowly seaward on that vast floating shelf and yearning for a proper burial.

"March gave way to April. We were alone, unfound, unsearched for, lonely, unsung. April became June, the shortest day, midwinter, time for celebration. The great dark colds of August embraced us, kept us dry, inviolate, hard as rock. Then came October, the waning darkness, the promise of rich low sunlight, counterclockwise, for our frozen eyes. In November the search party, retracing our tracks, four specks in the white blue-domed immensity, reached the depot, saw we hadn't been there, went south beyond it and—a miracle—spotted the tip of our conical tent at a great distance. It was young Wild, the glaciologist, who cried when I failed to include him in the polar-trek party, wearing spectacles as usual, who saw it first, now keen-eyed. We were lonely no longer.

"They uncovered us with hot spadework, sweat blinding them. The snow, pressured into ice, made heavy work. They were shocked to see us so haggard, bones, skin, unshaved, gray as frostbite, above all familiar, undecayed, former comrades, leader: Bowers, Wilson, me, all of us on our backs, my arm across Wilson's chest. Reading my messages aloud, they wept for our story, far from England. Watching them, we wept too. Dead though we were, the humanity was still hot in us.

"We wanted to embrace them but couldn't, our joints were stone. We wanted to shout but were voiceless though our flesh and sinews were intact that should have vaporized long ago. The search party, the daylight growing longer each day but the cold still awesome, having removed what they thought right to take to England, let the tent fall on us, covered us with snow-ice, built a cairn of blocks above us, read a service and, weeping, returned with frost-shredded faces and hugely blistered fingers to winter quarters at Cape Evans, the hut we had constructed so proudly and which would never house us again. Later they set a cross of Australian jarrah wood for us on the top of Observation Hill, laboring two days.

"We gave great sighs. We were at peace beneath our tent, our snow, our ice, our cairn. Though not land-buried, though still heading for the sea creatures who would eat us—leopard seals, Weddell seals, crabeaters, killer whales, and all the smallfry krill, not to forget the skuas, the penguins, the varied fish—we had had our funeral. Our story would be known, at least in England. I never dreamed it would travel worldwide, truly I didn't."

There was a long pause.

"Judge us fairly, Joel," he said, then turned away and strode with heavy, lame steps into the whiteness.

34

Suddenly, in bright flashes that lasted fifteen to twenty seconds, I had an extreme revelation: Erebus was a hypnotizing, seductive, malevolent force at the world's nether end, the planetary anus spewing the fires of earth's indigestion. The events I had been brooding about came tightly together. Erebus caused the DC10 crash. The helo crash. All the deaths connected with them. It caused the madness in Scott's polar-trek last-minute decisions. And his fate.

I crawled inside the tent—it felt spacious now—got into the sleeping bag and resumed clapping my hands. How soon would Usher return? What if something happened to *his* helo? What if the weather socked me in again? Why hadn't I asked for some liquid, at least for something hot? Or for matches, McIver's lighter? However, Van no doubt still had *his*. What would I burn? What to catch water in?

Restless, I went outside and stared toward the summit. Would the weather hold? What had caused the break in the cover? Hot gases boiling up from the crater? Why was Erebus angry with me? What had I done to offend it? I had been the sole survivor. Now I was the one least likely to survive.

Going to the cabin, I paid my respects to Don Lynn, chaplain, fellow Protestant. I stood beside him awhile and wanted to cry about his death but was too worn out. In the cockpit I checked the outside temperature: it was minus thirty-nine Centigrade, or roughly minus thirty-eight Fahrenheit. I went to the boulder and paid my respects to Van, tosser of flares, stabber of helos. He looked mysterious in the long mitts, with his arched head, making me think of figures from El Greco. I found the lighter but left it in his pocket.

Stumbling, dangerously cold, I paid my respects to the ice fumaroles, those monkish cowls with their deadly vapors. Finally I went to the lichen, the bit of life with which I had much in common now, we were the sole residents on this Erebus plateau. How had it managed to survive the volcano's wrath? By supreme cunning?

I returned to the tent and spent some time nursing my hands, after which I tried to drift off, but I still had altitude insomnia. I lay there vegetating—until I realized I hadn't taken accident photographs of the craft. An accident investigation was inevitable, but it seemed unlikely that lives would be risked to photograph the damage. I went out and photographed it methodically.

At last Usher's helo came. I fetched the cardboard box and carried it with my professional gear to the helo. I handed the box to the red crewman. It was a high step to the cabin floor. With gear hanging from my shoulders and cameras from my neck, I fumbled to climb aboard. My knees were weak, my hands couldn't clutch, my gear was pulling me backwards toward the rock. The crewman reached out above me, grabbed my armpits and with a tremendous jerk hauled me aboard.

I removed my gloves, fumbled with my seat belt. Noticing I was having trouble, he belted me in. My hands were dead white, especially from the knuckles to the nails. To the left of my seat I felt a current of warm air. I hung my left hand in it. He bent over to increase the air flow. I warmed my hands in it alternately until they hurt very badly and I knew they would be all right.

He handed me coffee in a paper cup. Now and then he glanced almost lovingly at me. He was older than the usual crewman and looked mellower, wiser, perhaps also sadder. Usher called him away, and after awhile the two of them, breathing heavily, carried Don Lynn aboard and gently set him down on the middle of the floor. I felt the warmth returning slowly to my body.

Stepping down at the helo pad at McMurdo, where it was startlingly warm and bright, I glanced at my watch. We had crashed at about 2:30 P.M. It was now several minutes past four in the morning. I looked for Kate. She was there.

I remember the extraordinary emotion I felt at that moment. I had expected McMurdo to be the ghost town it usually was at that hour. What seemed a wave of human bodies slowly, deliberately, moved towards me, surrounding me silently, observing me strangely, as if I were a ghost. Many people had apparently been unable to sleep. They wanted to be at the pad when we got back.

While on Erebus I thought the helo crash didn't really get to me. Maybe this too was part of being cunning. A phone patch to Morgan the morning of the rescue changed my mind. I was reluctant to call my daughter. However, I had been told that news releases had already gone out, and I decided if she must learn about what had happened, it was best she hear it from me and as soon as possible. Would I behave well with her? The distance between us was great, phone patches were hard to come by, I must make my point casually and well. If I wasn't up to it it was better not to call her at all.

The phone rang. It was near my room in the corridor of the Lodge.

"Professor Stevenson? Stand by, please. Don't hang up," the ham operator said.

My hands went cold as I waited. I felt naked in the corridor. I hoped no one would come along during the call. Then she was on, that voice I knew so well.

I should explain that a phone patch is a combination of short wave radio and telephone, and that it doesn't permit you to speak simultaneously.

I said, "Dear, if you hear or read about a helicopter accident down here and my name is mentioned, don't be concerned. I'm fine. Five of us crashed near the summit of Mt. Erebus. Two killed. The other three of us were rescued after twelve hours and all are in good shape. So you're not to worry about me. Okay? Over."

"Daddy, I'm flabbergasted! Can you give me some details? Over."

I provided them. When I told her about my hands and glanced at them, my heart grew cold, I felt I was melting away, my voice dropped in pitch, it sounded unlike itself, my throat trembled, I didn't dare to speak.

I struggled to regain control. My jaws clamped shut, my eyes grew moist, something threatened to babble out of my voice box, and I grew icy with fear. I must above all carry the patch off well and not let her suspect there were unresolved forces fighting inside me, trying to overwhelm me. The sole purpose of this call was to spare her anxiety, yet I was in danger of doing precisely what I wanted to avoid.

There were moments of hard, brittle silence when I lost my voice and something terrible seemed to be menacing me. The silences terrified me. They mustn't be allowed to give me away. She mustn't realize that I was wrestling with something tremendously powerful, that at one moment I was calm, objective, serene, then suddenly I was beset, especially when I spoke about myself in some detailed way. She mustn't be permitted to grasp the horror of the wrestling match I was so unexpectedly going through. I fought, rescued some semblance of a voice.

"Daddy, you all right?"

"I've been drinking, dear. Guess I've drunk a right fair amount," I replied, relieved to have an excuse.

Just as my heart on Erebus had throbbed wildly in a rhythm all its own, so now my voice and jaws deserted me for urgent tasks and messages, they needed to cry out something with enormous strength which I was convinced would shame me. I knew my task if they didn't. It was to handle this call gracefully and with only one objective: her peace of mind. If I failed, she would be badly upset, would decide I was covering up a serious injury, and I wouldn't get another patch for some time, and a letter to her to set things right could take a long while reaching her.

"Aren't we going over our time?" she asked, perhaps glad to change the subject because of what she may have suspected.

"No, this is a high-priority patch."

"My God, Daddy, you'd better come out of there. I don't want you there any longer."

"I'm all right, honey."

"Well I'm *not*."

She began to cry.

"Honey, I'm fine," I assured her.

"*Two crashes*! You come out of there, Daddy! I *hate* that place!"

"I'll be leaving soon."

"Promise?"

"Promise."

Some merciful force appeared from nowhere to help me. I steadied myself and at last managed to sign off decently. The wrestling ended once I hung up.

I went to my room, lay down, closed my eyes and listened to echoes of the conversation, feeling I had come through by the skin of my teeth. Exhausted, gathering my forces as well as I knew how, I was no longer prepared to believe I had been emotionless on Erebus.

35

I closed the drapes, removed my clothes and fell asleep. Awaking, I sensed I had slept enough but a glance at my clock showed I had slept only about three hours. I went across the corridor to the head. Since I was here last—on Wednesday, yesterday, but it felt like several days ago—broad ribbons of masking tape had been stretched across the two toilet cubicles and the two urinals. On them had been hand-printed: SECURED. WATER HOURS. The water-making system had apparently broken down. The four wash basins were free, however.

As I washed, my finger ends were strange to me. They felt fat, calloused. They were swollen. They tingled in an unpleasant way and felt dangerously slow and stupid in hot water. The middle finger of my right hand was curved like a hook. The knuckle was swollen and very sore. I had no idea of what had happened to it.

After dressing I went outside. The sun shone. It was always gleaming and glaring somewhere.

I thought, "Anybody fearful of the ghosts of night might do well to consider the advantages of a place where the nights are brilliantly sunlit. God, how beautiful. How I love this place, those mountains, that ice, that sky, this air so dry it cracks your fingers to the quick out in the field."

I went to the Dispensary, where Mike the paramedic said there had probably been nerve damage to my fingers. Sometimes it could take as long as a year for the sensation to return. Or it could come back in a matter of months. He straightened and splinted the injured knuckle and said I couldn't go camping with my hands the way they were. There was no sign of Kate. I assumed she was catching up on sleep. It was frustrating to write in my journal with a splinted hand.

Later the same day I learned from Dave Breslin two stunning facts, which he had gotten from Brian Edwards, the Scott Base leader, within the hour and which Edwards had received by telex from New Zealand. The first explained the DC10's being off course. The second revealed that the craft's radar had indeed been functioning and made clear why it had failed to show Erebus's looming presence on its screen.

The first fact. The coordinates for McMurdo which Sam Ogilvie had been given at the pre-flight briefing in Auckland and which he had carefully written down—as he had jotted down the coordinates of all the flight's waypoints—were 164°48′E and 77°53′S. These placed McMurdo not in its true position but two degrees and ten minutes of longitude, or about twenty-seven miles, to the west. It turned out that the station's false position had been in the airline's ground computer system for almost fifteen months without being discovered. As it happened, there was a beneficial side to this error (an error which may have been deliberate), for, placing McMurdo at the head of McMurdo Sound, it caused the nav track's final lap, of some fifty miles, to proceed over the safe (because flat) terrain of McMurdo Sound in an area threatened by Erebus's towering, massive height. As we know, the Sound, about forty miles wide, lies between Ross Island's western coast and the eastern coast of Victoria Land.

What Ogilvie didn't know when he took off for McMurdo was that at 1:10 A.M. (almost six and a half hours earlier), someone in the Flight Operations Section of Kiwi Airways had discovered the error and had corrected the McMurdo coordinates in the ground computer and in the plane's nav track, thereby changing the track from the safe area of the Sound to an overflight of Erebus and thus to a potential collision course with the mountain. The cockpit crew had not been informed of the crucial change, consequently the aircraft's high technology, which Ogilvie was so proud of and on which he had staked his life, had been defeated. When, at the end of his second orbit, he armed the nav mode it locked onto McMurdo's coordinates and sent the plane hurtling toward the station regardless of the fact that the great mass of Erebus barred the way.

The radar. The radar equipment on the plane was designed primarily to detect moisture and variations in moisture—to detect air turbulence. But because the Erebus slope was extraordinarily dry, and because the ice absorbed the radar's radio waves, nothing was echoed back to the plane, and the radar screen remained empty. Self-evident? Hardly. It was discovered only after much investigation. When, desperately trying to convince Ogilvie to turn back, I had said, "Then there's something wrong with the radar!" I had been only partly right—the radar was functioning, but it was disastrously inadequate in dealing with the ice-sheathed slope. So much for the casual assumption that Antarctic conditions can be safely encountered simply by the use of fine equipment and by extrapolating from temperate region experience.

What a chain of events!

(1) Someone may have made a deliberate error regarding McMurdo's true coordinates.

(2) Fifteen months later someone corrected the error.

(3) Someone may have failed to inform the cockpit crew of the correction.

(4) Bad weather prevented Ogilvie from seeing he was off the safe course.

(5) The remarkably dry surface of the Erebus slope hid the mountain from the plane's radar screen.

(6) And the inexperience of the cockpit crew with Antarctica, together with (7) Ogilvie's absolute reliance on his high technology, sealed the fate of 248 persons.

Improbable? Highly. Yet it happened.

The idea of improbability possessed me. Even a single air

crash on an active volcano (of all the many mountains available in the region) seemed improbable. Yet there were two such crashes. And within weeks of each other.

The helo crash itself seemed improbable.

(1) An immense cloud cover hovered over Ross Island and its environs.

(2) The pilot was a greenhorn in Antarctica.

(3) He left the prescribed safe course.

(4) He went so high that his engine air-starved.

(5) He blundered into the downdraft.

(6) The craft's four survival packs were missing.

(7) Of the five persons on board, only one had brought survival gear.

(8) That gear included a survival tent and cot mattresses.

Thinking back to Scott's historic polar trek, it seemed to me that there too I saw remarkable improbabilities.

He had meticulously planned the polar party for four men.

The tent held four.

The rations were made up for four for each week.

The cookers held four mugs, four pannikins, four spoons.

Yet at the last minute and without explanation (a mysterious decision that is still being debated) he added Bowers—Bowers the shortest among them by far (my memory said five foot four), with a short stride, and the only one of the supporting parties without skis, so that, unlike the others of the polar party, he was obliged to walk, and at times to slog, not ski, to the Pole.

Scott soon discovered he had miscalculated in at least one respect by taking Bowers along.

"Cooking for five takes a seriously longer time than cooking for four; perhaps half an hour in the whole day," he wrote in his journal on 5 January 1912, two days after his decision regarding Bowers.

This meant a half-hour lost from marching or sleep. In the perilously close margins by which the party proceeded, and for the length of time in which they had to endure, the daily loss could prove serious indeed. Between 3 January and 16 February, when

Evans died at the foot of the Beardmore Glacier, the loss amounted to twenty-two hours, or more than two man-hauling days.

Toward the end Scott was much beset by improbabilities. In fact, they were killing him.

In his "Message to the Public," written as he lay dying, he noted, "But all the facts above enumerated were as nothing to the surprise which awaited us on the Barrier [ice shelf] . . . . Our wreck is certainly due to this sudden advent of severe weather, which does not seem to have a satisfactory cause . . . and to a shortage of fuel in our depots, for which I cannot account, and finally, to the storm which has fallen on us within eleven miles of the depot at which we hoped to secure our final supplies. Surely misfortune could scarcely have exceeded this last blow. We arrived within eleven miles of One Ton Camp with fuel for one last meal and food for two days. For four days we have been unable to leave the tent—the gale howling about us."

Not the least of the improbabilities surrounding him in my mind was that although he was the oldest of the party, he was the last to die. At the end of 1911 he was forty-three, Wilson thirty-nine, Evans thirty-seven, Oates thirty-two, Bowers twenty-eight.

Finally, there were perhaps the greatest improbabilities of all—I had survived both crashes and, to top it off, had escaped hypothermia and even frostbite as I lay unconscious on the Erebus slope.

As I thought about all this it began to dawn on me that it was *too* improbable. My mind cast about for a revealing single cause, a common denominator, and one which would, furthermore, explain why Amundsen had been so easily successful in reaching the Pole whereas both Scott and Shackleton had had such a terrible time of it.

Shackleton had declined the Bay of Whales as winter quarters and followed in Scott's steps by basing himself on Ross Island—Cape Royds, to be exact. He had made it back by a hair from his farthest southing, which was within ninety-seven nautical miles of the Pole. Amundsen, after conquering the Pole, said that if Shackleton had based himself on the Bay of Whales (as Amundsen had done) *he* would have been the Pole's discoverer, the Bay of Whales being some seventy or eighty miles closer to the Pole than Royds.

Was Shackleton's near disaster a warning to Scott? If so, had Scott failed to read it? He had followed in Shackleton's steps by using the Beardmore Glacier, which Shackleton had discovered, as the highway to the polar plateau and the Pole. Why? And why had they followed each other in such a tortuous way?

You have no doubt caught my drift—that Erebus was behind all this witchery. As the end closed in had Scott glimpsed at last if only fitfully the true nature of Erebus and realized he had been bewitched by it, as he had been bewitched to a less focused degree by Antarctica? And had he understood that his strange decision regarding Bowers had been caused by that witchery? And that he was responsible for Bowers's death?

He had written to Bowers's mother, "The ways of Providence are inscrutable, but there must be some reason why such a young, vigorous and promising life is taken," as if he had had no part in the chain of events which led to Bowers's death. Privately had he sensed a different truth? He had written not at all to Evans's wife or Oates's next of kin. Why? Because of guilt?

Was it possible that Amundsen had been graced because the Bay of Whales was far from Erebus, and that Scott and Shackleton had gotten their comeuppance because they had based themselves in close sight of the volcano? Had Scott, near the end, suddenly realized, if perhaps dimly, what had brought about his fate? Was he hinting at something metaphysical when he wrote of the severe weather, "which does not seem to have a satisfactory cause," or when, mentioning the shortage of fuel in the depots, he wrote, "for which I cannot account"?

If so, would it show in his face? I had often wondered what it would be like to study his face. Now I was possessed, as if I were destined to discover his inmost secret in it—whether he knew, finally, what had spooked and killed him. Although normally I was humble about such things, I felt certain now I could read his features with great prescience, much more profoundly than any mere gypsy reading tea leaves (I thought of Pamela Mansfield's grandmother with her gypsy blood).

For years I had thought it would be worth recovering the still-preserved bodies of Scott, Wilson and Bowers before they drifted out to the carnivores of the Ross Sea, and interring them in Westminster Abbey. The tent contained metal: hobnailed boots, pannikins, spoons, mugs, a primus. And the rate and direction of drift of the ice shelf in the tent's sector were known. Scientist friends of mine thought that modern airborne magnetometers were capable of detecting the metal even though the tent by now was probably buried deep in the shelf. But no one I had spoken to thought such a project had enough scientific research merit to warrant funding.

36

By next afternoon the cloud cover had lifted and I flew to the DC10 site. Kate and Billy Blackburn came with me. Opening the cardboard box with my sheath knife, I slit open the individual plastic bags and let the gray-white, fine material gently sift out. I felt I should be feeling more. But I was too tired to feel much, even to be afraid of the Site.

"Earth to earth, ashes to ashes, dust to dust. . . ."

The light wind gusted, causing a spray of ashes to fall on one of Blackburn's boots. Was it an omen? Later, when I heard he was badly burned in the helo crash the following season, the one in which Hank Dana was killed, I recalled that moment.

The following day, Saturday, I rested or packed. I was alone with Kate most of the day. I had a greater sense than ever that with her I could fulfill my need to love and be loved, which had been blocked for a long time. We felt a special closeness despite the difference in our life styles, ages, backgrounds. How lucky we were to have gotten to know each other intimately in a mere seven or eight weeks.

We agreed to meet in California in less than a month, and to see each other as often as we could. I would look into the possibility of finding a position at the University of California in Berkeley, where I had been offered a job two years previously. She said that for some time she had been considering resigning her commission to go into private practice.

Alas, when we were back in the States it wasn't as simple and easy as it seemed then. Despite Kate's urging, I couldn't make up my mind to get psychiatric help—I wasn't convinced I needed it. Nor could I decide to get a divorce. The distance between Kate and me, at first mostly geographical, lessened my need for a divorce. Before long our relationship seemed to be unraveling. In the "real" world, the temperate one, we appeared to have less in common than before, to be less compatible. Still, sensing the potential long-term importance of our relationship, we both struggled to save it. In one respect I *was* decisive: I made the move to Berkeley. But we continued to live apart.

What was the matter with me? Why couldn't I see what was necessary for my well-being? I lived in an emotional fog most of the time, possibly all of it. The "Grab your ankles!" phase had passed but I was unwell, I felt remote from people, remote even from myself, and at times needed to injure myself—preferably physically, or if not that, emotionally, psychologically. Yet I resisted seeking help.

Meanwhile I continued working on my Antarctic history. I decided to interview the leader of the search party which had found Scott's tent in November 1912, some eight months after the tragedy of One Ton Depot. He was Sir Henry S. Wild, eighty-eight, and was living with a daughter on Saltspring Island, one of the Gulf Islands off Vancouver. Although my work in progress was about American activities in the Antarctic, I had to deal with Scott and Shackleton because they were the Americans' predecessors on Ross Island.

"Well," I thought, "if I can't see Scott himself in the frozen flesh, I'll do the next best thing and discover what Sir Henry can tell me about him. Possibly he has some important insight into what spooked Scott."

As you see, I no longer thought there was any question that Scott *was* spooked.

I flew to Vancouver, where I put up for a night at the Georgia. In the morning I took the ferry from Tsawwassen to Saltspring Island, where I visited Sir Henry and his daughter Meg for two days, talking and taping.

He was very old, a bit hunched over, but his face was

youthful for his age, and his nose was prominent in a gentle way. His thin white hair was close-cropped. A cowlick fell to the right. His face was longish, with dewlaps, his eyes ready for humor, at times twinkling with it. He had a pensive look and smile that seemed a bit disturbed, as if from long-faulty vision. He wore spectacles in flesh-colored plastic frames. His large hands, brown, gnarled, with huge age spots (pathetic hands, once youthful, working in the Antarctic), had an old habit, the left one enfolding the knuckles of the right, and the thumbs cuddling each other. They had another habit too, stroking each other lengthwise, one above the other. They had much extra, paperlike skin that he sometimes pursed into mountain ranges, then, catching himself, smoothed out. Occasionally, when he laughed, the tip of his pink tongue showed between his teeth and lower lip.

He wore a boldly checked sports jacket and brown loosely hanging trousers. His blue tie had a little penguin motif. The collar of his plaid red shirt was unbuttoned. A white kerchief graced his lapel pocket.

It was a rustic setting: a small, simple house in a grove of arbutus near a saltwater pond. At times I heard chickens muttering and a rooster crowing. One of my first and most vivid impressions of the place was of a large sepia print of the famous photo by Herbert Ponting of Scott seated at his collapsible desk in his cubicle in the Terra Nova Hut on Cape Evans. Above and to the left of it was a large print of young Wild on his knees, peering upward through a theodolite. I became aware of other memorabilia: rare first editions, even rarer photographic scrapbooks, a bookcase made of a Nansen polar sledge cut in half, a penguin-shaped menu from the last midwinter's feast of the Terra Nova Expedition signed by many of the expedition members, a beautiful watercolor of Erebus by Edward Wilson.

We covered much ground about those old days though his fading voice was a problem. He corrected it by drinking plenty of rye when we rested. It did seem to improve his voice considerably. At first I was careful not to say anything that might put him off, cause distrust. He was very alert and easily remembered details of those sledging journeys of long ago. I was about to mention my idea of searching for Scott, Wilson and Bowers when I asked him, "When you first went back to Ross Island and saw the Discovery Hut there, with the modern storage tanks nearby, were old memories stirred?"

"Well, naturally," he said. "The fact was that the hut, and Observation Hill, and the great cross that had been put up umpteen years ago—they didn't seem *very* different except there seemed to be more bare ground, less snow about."

"Was it depressing to be there and see the changes?"

"No, no, not at all. But I'll tell you one thing that gave me a frightful shock. I gave a talk once—at McMurdo, it was—and at the end of it one of the chaps got up and said, 'Could you have got the bodies of Scott and his companions back?' I said, 'Of course.' And then I realized what it was all about. There's a fundamental difference between the American attitude and the British attitude. American casualties have been brought back from all over the world and been planted at San Diego. It's quite amazing, it really is a strange thing to my mind. I'm sure there was not a single one of our party would have thought of it. This was the place where they had done their *best work*. *Leave* them there! Gosh! I got such a shock!"

He chuckled as he thought back.

So much for mentioning my idea of airborne magnetometers and a burial in Westminster Abbey.

"According to Cherry-Garrard, you were the very first to spot the signs of the tent during the search," I said.

"I want to explain this," he said. "Atkinson was in charge of the overall party, those of us left in winter quarters. It was decided during the winter that the right thing to do was not to try any more to relieve the northern party. At any rate we decided that we'd spend all our efforts at first to find out what had happened to

Scott. We all had in mind what had happened on the first Scott expedition, when the Royal Navy sent down half a fleet''—he chuckled—''to help free the *Discovery* from the ice, and all unnecessarily. We were afraid that this sort of thing would happen unless we cleared it up. Well, Atkinson was in charge, there were thirteen of us left, and two were left back at winter quarters because they had been injured in an accident. We had some mules sent down and we had a few dogs left. Cherry and Atch and Dmitri were with the dogs, and I had the navigating business and was in charge of eight mules, I think. The dogs weren't awfully good, you know, they came from Siberia and used to be used on the postal services. Their route was always on a road and they hadn't been trained, like the Greenlanders, just to go blindly ahead if you told them in what direction to go. They had lost an awful lot of heart, they were not in very good shape after the previous summer, and they followed up after us.

''You see, on the way south, every lunchtime we built up two cairns, and one cairn when we stopped at night. This was in order to help on the way back in case we didn't see the sun and couldn't get a bearing. But the plan of the search party was to go along, following as nearly as possible the route that they should have taken back, until we found a cache which had been picked up by Scott. And then backtrack, and on to the next cache. I was certain we'd find them, all right. I had a little map—I guess I've got it there''—he motioned with his hand—''showing where the cairns were on the way south. And to actually find this little bit of tent sticking out of the ice was no problem. They were on line coming back. If they hadn't been we'd have gone on to the cache, the depot, before, you see, and then come back. We couldn't have missed them.

''Well, I don't pretend to say that I was the first who saw it. How can one? But nobody—if anybody else did see it first, well, I don't know, it didn't occur to me to inquire, I saw the damn thing. It was a black spot on the ice on the starboard bow and, not knowing what it was except that it shouldn't be there, I had it all nicely laid out where the cairns were, you see, there was something black out there, so I went out on skis to see what it was, and told the party to carry on to the south. We were fitted out to go as far as the top of the Beardmore and have one day for research there. We didn't have much left, you see. At any rate, I went on, and I don't quite understand myself, really, but when I saw it was the tent I signaled the party to come in and I couldn't make them understand and I didn't feel it was right to shout, and this is the first funny thing, you see, I didn't think it was all right to shout, like being in a cathedral. Finally I made enough signs to make them see what I wanted.

"The second funny thing was it didn't seem to me to be right to make our camp too close to the tent, so I made it about a hundred and fifty yards away. And then there was some discussion, I think, as to what we should do before Atkinson came up. Well, I wasn't having any of that, Atkinson was in charge and Atkinson had to be there when the tent was opened. So we did just that, and Atkinson came with the dogs about an hour later, I guess, I don't remember that, I don't remember it at all. So at any rate we waited for Atch and he opened up the tent and he and Cherry and I went in and had a look at the party of three—Scott, Wilson and Bowers—and closed it up again. Atkinson had taken out Scott's diary, and he read certain parts of it to everybody, the parts that made it clear that Evans had died on the Beardmore and that Titus Oates had walked out into the blizzard, and so on—explaining why there were only three there. And then we got the bits of rock they had brought back, and collapsed the tent on them after taking away the chronometers they carried. I got the idea that we'd get into trouble if we didn't bring these back to Greenwich, so I suggested to Atch, 'Well, I think we'd better take these back, hadn't we,' you see, so Atch dealt with Scott's chronometer, Cherry dealt with Dr. Bill's, and I dealt with Birdie's. And then we collapsed the tent on them and built an enormous cairn on top."

"Did you examine the bodies?" I asked.

"No."

"Was it easy to identify each person?"

"Oh, heavens yes. They were very thin and so on, but they looked as though they were asleep. They were in their sleeping bags, except that Scott was half out of his bag and sort of leaning toward Uncle Bill's bag. They had simply frozen to death."

"Do you feel you still remember these moments? Or are they memories based on your journals?"

"Oh, I remember this very well indeed. I was so surprised at myself. Why should I be diffident about shouting out and telling the party what to do? That sort of thing. Oh, it's very clear in my mind—if only because I couldn't understand myself."

"You undoubtedly thought many, many times about the possible motive Scott had for at the last minute taking Bowers along on the polar party which was set up for a group of four."

"I don't understand it," he said. "The whole thing seems so queer. Quite obviously, as Birdie had left his skis behind—a little beforehand, they didn't go back to get them, you see—it looked as if Scott had chosen his four and told them so. And then, somehow or other, something must have happened and he had second thoughts and took along a fifth man. It's very strange."

There was a long pause.

"It doesn't make sense to me at all," he said. "I can't imagine what kind of argument Birdie must have made with Scott to take him along. I can't think. . . . In fact, if he'd been in the Royal Navy I can't see Birdie even daring to do it. But I can't see what form of argument he introduced that would enable Scott to make such a strange decision. I can't understand it."

I had a sense he was withholding something but I was reluctant to press him. And having barely missed making a fool of myself by talking about magnetometers and Westminster Abbey, I avoided raising the subject of Erebus in any but a straightforward way.

"Sir Henry, do you believe there's such a thing as an Antarctic addiction?" I asked.

“It’s really a queer thing, but you know, you see those sunsets, perfectly lovely things. Makes you feel as if you’ve swallowed a rainbow. And sometimes Mount Erebus is so beautiful, stops you in your tracks! You feel you’re part of nature is probably the best way I can explain it. But you know, not everything is explainable. There are things. . . .”

His voice drifted off.

Very early the next morning—it was still dark—he and his daughter Meg, a woman in her sixties, drove me to the ferry slip in Long Harbour.

As we stood around waiting for the departure, he said, “I’ve learned something from your visit. It’s made me think. I hadn’t thought of the psychological aspects. It has stirred many memories.”

A little later, when Meg was standing apart from us, he suddenly said, “I’ll tell you something I’ve never told anyone. When we went into the tent, Scott’s left eye was slightly open. The effect was extraordinary. I have never forgotten it. It looked alive, you see. It was uncanny. He was a remarkable man, quite unpredictable in some ways, but I hadn’t expected anything like this. Dr. Bill’s and Birdie’s eyes were closed. But Scott, with his eye half open, looked. . . . He was haggard, skeletal, bearded, terribly frostbitten . . . and he looked . . . haunted. . . . I thought so at the time and I think so now. Haunted. . . .”

It was time to part. I thanked him and Meg for their wonderful hospitality.

It was only after the ferry had gone around a bend and we were out of sight of the island that I realized his last word also described me. “Haunted.” I heard him, again and again, saying it. “Haunted.” The word echoed louder and louder in my mind, riveting me.

I too was haunted. This came with the force of a sudden revelation. It was then I fully understood I was still possessed. Possessed by the scenes on Erebus. And by my guilt. I understood then how badly I needed help.

I resolved to get it. Without it how could I hope to free myself from the Erebus figures, alive and dead, the Erebus ghosts? And from a guilt that increasingly felt bottomless? Without it, too, how could I hope to free myself for a fighting chance to save my relationship with Kate?